THE
RULES
OF
ROYALTY

ALSO BY
CALE DIETRICH

The Love Interest
The Friend Scheme
The Pledge

WITH
SOPHIE GONZALES

If This Gets Out

THE
RULES
OF
ROYALTY

CALE DIETRICH

WEDNESDAY BOOKS
NEW YORK

First published in the United States by Wednesday Books, an imprint of St. Martin's Publishing Group

THE RULES OF ROYALTY. Copyright © 2024 by Cale Dietrich. All rights reserved. Printed in the United States of America. For information, address St. Martin's Publishing Group, 120 Broadway, New York, NY 10271.

www.wednesdaybooks.com

Designed by Devan Norman
Emoji art © Cosmic_Design/Shutterstock

Library of Congress Cataloging-in-Publication Data

Names: Dietrich, Cale, author.
Title: The rules of royalty / Cale Dietrich.
Description: First edition. | New York : Wednesday Books, 2024. |
    Audience term: Teenagers | Audience: Ages 13–18.
Identifiers: LCCN 2024029412 | ISBN 9781250887771
    (trade paperback) | ISBN 9781250887757 (hardcover) |
    ISBN 9781250887764 (ebook)
Subjects: CYAC: Princes—Fiction. | Friendship—Fiction. | Family
    life—Fiction. | Gay men—Fiction. | Romance stories. | LCGFT:
    Romance fiction. | Novels.
Classification: LCC PZ7.1.D543 Ru 2024 | DDC [Fic]—dc23
LC record available at https://lccn.loc.gov/2024029412

Our books may be purchased in bulk for promotional, educational, or business use. Please contact your local bookseller or the Macmillan Corporate and Premium Sales Department at 1-800-221-7945, extension 5442, or by email at MacmillanSpecialMarkets@macmillan.com.

First Edition: 2024

10 9 8 7 6 5 4 3 2 1

TO DAD

PART
ONE

As a leader, one must put the nation's needs above personal wishes. Although it is a sacrifice, it is necessary for the greater good.

—QUEEN KRISTINA

CHAPTER ONE

JAMIE

I don't like birthdays.

Don't get me wrong, there are some good parts about them. I enjoy presents, because who doesn't, and I'm never going to turn down cake. It's just that, given the complicated nature of my family, birthdays have a way of bringing up feelings I'm usually able to keep shoved down in the deep, dark recesses of my soul, where they belong.

My best friend, Max, nudges me. We're sitting at our booth at our favorite restaurant, Anchor Bros diner. I look up and see why she got my attention.

A ridiculously cute guy is looking at me.

My friend group's overly lively conversation, which has been trying to lock down a definitive ranking of the Studio Ghibli films—*Spirited Away* is number one, obviously—is halted by a cute boy, which is admittedly the best way anything can be halted.

Said cute boy, who has sandy-blond hair and blue eyes and is therefore the epitome of my type, has emerged from the kitchen, even though I've never seen him before. Given how much time my friends and I have spent here, it means he must be new. He swings into an empty booth directly across the diner from us, pulls his phone out of his pocket, and starts scrolling.

But then he looks directly at me and smiles a little. And it's like: hello, eye contact. I get that I'm not exactly inconspicuous at the moment, given my party hat and the BIRTHDAY BOY ribbon stuck to my chest. Still. Sometimes I'm oblivious, but even I can't miss his flirty expression.

Max nudges me again. I look back at the guy, and—oh shit. He has a Pokémon phone case, and it's not even of the ones everyone knows. It's of the latest generation. Be still, my heart.

"Go talk to him," whispers Max.

I nearly laugh. What, go up and talk to a stranger? Who does that?

I shake my head and sip the mint milkshake I'm currently halfway through. Earlier, my friends and I had a discussion about the difference between shamrock shakes and plain old mint shakes, and I decided that it needs to be near Saint Patrick's Day for it to be called a shamrock shake.

Anyway, I, Jamie Johnson, am a lot of things. I know way too much about movies, video games, and mint shakes, apparently. I'm also weirdly good at soccer for someone otherwise spectacularly unathletic and like to think I can occasionally crack a good joke. What I'm not is the type to talk to strangers, especially ones of the hot variety, which this dude clearly is. It might be particular to me, but the modern Pokémon phone case? I can't imagine anything hotter.

"What about your challenge?" asks Max. Sometimes, okay, all the time, I wonder how I got lucky enough to have a best friend as cool as future punk-pop superstar Max Delgado. Not only is her future so exciting, but she's also ridiculously kind and takes no shit from anyone. She's my hero, truly. "Don't you want to get out of your comfort zone?"

"Yeah," I say. "But there's that and there's bothering someone at work."

"You wouldn't be bothering him," says Ren, one of my other best friends. He's tall and kind of gangly and is always overly animated. His black hair is cropped short, and he has an earring shaped like a dagger dangling from his left ear. "Every time you look away, he checks you out."

It's still a no, but now I'm at least entertaining the idea. I do want to push myself out of my shell now that I'm seventeen. I don't want to be known as the quiet guy forever. I want a lot out of life, and I'm starting to think that won't happen if I don't go for it. Maybe I *need* to push myself out of my comfort zone, and going over and talking to that guy might be the perfect first test. What's the worst that could happen?

I imagine him laughing in my face, and suddenly the stakes feel impossibly high.

I grab a french fry from Ren's plate and glance out the window. It's pitch-black outside, and the diner is only half-full. Classic rock is coming from the jukebox, "Always" by Bon Jovi, which I recognize because my stepdad, Mike, is a chronic classic rock fan. It's basically all he listens to.

In my pocket, my phone starts ringing. I check, and it's from Mom. I flip my phone back so it's facedown. I'm sure it's nothing major. She knows I'm with my friends and she also knows I'm not the type to lie about what I'm doing. I've been to a few house parties so I'm not totally inexperienced when it comes to being around alcohol or drugs, but I've always told Mom the truth. It might be my birthday, but I'm spending it exactly the way I want to: sober, with my closest friends and nobody else.

"Anyway," I say. "Everyone's free to come over tomorrow to watch the video, right?"

I'm referring to Max's music video we have spent most of the past week shooting in Spencer's mansion and some of the landmarks around Providence. It's for Max's first-ever single, "Ashes." The video has been a group effort. I have all the clips we filmed on my phone, and it's my job to assemble the whole thing.

"I will be," says Max. For the shoot she dyed the ends of her blond hair a pastel pink, hoping to create a branded look. She's spent a fortune on this single: booking studio time isn't cheap, and she didn't want her song to seem low-budget or too indie, even though it's both those things.

The music video is a bonus. According to Max, all people really care about is the song. Still, we have all put an absurd amount of effort into it, because we love Max, and being a musician is her dream. I will do anything to make that a reality.

"I can't wait," she says.

"Same," says Amara. She proudly told me earlier that her entire outfit was thrifted, and she told me the exact amount of pollution her decision has saved. Honestly, if Amara Eze winds up saving the entire world one day, I won't be shocked. "People are going to freak out when it drops, I know it."

Max knocks her knuckles on the table.

According to Max, most agents now want either nepo babies or musicians with an already sizable online following. Given the former is sadly off the cards, she needs to do it the hard, grassroots, "throw yourself on the mercy of the internet" way. The plan is to post the video to YouTube, the song to Spotify and Apple Music, and then to post a bunch of TikToks about it. Our summer will be spent making Max a bona fide star, and I wouldn't have it any other way.

"Who cares about the video right now," says Ren, keeping his voice low. "No offense, Max."

"Some taken," she says. "It's just my dream, but whatever."

"One of the finest guys I have ever seen is checking out my boy," says Ren. "And everyone knows Jamie desperately needs to get some."

"Hey," I say.

"Truth hurts, buddy," says Ren. "You're cute, you're smart, and you're a good person." He puts his arm around me. "You have so much potential."

"Ren," says Amara, in the tone she only uses to playfully scold him. "Jamie is perfectly capable of deciding when and if he wants to start dating."

Ren recoils in disgust. "I was talking about a hookup, obviously."

I glance across the diner, and the boy is actually checking me out again. Like, he truly is.

"Do you think I should say hi?" I ask.

"Yes," say both Ren and Max emphatically. Amara says, "No."

We all turn to Spencer. He hasn't spoken in this conversation, which is actually pretty normal for him. As opposed to me, he's the cool kind of quiet: he only speaks when he wants to. Like Max, he dyes his hair, so now it's a bright shade of platinum blond.

"Sure," he says. "He'd be lucky to meet you."

Three to one. I should do this. Okay, Jamie. If Max is brave enough to put her music out into the world, then I am brave enough to talk to a cute stranger. I'm seventeen now. Practically an adult. I can do this.

"Excuse me," I say.

"There he is," says Ren, clapping me on the shoulder as I pass him. "You've got this."

I get up from the booth and start making my way toward the guy. He's returned his attention to his phone, so he hasn't seen me approaching. My doubts are starting to grow stronger. What am I doing? Just because he looked at me a few times and smiled doesn't mean he wants me to introduce myself. Plus, this is his place of work, which happens to be the place my friends visit all the time. If I screw this up, it could ruin Anchor Bros for all of us.

At the last second, I swerve and go into the bathroom. Like the rest of the diner, this bathroom is decorated with anchors, buoys, and other nautical stuff. We like it because it has the best burgers and shakes, and it's cheap. All of us, save Spencer with his mega-rich doctor parents, have jobs, but they're minimum wage, and my shifts at Cinnabon have been sporadic at best. I've liked the reduced hours because I've had exams to focus on, but it hasn't been great for my bank account, which is hovering at around thirty dollars at the moment.

My phone starts buzzing. Mom again. I frown. It's strange for her to call twice in a row. She usually texts if she wants something.

I swipe and answer the call.

"Where are you?" she asks. She sounds stressed. My blood goes cold. Has something happened?

"At the diner, why?"

There's a pause.

"You're out later than I thought you would be," she says.

I check my watch. It's past ten, which isn't that late. Still, the worried tone in Mom's voice is fairly concerning.

"Is that okay?"

"It's fine," she says. "I was hoping I could talk to you tonight. There's something I need to tell you."

I'm getting a strong sense it's nothing good. I struggle with anxiety, but this seems like one of the rare cases where I'm not simply imagining the worst. This time, something has actually happened. There's no way she'd use the phrase "there's something I need to tell you" otherwise. That is saved for emergencies.

"What's going on?" I ask. "Is everyone okay?"

"Everyone's fine, but I need to tell you this in person. I don't want to ruin your birthday, we can talk when you get home."

"Okay, I'll come home now. I'll see you soon."

I end the call. My nerves are in overdrive. Mom has never talked to me like that. It's not like her, and we're very close. It was just us before she met and fell in love with Mike six years ago.

Few people know this, but she's not my biological mom, who passed away when I was a kid. That whole story is complex, but the gist of it is that Mom was my bio-mom's best friend. After my bio-mom passed away when I was one, Mom volunteered to adopt me, and the rest is history. People are sometimes weirded out that I don't know all that much about my bio-mom's past or family, but it's not like I don't have family. Mom legally adopted me, and I have my grandparents, a few aunts and uncles, and a bunch of cousins. And for the past six years, Mike, who is about as perfect as one could hope for, for a father figure. I have more than enough.

I leave the bathroom and go back to the table.

"Classic Johnson." Ren grins, showing off the dents of his Invisalign. "Terrified of boys."

"Is everything okay?" asks Max, her eyes filled with concern.

"I just got this weird call from Mom," I say. "She wants me to come home."

"Do you want me to drive you?" she asks.

"If that's okay?"

"Of course," she says, grabbing her phone from where it was resting on the table. "I'm not going to make you take the bus. Let's go."

We say our goodbyes to the group and then leave the diner. Even though it's dark out, the giant neon-blue sign on the top of Anchor Bros lights our path, and we go around the block to her car. It's a small red Honda that first belonged to her mom, then her older sister, and now, finally, her. It's always in danger of breaking down, but Max will keep driving it until it dies. I'm sure Max would spend any money for a new car on music instead.

"What do you think your mom wants to talk about?" she asks as she starts the engine.

"I don't know."

"Whatever it is, you know I'm here for you, right?"

"I do."

It's the truth. Max will be here for me no matter what. I wonder what I did in a past life to have a best friend like her. We've been pretty much inseparable since the first day of fourth grade, when she stood up to a guy who had made fun of me for reading during lunch. After scaring him off, she sat with me and asked about the book. Ever since then, she's been my best friend and protector in equal measure. She's the first person I ever came out to, and the person I'm closest with on the entire planet.

We go over a speed bump a little too fast, and the car bounces. She takes a right turn, and we're in the suburbs, surrounded by houses.

"I'm sure it'll be fine," she says. She drums her fingers on her steering wheel.

"I hope so."

I pick at my fingernails, a habit I thought I'd managed to grow out of. When we reach my house, she parks behind Mike's car.

"I love you," she says.

"Love you, too."

She leans across to hug me. "Whatever it is, you can handle it."

"I'll text you once I know what's going on."

"Please do."

I unclip my seatbelt, open the car door, and step out into the night air.

The sprinkler is on in our lawn, so I move around it to reach the front door. I unlock it and go inside. Our cat, Coconut, comes up and runs a few laps around my legs. I know cats are supposed to be aloof, but my dear Coconut forgot that memo—he's the neediest thing I've met in my life.

"Hey, boy," I say, giving him a scratch between his ears.

The lights are on, but the house is quiet. I pause for a moment before I put my keys in the bowl by the doorway and go to the dining room. Coconut trots behind me.

As I go through the house, I sense something is wrong. Nothing is out of place, but something feels seriously off. It's like the house is a few degrees colder than usual, nearly impossible to miss.

I wish I could pause time because I know I won't like whatever I'm about to be told. These feel like the last few moments before whatever Mom needs to say to me completely changes my life.

I reach the dining room. Mom is sitting at the dining room table, which is still decorated for my birthday. There are balloons all over the floor.

"Take a seat," she says. Up close, I notice there are tears in her eyes. "I need to tell you something I should've told you a long time ago."

Chapter Two

ERIK

"I need to tell you something."

Nate and I both stop. This isn't normally how our hookups go. Usually by this point we're making out, not talking. I do enjoy talking to Nate, but I was under the impression that I came to his dorm room for, ahem, other reasons.

"Can it wait?" I ask.

Nate kicks his dorm room door shut, and then pulls his shirt off over his head. "Fine."

He presses me up against the wall, and then starts kissing me. "You're so hot." He starts unbuttoning my shirt. "Sorry. You're hot, Your Royal Highness."

I narrow my eyes at him, pretending to be annoyed.

His joke reminds me I only have a few hours before a car picks me up to take me to the palace. I don't want to think about that right now. I can't stop, though, and now instead of being here with Nate I'm thinking about how, very soon, I'm going to visit Gran for our traditional end-of-school-term tea visit. No one wants to think of their grandma while they're making out. No one.

Even if she is the queen of Sunstad.

To push the thoughts away I kiss Nate harder. His fingers trace down my chest. Gran, AKA Queen Amalia, hovers around the corners of my vision with her snow-white hair, wearing a necklace covered in glittering dark blue jewels.

Why, brain. Why.

Nate finishes unbuttoning my shirt, then he runs his hands up my chest to both sides of my face. Finally, I'm totally present, exactly where I want to be.

Right now, I'm not a prince, with all my responsibilities. I'm just a guy, making out with another guy. Specifically, Nate Saitō, one of the smartest boys at West Hill. Friend for years, friend with benefits for the past few weeks, after we finally figured out we both want the same thing: a guy who won't make things complicated. He's going to be one of the best lawyers in the country. Me? I'll fulfill my duties as Prince Erik of Sunstad, Count of Norgard, the way one born into my family should. I know I've been pretty lucky in life, and I haven't been as supervised as a lot of my family members. I've put that down to two things: one, I'm the spare. Second, I'm gay, and a lot of the more old-fashioned people who advise my family don't know what to do with that. Sunstad is an extremely progressive country in regards to LGBTQIA+ rights, but some people still have a hard time wrapping their head around the whole queer prince thing.

"What?" he asks.

"Nothing," I say. I slowly lower myself down to kiss him. He grabs my wrist and pulls me to the bed.

Nate and I make out for a while, lying side by side. It's fun enough that for a few moments, I actually do start to forget about who I am and all the pressure on me. I've always heard that the responsibilities placed on people from my family increase dramatically once you turn seventeen, which is the age I am now. I am expecting everything to change at any moment.

My phone alarm starts blaring, pulling Nate and me out of our makeout trance. How is it time to go already?

Nate stops and rubs my arm. "Duty calls?"

"Yeah," I say, silencing my alarm and shoving my phone back into my pocket perhaps a little harder than I need to. "Sorry."

"Don't be, this was fun."

It takes all my willpower to push myself off the bed. What I want to do is to say "screw it" and return to what we were doing. But that wouldn't be me. I do everything perfectly. I'm never late, and I'm never unorganized. I may not be as much of a golden boy as my older brother, Stefan, because he never does anything wrong. But I try my best. The least I can do is show up when I'm asked.

"Where are you going, anyway?" asks Nate. He's grabbed his phone from his bedside table and is already scrolling. I take him in. Short black hair, tanned skin. God, I wish I weren't a prince right now. I love Gran, and want to see her. I would just prefer to make out with Nate.

"Tea, with Gran," I say.

He lifts a perfectly groomed eyebrow. "Well, give the queen my best."

"I wish I could stay, but I don't really have a choice."

"I mean, you do," he says. "You don't have to do everything they tell you."

He has no idea that's not true.

"Wait, where did my shirt go?" I ask as adrenaline kicks in. I really shouldn't be here. I should be in my room, dressed and ready to go by now. Not shirtless in another boy's room. My meeting with Gran starts in half an hour, and I doubt she would appreciate me showing up without a shirt. Even then, she would probably prefer that to me being late. She's a stickler for that. Nate gets up, retrieves my shirt from his desk, and hands it to me.

"Thanks," I say, as I pull it on. A blue crest is stitched into the chest of a raven holding a book and a torch, and beneath it is the school's motto: "Innovate. Inspire. Achieve." I think a fairer motto would be "nepotism is key," but hey, I'm not the one who comes up with this stuff. Plus, I know I'm not the right person to complain about nepotism.

"So, about that thing I need to tell you," Nate says. "Can we talk?"

I freeze. I feel my heart beating. No good can come from those words. "What's on your mind?"

"This is a little awkward, because I know we were never official or anything."

I'm completely silent. Does he want to be serious with me? It surprises me that I don't hate the idea. It will certainly be complicated—dating in my family always is. I am often reminded that in order to get married, I need to get the consent of both the monarch and the government. They literally can and will control who I love. Not that I even want to marry Nate, or anyone else at the moment.

"But the thing is," says Nate. "I've met someone."

I go quiet. I get the sense that this isn't a conversation. Nate has rehearsed what he's about to say to me, and now he's getting it out.

He folds his arms over his chest. "This was sort of a last-hurrah kind of thing. Wow, I can't believe I said hurrah. Sorry."

I lean against the doorframe. "For saying hurrah or the dumping?"

"I'm not dumping you," he says. "I'm strategically ending this. You did say you didn't want anything serious."

He's right, I did. This should be fine. It is fine. And I don't want anything serious. It would be too much of a headache to navigate royal dating while also dealing with school and everything else in my life.

"You're right, I was joking," I say. "I just liked this."

"I liked it, too. But I think it'd be easier if we end it now." He drags his teeth along his bottom lip. "Sorry."

"No, don't be. It's totally fine. Um, not to seem like a huge jackass, but I really need to go." I feel lucky that the car will actually be here shortly. I shouldn't leave the driver waiting.

"I'll message you later?" I ask.

"Sure. But so we're clear—"

"We're done, yup, got it."

I step into my shoes. This hurts, sure. I liked hooking up with Nate. I liked it a lot. And even though I never wanted it to be a relationship, it was still a fun escape, one of the few things in my life that felt indulgently mine.

And now it's over.

I leave his room and check the time on my phone. The conversation took longer than expected, and the car will be here any moment.

I'm going to need to run.

I breathe in musty air as I fly down the stairwell as quickly as possible, my hand hovering above the railing because I refuse to be known as the prince who died falling down the stairs.

Once I reach the bottom I race outside. Even though the school term has just ended, it's been summer for a week already, and you can tell. The sky is clear blue, and the sun is blaring. It never gets too hot here, but it's pleasantly warm out, a sort of dreamy, perfect temperature. I wish I could sit for a while and take it all in, maybe write in my journal.

I pass by tall structures made of reddish-brown brick, and meticulously maintained gardens. I've lived in palaces my whole life and I still think this is one of the nicest places I've ever seen. I dash past an enormous oak tree with sunlight dappling through its leaves, totally picturesque. I catch the attention of a few younger students, all enjoying their last few hours on school grounds before returning home for the break. They pause what they were doing to openly stare at me.

I don't mind. I'm used to it. It's not like I blame them, either. I'm sure a prince, even a spare one, wildly running across campus is quite the sight.

I go past the science building, one of the most modern-looking

on campus, then enter the main quad that leads to the front gate
of the school. The iron gates are open. I jog out onto the sidewalk.

The streets are bare of waiting cars, but there's another problem. I'm sweaty and out of breath, and my heart is pounding. I
know it's ridiculous to worry about appearances, but I really can't
be seen like this. I take a folded handkerchief out of my pocket.
It has my family crest in the middle, a perched falcon surrounded
by roses.

I lean forward, resting my hands on my thighs, and suck in
some much-needed air. I manage to calm myself and check my
phone again: 4:00. I'm right on time.

A black car appears around the corner. It parks in front of me,
and a driver steps out and opens the door.

The back of the car isn't empty.

I'm greeted by the crown prince, Stefan. The future king of
Sunstad.

I climb into the car and give him a hug, and he squeezes me
back. Us traveling in the same car is breaking a rule, but I'm so
happy to see him I don't really care about that.

If you picked up a magazine, you'd think the Lindstrom brothers were bitter enemies. I'm apparently jealous of him, which
couldn't be further from the truth. I barely feel like I'm handling
the royal duties I do have, and I know the pressure is nothing compared to being the crown prince.

The truth is I love my brother. We've had disputes over the
years, and yes, it has been difficult for me to be consistently considered second fiddle, but that's not his fault. It's the hand we've
been dealt.

"You look well," he says.

People often say Stefan and I look alike. We have a lot of the
same features: pale skin, blue eyes, light blond hair. The biggest
differences are my longer hair and the thirty extra pounds he has
from the weights he lifts.

His engagement ring catches the sunlight. The wedding, which is expected to be the event of the year, is only a few weeks away now, at the end of summer. I'm both excited and nervous in equal measure.

I'm excited because it's my brother's wedding to the brilliant woman he loves.

I'm nervous because hundreds of thousands of people are going to watch. Even with all my training, I'd be lying if I said I wasn't nervous about making a mistake.

As the car pulls away from the curb, my phone starts to ring.

My eyes go wide at the name on my phone.

A king is calling me.

CHAPTER THREE

JAMIE

I don't want to, but I force myself to sit down in front of Mom. I know bad news is coming, I know it with every fiber of my being. Time feels like it's slowed down, and with every passing second, I try to figure out what, exactly, Mom wants to tell me.

It has to be major for her to be acting like this. I seriously doubt she would sit me down to tell me something like she's decided to become vegan.

"Where's Mike?" I ask. My voice comes out shaky.

I'm terrified she's about to tell me she and Mike are splitting up. That would be really messed-up timing. Why would she tell me on my birthday?

"He went for a drive," she says. "He wanted to give us space to talk."

What does that mean? The only thing holding me together is the hope that I'm wrong and Mom isn't about to tell me they are separating. I don't want them to get divorced. That might be selfish of me—I want the two of them to be happy, and if they are making this decision, then there must be things about their relationship I haven't seen.

But wait, Mom said that she wanted to tell me something she should've told me a long time ago. Have Mom and Mike been separated for a long time? That doesn't make any sense, but I can't think of anything else that could make her look this worried.

I've always thought of her as fearless, probably because she is. She traveled a lot when she was younger, primarily by herself, so there are pictures around the house of her adventures skydiving, bungee jumping, and driving quad bikes over dunes. In each of them, she's smiling, clearly not afraid at all, even as she is plummeting to the ground. She also has a sleeve of tattoos even though she's afraid of needles. She seems to operate under the idea that if something scares you, it's worth doing.

It's clear whatever she's about to tell me scares her more than anything else. She's a few shades paler than usual, almost ghostly white.

"It's about Emilia," she says.

All the air gets sucked out of the room.

She's going to tell me about my bio-mom?

I don't know much about her. All I have is a physical photo album of pictures and a few stories Mom's told me. Emilia was clearly on the run from something when she came to America. She had no family and wouldn't tell Mom anything major about her past. I've been told she was from a family of bad people, and I shouldn't go digging for information.

"What about her?" I ask.

"The first thing you should know is I was trying to honor her wishes," she says. "All she wanted for you was to grow up differently than she did."

It slams into me with a metric ton of force. Does she know how Emilia grew up? If so, why hasn't she told me?

We've had long conversations about this a bunch of times. I've told her how it feels strange to have an entire side of my family I know nothing about. I've come to terms with it now, but when I was younger, I really struggled.

Tears prickle in Mom's eyes. "I'm sorry, Jamie. I've always known what I was doing was wrong, but I couldn't get myself to break my promise to her. I'm so sorry."

"So you know about her family?"

Mom nods. "I'm the only person she's ever told about them."

This is too much information for me to process right now. What does this mean? I'm so curious to find out more, but at the same time I can't really accept it. How could she possibly know things about Emilia and not tell me? Actually, it's more than that. She's told me she doesn't know anything about Emilia, that in their entire friendship she never spoke of her past: only hinted that it was a dark time. That means my mom has done more than simply keep things from me. She actively lied.

I ask what feels like the biggest question of my life.

"What do you know about her?"

"She is from an aristocratic, powerful family from Mitanor. But that's not all I've kept from you, Jamie. Because I know who your father is, too."

The room is quiet for a second, stretching out far longer than it should.

"I thought he was a random guy?" I say. "You said there was no way to track him down."

"I know I did, and I'm sorry I lied. There's a reason, Jamie, and if you let me explain, it will all make sense. Your mother is a member of the Alcaron dynasty: an incredibly wealthy and connected family in Mitanor, the type who run in powerful circles. Your father is, well . . ." She pauses. "He's well known."

"Well known how?"

None of this makes sense. I was told that he was a one-night stand to my bio-mom, and that they had fallen out of contact by the time she realized she was pregnant with me. By that time she was already living in America, and had a totally new life. I didn't even know Emilia was from Mitanor. Mom always said she'd never told her where exactly she was from.

"Your father's name is Alexander Mortenallo."

Alexander. My father's name is Alexander. One of my life's

biggest mysteries, answered in one sentence, in one word. Alexander. So, not Alex. That makes me think he's a more serious kind of guy, some sort of professional. I try to picture him, as I have many times before, and envision a suave man in a suit, sitting at a bar.

"But he goes by his title," says Mom. "Which is His Majesty King Alexander."

Did she seriously say that? For a moment I think I must have heard her incorrectly.

Did she just say King Alexander?

"What are you talking about?"

"That's what I'm trying to tell you, Jamie. Your father is the king of Mitanor."

I'm sure a whole variety of emotions is showing on my face right now. The biggest one is confusion. Because what in the world? She can't be serious. There's no freaking way. I'm a completely normal guy. There's nothing royal about me. I go to public school and work at Cinnabon part-time. I have friends and a normal life.

I wait for a moment for Mom to smile and say she's joking. But she doesn't. As the seconds stretch on, I find myself more and more confused. She just told me that my biological father is a king. That just happened.

I laugh. "Good one. What is this, some sort of birthday prank?"

"It's not a prank, Jamie."

"Yeah, right. So I'm a prince."

"You are."

A moment passes.

And then another.

A million thoughts are going through my mind, all at the same time. I wish my brain would shut up for a second so I could figure this out. Just. Shut. Up.

I laugh again. "You've really committed. You nearly had me, but let's stop now, okay? I'm not a prince, and this is a joke."

She puts her hand on my arm. "I'm sorry, Jamie. But it's the truth. King Alexander is your father."

She looks serious, but there's no way what she said is the actual truth. There has to be some other explanation, it's just that I can't figure out what it is right now. I'm not, and I never will be, related to a king. It's not possible.

"I promise you," says Mom. "I'm telling the truth. Your father is the king of Mitanor. Your mother slept with him while he was briefly separated from his wife. Emilia left the country shortly after. She told me she wanted a different life for you, one away from the pressures her family put on her. She thought if you were raised as a prince, you would be molded into who they wanted you to be, the way her family did to her."

I can't think of anything to say.

"You're a prince, Jamie," says Mom. "I've kept this secret long enough, and now that you're seventeen, I thought you deserved to know."

I get up from my chair.

"I don't like this," I say. "It's not funny. I'm going to go now, okay?"

"Jamie, wait. We should talk about this more."

"I don't want to!" I say. "I need to, yeah, I'm going."

I go straight to my room and close the door.

I can't be a prince. Something else must be going on, I just don't know what yet.

It's the only explanation that makes sense.

CHAPTER FOUR

ERIK

"Well, go on," says Stefan. "Answer it!"

I look at the screen of my phone.

On the other end is King Alexander of Mitanor, one of the most powerful people in the entire world.

I shouldn't ignore his call. I *can't* ignore his call.

I know what will happen if I do, and it won't be good for me. I'll be hauled into Gran's office and given a firm reminder of my station, and how my actions represent my family and my country.

And yet, something is stopping me from answering. How many rings do I have until he gives up? I think my hesitation has something to do with nerves. What could he possibly want to talk to me about? Yes, I'm a prince from Sunstad and second in line to the throne. I'm also seventeen and have yet to properly step into any official royal roles. I'm not the kind of person a king calls out of the blue.

And yet, that is what is happening.

I seriously doubt it's a friendly chat. I try to think of something I might be in trouble for—my hookups with Nate are my only real secret, and I doubt they will cause international scandal. It's no secret that I'm gay, but then again, they might not approve of me kissing boys simply because I think it's fun.

My point is that unless something has happened that I'm completely unaware of, I don't think I am in trouble.

Across from me, Stefan's eyes are wide. I get it. I've left the king hanging for far too long.

I swipe and answer the call. King Alexander's face appears on my screen. He's basically the epitome of tall, dark, and handsome, with piercing eyes and the sort of jawline that meant he could model, if he wanted. His dark hair is swept back, long enough that it curls past his ears.

"Your Majesty?"

"Erik, hi," says King Alexander. I've always loved the Mitanorian accent: every word sounds graceful, and the way the words flow together is beautiful. The accent of Sunstad is short and sharp, nobody's idea of a nice accent. It's too harsh. English, truly the Times New Roman of languages, is King Alexander's second, and I can see him thinking before he speaks. "Is now a bad time?"

I look out the window at the passing gray, monotone streets. They're pristine, yes, and do have a harsh beauty to them. But they're lacking in charm compared to some of our more colorful neighbors. There's a reason a lot of sci-fi movies are shot here, taking advantage of the uniformity of the buildings, usually to show a futuristic alien city.

"No, I can talk."

"Are you alone?"

This is getting weirder by the second.

"No, sorry. My brother is here."

"Ah, Stefan, how are you?" asks Alexander. "Excited about the wedding?"

"Can't wait," says Stefan, flashing a grin.

Alexander nods, then turns back to me. "Now, Erik, I'm calling because I have a proposition for you."

We enter a roundabout. We're near the heart of the city now, and cars are everywhere. In the far distance, the Sarde River glimmers.

"I'm about to tell you something very private," he says.

"Something you cannot tell anyone outside of your immediate family, all right? You, too, Stefan."

I frown. This whole conversation feels extremely confusing. I've only spoken to Alexander on the phone once before. He called me to show his support after I came out of the closet publicly. I've never forgotten that, and I never will. It felt like he called because he truly cared, not because of PR reasons.

And now he wants to tell me a secret?

"The secret is," he says, "I have a second son. An American, to be precise."

He has a second son? I know his other son, Tomas Mortenallo, who's a nice enough guy, but we don't have much in common. I've chatted to him at events a few times, but that's it.

"Okay," I respond. I don't know what else to say. This is huge, truly world-altering information.

I have so many questions, the biggest of which is: How? Keeping a secret like this is a monumental task, especially given how hungry the press are to know anything about royal lives. Then again, I have seen firsthand how much a royal family can accomplish if they set their minds to something. If keeping his son a secret is what he wanted, then Alexander and his family certainly have the power and wealth to have done so.

"I kept him a secret because of his late mother's wishes," continues Alexander. "We knew we would have to tell him eventually, but it was decided seventeen would be old enough for him to fulfill her desire for him to have a normal childhood. Today is his seventeenth birthday, and he has just learned of his connection to the throne."

Wait, the boy didn't know he was royal? I want to ask more about that, but I don't want to be impolite. I can't even imagine what it would be like to be in his shoes, thinking he's perfectly normal until one day he gets surprised with this information. How can one possibly hope to handle that?

If and when this were to reach the public, there would be global repercussions. A secret American prince of Mitanor? I'm hearing about the biggest scandal of my life in real time.

"What would you like me to do?" I ask.

"I thought it would be good for him to have someone he could speak to about his new life," he says. "Someone who knows exactly what it's like to be a young prince. All I ask is that I give him your details. He can decide if he wants to reach out. What do you say?"

I feel like I'm on shaky ground. I may have been a royal my whole life, but I don't know how I feel about being someone's first point of call. I struggle with this side of my life sometimes: the pressure and expectations and the number of rules I must follow. I'm not sure I'm the right person to be anyone's royal mentor.

Someone like Stefan would be perfect. Someone who has adjusted to royalty with effortless ease. I try my hardest, but it's not without effort.

Then again, this is a request from a king. I basically have no choice.

"I'll do it," I say.

"Excellent," says Alexander. "I will pass on the word. Thank you, Erik. I won't forget this."

The call ends.

I glance at my brother as the information sinks in.

Alexander has a second son.

And he's *American*.

Chapter Five

JAMIE

Dearest Jamie,

First of all, happy birthday. I hope you have had an excellent day and have been spoiled in every way. It's what you deserve.

I cannot express how difficult it is for me to put this into words, and how long I have waited for this day to arrive. But now that it is here, I find that I'm beside myself with joy and excitement.

Over the years, your mother has given me updates on your life, and I know that you have grown into an intelligent, articulate young man who cares deeply for his friends and the world around him. I cannot be prouder of the man you have grown into, and I am overjoyed at the prospect of getting to know you now that the secret keeping us apart is no more.

I must also apologize that you are only discovering this information now. I confess, I have wished to tell you for years, but have not wanted to ignore the wishes of both Rebecca and Emilia. Thus, I kept my distance. I understand forgiveness might be too much to ask, but you have my sincerest apologies.

That said, I would like to extend an invitation to you and the rest of your family. I have been made aware that you have a short break from school coming up. I would love for you to visit Cristalia Palace, where Maria and I will be spending this summer. You would be our guests of honor, and if you would like, I could teach you what it means to be a prince of Mitanor.

One final thing: I am sure that this transition is quite a shock. If you would like to speak to someone about everything you have been going through, call this number +89 1555 322049. They'll help you.

Your father,
Alexander

I reread the email for what has to be the millionth time.

It's been around two hours since Mom broke the news, and time hasn't helped as much as I hoped it would. I'm still freaking out, but I'm slowly starting to accept that what she told me is the truth, and that I am King Alexander's son.

I'm starting to accept that I might be a prince.

I swipe across my phone screen, and load the image search I did for Alexander. A wall of pictures appears. He's classically handsome, with dark hair always neatly combed. On his cheeks is some salt-and-pepper stubble. I still can't grow anything close to a full beard, but aside from that, it's very easy to see the similarities between us. Our faces have a nearly identical shape and our eyes are the same shade of light brown.

Putting us side by side, there's no missing that we're related. In fact, if I swept my hair back and wore a fine suit, I'd look just like him from around twenty years ago, back when he was a prince.

A knock sounds on my window, startling me out of my thoughts. I get up from my computer chair and pull open the window, letting Max inside. It took me a little while to get my bearings, but now that time has passed, I've decided I really need to see Max and talk to her.

Silently, I pull her into a hug. She squeezes me back.

"Are you moving?" she asks.

I shake my head. How does one even start a conversation like this? Like, hi, Max, remember that thing that Mom wanted to talk to me about? Well, apparently, I'm a freaking prince of a small European country. Surprise!

"What happened?" she asks.

"It's about my bio-mom," I say. "Apparently Mom has known stuff about her this whole time."

Max's mouth drops open. "Shit, really?" She sits down on my bed. "Okay, tell me everything. What did she say?"

I run a hand through my hair. I've done it so many times tonight I'm sure it's a total mess. Good thing my appearance is the least of my worries right now. "She also knows who my father is."

"All right, I'm not following. Why would she say she doesn't know anything about them?"

I don't know how to say the words. I need more time, and there's still a part of me that thinks this still has to be a prank. How do I tell Max I'm a prince, that Mom lied to me, that I have an email from a king open on my computer?

"You're freaking me out," says Max. "What's going on?"

I decide I may as well say it. "Apparently my father is the king of Mitanor."

She lifts an eyebrow. "The what now?"

"King. Of Mitanor. You know, that country near Spain?"

"Mitanor isn't the issue right now. You said your father is a king."

I get it. Max and I have spent so much time in my room, and we've talked about our true feelings on pretty much everything. It's normal for us to talk about crushes or worries about the future or the horrors of late-stage capitalism. But this conversation is so clearly different. "Yeah," I say. "That's what I'm struggling with, too."

"Holy shit," she says. "I need to sit down."

"You're already sitting."

"And you're sure this isn't a joke or something?"

"It's not, no. Look at this."

I open the image search I did for King Alexander on my phone, and hand it to her. "He looks like me, right?"

She looks at the picture, then at me. Then she lifts my phone and holds it beside my face. She switches her focus between the two of us a few times.

"Jamie," she says. "You're a *prince*."

"I think I might be."

She jumps up and lets out a little shriek. "This is amazing! I feel like I'm in a movie! And you're not moving because your mom got a new job? I was so sure it was that."

"Nope, her job's fine, as far as I know. It was just the prince thing."

"Well, phew." She picks at the bracelet on her wrist. "How are you feeling?"

"I don't think I've processed it yet."

"That makes sense," she says. "How are you even supposed to process this? Like, you're royalty!" She starts pacing a circle around my room. "What does this mean? Do you have a claim to the throne? Are you rich now?"

"I don't actually know."

"Then look it up, damn!"

She sits down beside me, pulling her phone from her pocket and googling "Mitanor royalty law of succession." She finds a Wikipedia article, and taps on it.

"Apparently you do have a claim," she says. "Were you born out of wedlock? Actually, it doesn't matter. Wait, if your dad is the king, then who's Emilia?"

"She was from a noble family, apparently," I say. "I guess Emilia wanted me to be able to make my own choices."

Max is barely listening, as she's focused on reading the rest of the article.

"Are you learning anything?" I ask.

"Yeah, a lot. Sorry, Mitanorian law is interesting. Apparently, any child with blood of the royal family has a claim to the line of succession, even if they haven't been marked as official members of the family by the monarch or the government. Most of their rules are actually quite liberal. Like, women have been able to hold the throne for nearly a century."

"You're taking this better than I thought you would," I say. "I still haven't gotten past the 'is this real' stage."

"Oh, I'm sorry," she says. "I know this must be a lot. But this is a good thing, Jamie! How many times have you told me that you wished you knew more about your bio-mom and her family?"

"So many times," I say.

"Hey, this might not be what you imagined, but it's still incredible. So, big question: Do you think you'll, like, be a prince?"

"What do you mean?"

"Will you accept your title? Princes aren't like normal people, they don't get regular pleb jobs. They're always working for the crown or doing humanitarian stuff or giving interviews on TV. Is that something you'd like?"

I have not thought anything even remotely close to that yet. I'm still getting over the fact that I now know who both my biological parents are. I think I can leave the details of my status for a later time.

"I don't know," I say.

"I do," she says. "You'd be really good at it. I know you would."

I finally start to smile. I knew talking to Max would make me feel better. But a different thought creeps into my head. One about me being a prince, like I've seen on TV. They're famous. The press always follow them everywhere, and their every move is scrutinized. What if that happens to me?

I am in no way built for that sort of attention. I get stressed every time I need to speak in class, and I agonize over every single post I make on social media. And I've been on the internet, I know how people online treat celebrities. Royals sometimes have it even worse than regular famous people. Some of the most vitriolic stuff I've seen on the internet has been aimed at royalty.

Also, I'm not supposed to be the one who becomes famous. Max is.

"Please tell me I'll be okay," I say.

She puts her arm around me. "You'll be okay."

Her confidence makes me think she might actually be right. I'm not sure what I was expecting from Max, but her excitement is slightly infectious. Like, yes, this is so out of the blue, but it's not the worst news. In a lot of ways, it's incredibly exciting.

"So, what now?" she asks. "Are you going to meet Alexander?"

"I got an email from him," I say. "Can I show you?"

"Of course!"

I open the email on my phone, and let her read.

"That's sweet," she says. "Why haven't you replied yet?"

"I haven't figured out what to say."

"Um," she says. "You're obviously going."

"Am I? We have plans this summer. I can't drop everything."

She gives me a blank stare. "Jamie. You just found out your father is a king, and he invited you to spend the summer in a palace with him. That's not something you turn down."

"But your video," I say.

"Don't worry about that," she says with a wave of her hand. "I'll get Collins to do it, it'll be fine." She's referring to Spencer—sometimes she calls him by his last name. "These are special circumstances. By the way, are you going to call that number?"

"What number?"

"The one in the email. It's fairly cryptic, right?"

Oh, yeah. That number. I am curious about it, but it's taken a back seat to everything else I've been thinking about. Then again, Alexander said whoever is on the other side of that line could help, and I could use a little guidance right now.

"Should I?" I ask.

"Up to you," she says, then she starts grinning. "Your Highness."

I groan and flop backward onto my bed.

CHAPTER SIX

ERIK

As always, Gran is waiting for me in her tea room.

For such a huge presence, both in my life and in the country, she's rail thin and only five feet two. Her hair is a bright shade of white, and she wears it short so it only reaches her ears. Around the room are vases filled with purple hydrangeas, her favorite. Today she's wearing a necklace studded with light blue jewels.

Waiting for us is a table of cream tea. The irregular shapes and sometimes inconsistent baking of the scones remind me that she took time out of her day to make something just for the two of us to share. Given how busy she always is, I know how big of a gift that is.

Gran looks up from her book, one of the mass-market paperback mysteries she loves, and her blue eyes light up. Her executive aide, Timothy, a tall, gaunt, and always brutally polite man, guided me from the entrance of the palace to here. When I was younger I used to be scared of him, given his withering stare and fondness for the rules. Other staff members would let us get away with things, but Timothy never did. He bows and makes his way out of the room, quietly closing the door behind him.

"Will you *ever* stop growing?" asks Gran.

It's always a little strange seeing Gran. On one hand, she's family. On the other, I know she is the queen, one of the most influential people in the country, one who I need to be extremely careful around. Those things constantly clash together when I see her; the desire to relax and enjoy my time with her is incompatible with the knowledge that I need to be on my guard.

She rises from her seat and kisses me on the cheek. I have to bend down so she can reach.

"Hopefully," I say.

"It's quite remarkable," she says. "Next minute, you'll be through the roof!"

She lets out a sharp burst of laughter. It makes me laugh, too. I love when she is like this. The family business can feel serious so much of the time, so a break of fun, even if it is an overdone joke, is always welcome. Like she always does when she displays too much emotion, she settles her features quickly.

"Tea?" she offers.

"Yes, please."

She pours me my tea from an ornate teacup with a pattern of blue hydrangeas, a family heirloom. She adds a splash of milk, I take a sip. It's delicious.

"I hear Alexander reached out to you about the American," says Gran.

I'm stunned, even though I shouldn't be. The call was mere minutes ago, but this is pretty typical for Gran. She tends to know everything before everyone else. It's one of the reasons she's so good at her job.

"Yes," I say. "You know about him?"

"I do. It's been a closely guarded secret for years, one only a select few know. I take it you accepted Alexander's request?"

"I did. But if I may be honest, I'm a little confused."

"By what?"

"Why did he pick me?"

"Why wouldn't he?" she asks.

"Of all people who could advise this American, why me?"

"I think that will become clear, in time," she says. "You and Jamie Johnson have quite a lot in common."

We do? I try to figure out what that could mean, and then it clicks. There is one thing that sets me apart from practically all other royals, and that's being gay. Does that mean he is as well?

And Jamie? That's his name? I like it.

"Is he . . . ?" I ask, letting the pause fill in the blank for me.

Gran lowers her gaze. "That's not for me to say."

Her nonanswer practically confirms it. At least it makes a little more sense now. Alexander reached out to me to mentor Jamie because he's gay. Who better to mentor this new prince than someone very similar to him? Someone who has experienced what it is like to be both gay and a prince.

"This is a good thing," she says. "Alexander trusting you with something this important to him is an exceptional sign. If you do this well, you will do not only yourself, but our country, proud. I take it you understand the gravity of this."

"I do," I say.

"Good," she says, her expression brightening. "I don't mean to alarm you, but as I'm sure you're aware, our relations with Mitanor have been strained as of late. You and Jamie forging a connection could be the first step toward bringing our countries back together."

The royal family of Mitanor is much more down to earth. King Alexander used to be known as the playboy prince, and he was beloved for that, even. Nothing like that would be even tolerated in my family. Our differing philosophies have long caused tension, an effect that trickles over into public sentiment. It's a dangerous thing I know Gran and my parents want to keep a close eye on.

"A royal friendship could be precisely what we need." She smiles. I'm used to this sort of thing. She's always trying to figure out ways to best use relationships to strengthen both the crown and our country. I would be a fool to disregard her ideas, as she is the most insightful and intelligent person I know.

I enjoy talking to Gran, but I don't think she knows me all that well. She doesn't know how obsessed I am with the game *Arcane Realms,* how I love swimming, or how badly I want to get the highest grades of anyone in my grade because that would be something I accomplished, not something given to me.

She doesn't know the real me. Then again, few do. I'm not even sure if *I* know who I really am, given how much I've been shaped since birth. For my entire life I've known who to be, and I've often felt like I've had to bend and twist myself in order to fit. After doing that for so long, sometimes I'm not sure how much of my genuine personality is left.

I wonder where the American is right now, how he's handling his life changing so drastically. I feel for the guy. What he's going through must be incredibly, agonizingly difficult. I've had a lifetime of preparation to face a royal life. I have no idea what it must be like to have this sprung on him out of the blue. I'm assuming it's quite the shock.

"But enough about that," she says. "I want to know about you. Tell me about school. Your mother tells me you're at the top of the class in literature."

Mum is right, and I'm glad she told Gran. Literature is my favorite class, probably because my teacher is incredible, and she has a way of turning even the oldest texts we had to study, namely *Beowulf* and *Medea,* into things I'd want to read for fun. I have spent many hours in the palace library, reading classics and taking notes.

"I still haven't gotten my grades back from finals, but I will be as long as I do well in those."

She beams. "Just like me."

"You were first in literature?"

"You expected otherwise? That and a few other subjects. History, for one, and I can't quite recall the other. It wouldn't have been mathematics; I've always been dreadful."

I smile. "Me too."

"In any case, I'm very proud of you. Are you?"

"Proud of myself?"

"Yes."

"I think so. I've worked hard, so yes, I am proud."

"Excellent," she says. "I've heard your generation is having a crisis of confidence. It's the internet. Everyone knowing everyone's business all the time is not good for anyone."

"I couldn't agree more."

"So, Erik," she says, pausing to take a sip of tea. "Have you been seeing anyone?"

The scone I was eating goes down the wrong pipe, and I cough uncontrollably. I thump my chest, clearing my airway. My eyes sting and my face feels hot. My etiquette lessons kick in and I fight with everything I have to get myself back under control.

"Sorry," I say. I scramble to figure out an appropriate response. Am I seeing anyone? No. Nate did end things with me, so I don't even have a friends-with-benefits deal happening at the moment. "No, I'm single."

"We could help if you need," she says, cutting me off before I can tell her how I enjoy being single. "Quite a few fine young gentlemen have expressed their interest in you."

"They have?" I ask.

"Why the tone of surprise? You're a prince, Erik, and a handsome one at that. You're a catch."

It's a little weird being told that by my grandma, but she means well, so I'll let it slide.

"What do you say?" she asks. "Shall I arrange some dates for you?"

"Thank you, but I'd like to focus on school at the moment."

Gran's demeanor changes, her smile vanishing. "A relation-ship is good for a man your age. It shows you can be responsible and are able to control your desires."

As her eyes meet mine, I know that she knows about Nate. Of course she does, she knows about everything. I've always tried to be careful, but I'm a prince at a private school that runs on gos-sip. All it would take is for someone to see me slipping out of his dorm room, and then it could make it back to her.

I think about telling her my thing with Nate is over, but I doubt it will make a difference.

"Reputations are a dangerous thing," she says. "You can spend a lifetime carefully crafting one; all it takes is one scandal for it to all come tumbling down. The last thing I want is for the public to turn on you."

"I don't want that, either."

"You can't forget that the public likes stability from us. They want to know we're a steady, strong hand guiding the country, putting their needs above ours. A relationship with an appropri-ate partner is one of the best ways to show them that. I believe the wedding would be a good place to introduce this new partner to the broader public. We could arrange a few appearances prior, so it's not a huge shock."

I know what she's telling me. This is happening, whether I like it or not.

She's decided it's time for me to get a boyfriend, and it has to be within the next few weeks, before the wedding.

And there's nothing I can do about it.

"I know one young man, Sebastian, who could be perfect for you. Shall I organize a meeting?"

I play my part, the one I know I have to. "Sounds good."

"Good," she says. "We're going to the king's ball in Mitanor next week. I will try to get Sebastian an invite. There's something magical about first meetings at royal balls, don't you think?"

A knock sounds. The door opens, and Timothy enters. He bows to Gran first, then to me.

"I'm sorry to intrude, but you're needed, ma'am."

"We'll have to cut this short, Erik," says Gran, already rising from her chair. "Lovely to see you, and thank you for being so agreeable."

She kisses me on the cheek, and I follow her out of the room. She goes down the hall. I watch her walk away.

In my pocket, my phone starts to vibrate. I pull it out.

I'm getting a call from an unfamiliar number.

The region code tells me the call is from America. I'm confused for a moment, then it clicks.

I'm getting a call from the American prince.

CHAPTER SEVEN

JAMIE

"Hello?"

I'm not sure what I was expecting, but the voice on the other end of the call is male and young-sounding, and has a thick accent. Probably from somewhere in Northern Europe, given the way the word has a slight tilt to it. Maybe he's Swedish? I was expecting to speak to someone from Mitanor, but he clearly isn't.

Curiosity burns within me. Who is this guy, and how can he help with my new life?

"Hi," I say. "Um, sorry if this is weird, but I got this number off my father, er, King Alexander."

Did I really just say that sentence aloud? My father, the king?

"Yes, hi," he says. He doesn't seem surprised I've called him, which makes me think that whoever this is was told to expect a call from me. "You're Jamie, right?"

"Yup, that's me. Um, no offense or anything, but Alexander didn't tell me who I was calling."

"Oh, I'm Erik," he says.

He says it as if that is enough information for me, even though it totally isn't. Is he famous or something? He said his name as if he were, like, Beyoncé or something. No further explanation needed.

"Cool. Erik, well, nice to meet you."

I wince at myself, because I know I'm not technically meeting him. We're just talking on the phone.

"Nice to meet you."

On my computer, I google "Eric royal." Nothing comes up based on that search, but it suggests an autocorrect for the spelling "Erik," which would make sense given this guy's accent. I click on that, and I nearly drop my phone.

A grid of pictures appears, all showing an absurdly handsome blond-haired, blue-eyed guy. But that's not the biggest thing—that would be the pictures of him at royal events. There are a lot of him standing by a palace. There's even a royal portrait of him staring off into the distance, wearing a blue ceremonial jacket.

I think I might be talking to Prince Erik of Sunstad.

My words bunch up in my throat. I keep looking at the pictures, and I'm totally awestruck. Now I can imagine him on the other end of the phone, and it feels staggeringly real.

"Are you still there?" he asks. "Sorry, I'm in Hjornborg Palace, the reception here is terrible."

"I'm here," I say, my voice coming out croaky. Okay, I need to keep my cool. I'm talking to a literal prince. "Sorry, I'm kinda freaking out, I've never spoken to a prince before."

"It's all right," he says, and I think I can tell he's smiling through the phone. "I must admit, I've been waiting for your call."

"You have?"

"I couldn't decide if you would take up Alexander's offer or not. The uncertainty was getting to me."

"I get that. It's like, it's always better to know one way or another, right?"

"Exactly."

I feel hyperactive. I already can't wait to tell my friends about this. It would mean I would need to tell everyone other than Max, but it would be so worth it.

"So what can I do for you?" he asks.

Oh, right. The reason I'm calling, interrupting him when I'm sure he has a lot going on.

"I'd like some advice, if that's okay?"

"Of course."

His voice sounds steady, and reassuring. It's as if I actually can tell him about all of my anxieties and stresses.

"I take it this means you've heard what happened?" I ask.

"I have," he says. "I don't know much, but I have to say that what you're going through must be intense."

"Yeah, it's been a lot," I say. "Biggest shock of my life, easily."

"I'd be surprised if you said otherwise."

"I mean, the surprise birthday my friends threw for my sixteenth comes close, but this takes the cake."

He laughs. "So, what sort of advice would you like?"

I let out a puff of air, blowing a strand of hair away from my eyes. When my hair gets this long, it's usually a sign that I need a haircut.

I glance out my window at the night sky. It's nearly 2 A.M. here. I peer out. The moon is full, so it looks much brighter than it should be. I'm struck by how strange it is that I'm here, in what by all measures is a fairly standard American suburb, speaking to a prince who is literally in a palace. Even a few hours ago if I'd been told this was what I'd be doing there's no way that I'd have believed it.

"Anything you've got," I say.

"I think you might need to be more specific. I want to help, I just need to know what you're feeling."

"I think that's the problem. I don't know what to feel."

"Talk me through it."

"Well, it still doesn't feel real. Like, even though I know it is, I keep expecting someone to tell me this whole thing is a massive prank, even though I know it's not. I keep thinking the rug is going to get pulled out from under me, if that makes sense."

"That's understandable. I can't say I've gone through this exact situation, but whenever I get a big piece of news it always takes a while for everything to feel normal again."

"You're right," I say. "I think I needed to hear that, thank you."

"You're welcome."

Talking to Erik is actually pretty easy. I can tell he's actually listening and seems to genuinely want to help, and it's making opening up way easier.

"And then there's my mom. Like, I know I shouldn't feel bad about this, but she did keep a huge secret from me. And I don't know, I can't help but be a little upset about that. Do you think that makes me a bad person?"

"Not at all. As for my advice, I think you should go easy on yourself. You shouldn't feel bad about struggling to come to terms with all aspects of this, because anyone would."

Him telling me that instantly takes some of the pressure off. He's right, it is understandable to feel the way I do. Who wouldn't? Maybe that means I don't have to try so hard to control my emotions, or to get over this faster than I really need to.

I can simply breathe, and I'll come to terms when I'm ready.

"Wow," I say. "You're totally right. It's a lot, right?"

"I think it's perfectly human to find a revelation like this difficult to process."

A different, quieter voice sounds through the phone. "Erik, your car is here."

"I'm sorry, Jamie, but I have to go. If you have anything else you would like to talk about, you can message me anytime. Okay?"

It is okay. Still, I don't want this call to end. Even though we've only spoken for a short while, he's already made me feel better. Between this and my talk with Max, I truly am starting to actually get excited. It was a shock, yes, but it's not a bad thing.

This might be the most exciting thing that has ever happened to me.

"I will," I say. "And Erik?"

"Yes?"

"Seriously, thank you. I really needed this."

"You're welcome."

I end the call, and look at my screen for a moment.

That really just happened.

As I wake up, I wonder if the entire thing was a dream.

It only takes a few seconds for me to realize yesterday was real. Mom revealed to me that I'm a prince, and I got to speak to Erik. I roll over, so I'm facing my window. Sunlight is streaming in, and my room feels hazy and warm.

Even though I barely slept last night, I'm already full of energy.

And one thing has been decided. Max was right. I was given an invite by a king. As excited as I was for my summer plans, it's not the sort of thing a person ignores. I get out of bed and quickly get dressed.

After my call with Erik, I spent a good while researching Mitanor.

At least I now know a little about the country. The flag is maroon, with a small golden crest of a roaring phoenix on the left. Population: 430,000. It's nestled between Spain and France. An image search shows beaches, coffee, and the main royal palace in the middle of the capital city, Gran Alcázar, called Marabella Palace. They also have a few other castles dotted around the country.

I go to leave my room, then stop. I've told Max, but the rest of my friends deserve to know about this. I start typing a message into our group chat.

> Hey, everyone. So I got some news yesterday I wasn't expecting, but I wanted to tell you all. Simply put, my mom told me she knows about my bio-mom's past. Long story short, my father is the king of Mitanor. So, yeah. I'm processing as best I can,

**but it was quite the shock, as you can
imagine. Also, this isn't a joke. I know
how it sounds, but it's real.**

I hit *send,* then leave my bedroom.

As I reach the kitchen, my phone buzzes. Mike is currently
making pancakes, and Mom is sitting at the kitchen island, sip-
ping a coffee.

"There he is," says Mike. "How are you holding up?"

"Well enough," I say.

My phone buzzes. Distantly, I find myself wondering if the
message will be from Erik. I doubt it, I haven't messaged him yet,
but the prospect is still incredibly exciting. I take my phone from
my pocket. It's a message from Amara.

JAMIE WTF IS THIS REAL???

A message from Ren comes in a second later.

**YOOOOOOOOOOOOOOOOOOOO
PRINCE JAMIEEEEEE WTF**

Spencer replies with a simple: **Nice!**

I get a private message from Max.

**Do you want me to pretend I'm
only finding out now?**

> **It's fine, you can tell
> them.**

"Seriously," says Mike. Like usual, he's wearing a comic-book-
inspired T-shirt. This one has Wonder Woman on it. He has maybe

the coolest job on Earth, comanaging an arcade bar called Stronghold, which he runs with his best friend. They hold game nights and serve nerdy and gaming-themed drinks, like the Princess Peach Punch or the Sonic Screwdriver. "How are you doing?"

"Good, I think," I say. "I got an email from Alexander."

Mom and Mike both stop what they were doing.

"What did he say?" asks Mom.

"He apologized for keeping the secret, and said he can't wait to get to know me. Oh, and he invited us to Mitanor. He wants us to stay with him this summer. And if it's okay with the two of you, I'd like to go."

The pair glance at each other. Honestly, Mom and Mike have the best, healthiest relationship of any adult couples I know. A lot of my friends' parents seem like they despise each other, but Mom and Mike clearly love each other so much. It also means they are a united front, and if we're going to do this, I need the go-ahead from the two of them.

"I think that's a great idea," says Mom. "But flights are expensive, especially last minute."

"What if Alexander paid for them?"

"I wouldn't feel comfortable with that," says Mom. "Leave it to me, and I'll look into it. But is this what you want?"

"It is," I say, surprising myself by how confident I sound. Flights are expensive, but I want to stand my ground. "And if Alexander volunteers to pay for the flights, I think we should let him. He's rich, it'll barely make a difference, and I don't want to miss out because we can't afford it."

"You're right," says Mom, surprising me. "I'll see what I can do."

"It's settled, then," says Mike, clapping his hands together. "We're going to Mitanor. Now, who wants pancakes?"

What he said sinks in. This is actually going to happen.

We're going to Mitanor.

CHAPTER EIGHT

ERIK

Hey, can I get some advice?

I smile at my phone. Over the past few days, I've been wondering if Jamie would message me, or if our one conversation was enough for him. Secretly, I've been hoping he would. I've found my thoughts often drifting to him, curious about what he's doing and how he's handling everything. Seeing his name on my phone is enough to make me smile.

Of course, I message back. **Ask anything you'd like.**

Currently I'm in the living room of my apartment, getting a suit tailored for King Alexander's birthday ball, which is now less than a week away. I already have a closet full of them, but given my recent growth spurt, it was decided that some alterations were needed. I'm happy to do it, because I do want to look my best, especially if I'm going to meet a guy for a date.

Sebastian agreed to the offer, and is going to meet me at the ball.

"Spin," says the tailor, a woman named Adrianne who has worked for the palace for as long as I can remember. She's not exactly friendly, and has a habit of barking orders at me, but she's so good at what she does that I find myself often not caring about that.

As she measures the back of my leg with a tape measure, my phone vibrates. Adrianne raises an eyebrow, but thankfully doesn't ask me to put my phone away. She has done that before, so I wouldn't put it past her.

> Well, I've decided to accept
> Alexander's offer, which means
> my family and I will be spending
> the rest of the summer in Mitanor.
> I'm at the airport now.

My eyebrows lift. If Jamie is on his way to Mitanor, that means that I am going to meet him in person very soon, since I, too, will be traveling there soon.

We might even become friends, and not because Gran said that friendship could be an important move politically. Jamie seems like a nice person, and I could honestly use a bigger social circle. Now that my friends-with-benefits situation with Nate has ended and he's stopped messaging me, I've found myself craving some non-family interaction. It stings when I realize I haven't planned to see anyone from school over the summer break, nor has anyone asked me to do anything with them.

My phone vibrates again.

> I'm kind of freaking out about it.
> I mean, I'm going to be staying
> at a palace and even though I've
> read as much about customs and
> stuff as I can, I'm worried I'm
> going to accidentally offend
> someone by doing the wrong
> thing. Is this a legitimate concern
> or am I overthinking?

Overthinking? Possibly. Then again, most of my family take their traditions very seriously, and if someone were to ignore them, that would cause tension. I might not agree, as I would like to think that everyone involved would extend some grace to someone who has only known they were royal for a few days, but I've been in the palace long enough to know that's not always the case. I've seen grown adults get upset with children over perceived etiquette slights. It's usually the most unpleasant, insecure people who behave that way, but if Mitanor is anything like here, those people have ways of popping up everywhere, like a fungus.

> I don't think you should be too worried. What you don't want to do is come across like an entitled tourist. As long as you're respectful, I doubt you'll cause any problems.

Cool, thanks! I mean, I'm for sure going to try my best.

> Then you'll be fine. If you have any other questions, let me know.

I will

🙂

"What are you smiling about?"

Stefan has walked into the room. I slide my phone into my pocket. I don't know why I feel like he's interrupted something private. He knows I have been tasked with giving Jamie some advice to adjust to his new life. It's not a secret.

"Were you messaging a guy?" he asks. He's dressed in a dark blue suit. He must've come from a meeting. "Tell me everything."

Does he know about the talk I had with Gran? He might. It's often hard to tell with Stefan, because he's so good in his role as the crown prince. I'd be lying if I said that I've never wished that I could have him as a protective older brother rather than a man who also must consider everything through the lens of the crown and his future as ruler of the country.

"It was Jamie," I say. Adrianne is still here, so I can't say more than that, but Stefan nods.

"Ah. So that's going well?"

"I believe so."

He crosses his arms. "That's good. I have some free time, and was wondering if you were up for a friendly fencing match? Elise said she'd like to watch."

"We're nearly done here," says Adrianne, before I can answer. "Then he's all yours."

"Half an hour?" I suggest.

Stefan grins.

The foil swings toward my head, and I only just manage to bring my blade up to block it.

The palace's fencing room is a long, window-lined hallway with timber floors that always smells faintly of sweat, no matter how rigorously the room is cleaned. Which, if it's anything like Mum's standard for the rest of the palace, means meticulously.

Across the room, Stefan's fiancée, Elise, is keeping score, and I trust her to keep things fair even though I'm up against her fiancé. She will because she's a good person. I've known that from the first moment I met her. The press often say she was born to be royal, and I can see that. She's brilliant, one of the best medical researchers in the country. In addition to her royal duties as Stefan's fiancée and future princess, which she takes incredibly seriously, she works at a university, developing preventative drugs for type 1 diabetes.

Stefan swipes at me again, coming at me from the left this time. I was expecting it, as this is a combination our shared fencing teacher taught us, so I can easily block it. I push his foil away and start to smile under my mask.

"Nice one," says Stefan.

The compliment thrills me—game on, brother.

I move backward, dodging a horizontal strike. In *Arcane Realms,* sword fighting seems easy. Just press a button on a controller, and the blade swings with ease. In reality, though, it's difficult, and the exertion already has me sweating. Stefan takes a step back and gets ready to strike again, faster than before. He wants to get the point as quickly as possible.

It's good. It means he's tiring.

He jabs his foil forward, and I manage to raise my weapon in time. I step back, making my shoes squeak on the timber floor. Stefan pushes aside my weapon then jabs his foil toward me, earning him a point. Fair play.

On a scoreboard on the wall above him, it reads 3–7 in his favor. It seems dire, but this always happens in fencing matches with him. He always comes out swinging and spends most of his energy in the opening rounds. As long as I'm defensive and bide my time, he'll tire, and the win will be mine for the taking. Elise presses the buzzer, and Stefan swipes at me from my left. I react a second too slowly, and he gets another point.

Luckily for me, Stefan isn't the type to boast. It wouldn't fit his whole "perfect prince" persona. He could, though, because it might be crude, but there's only one proper way to describe what is happening right now.

He's kicking my ass.

"Go, Erik!" cheers Elise. "Don't give up!"

We get back into position. I am going to need to try something different. He isn't tired, and only a few points are left before the match ends. I don't care about losing; I feel like the fun is in the game itself, and trying to improve my technique. Still, I don't want to go down too easy. That would not be very pleasant, especially in front of Elise. She's so perfect, and I want her to think something similar about me.

I go on the offensive, first swiping at Stefan from his left, which he blocks, then I try again from the other side. He only just manages to catch my foil before my hit connects. This is what I want. I push his foil across, opening up his side. My tutor has made me practice this move countless times so I can do it almost effortlessly. He tries to move away, but I hit his side before he can escape: 4–8. I'm in a difficult position, but a comeback is still possible. It always is.

I go on the offensive, swiping at Stefan's left and right. As I do, I get a hit in and score a point: 5–9. I start to smile.

I feel it—a shift in the tide. I can come back from this. He's breathing heavily, I can hear it even through his mask.

We both get into position, foils raised, and then he rushes forward. I block, adjusting my weight to deflect his weapon with ease. He swipes again, and I block it, then lash out. He misses, and then strikes again, and for a moment I think he's going to get me, that I've underestimated him, but I manage to block that strike as well. His attacks are frantic and messy, and even though he has the lead, I know this match is mine.

Across the room, the doors to the fencing room open, and Mum walks inside. Stefan and I both pause. Only now have I realized how worn out I am, as my arm is tired and my lungs are screaming out for air. Mum crosses the room to sit beside Elise.

The match resumes. Stefan swipes at my side, and I block. Stefan attacks again; this time, I'm too slow, too distracted, and his foil hits me on the side. It stings even through my protective clothing. I know Stefan didn't mean it, but still. Ouch.

Mum claps. I rub my shoulder. I know she would clap for me if I got a point. She doesn't play favorites. She has just given

Stefan more attention. He needs it, because one day he will sit on the throne, and it's less likely that I will.

We get back into position, and the match recommences. It might be in my head, but Stefan seems more aggressive than before and doesn't seem to be tiring like he usually does.

I burn up all my remaining energy, trying to get a point back to stay in this. We move back and forth, metal clanging, neither making any mistakes. He blocks my attacks effortlessly, and I try one last move, one I know is desperate. I lunge forward, forcing him back a step. I miss and realize too late that I've overextended myself. I'm completely open. He could win right now.

But he doesn't. He hesitates.

He's going easy on me.

I swing my foil around and get another point. And then another. I know what Stefan is doing, I can tell. He lets me win a few points, until we're even.

"You've got this, Erik!" calls Elise. She whistles so loudly that the sound bounces off the walls.

"Aren't you supposed to be on my side?" asks Stefan, good-naturedly. I feel bad for the spike of jealousy I felt before. He's a good person, and I shouldn't be jealous of him. It's a poison that I need to be careful of. It will ruin my life if I let it. One of Mum's brothers, Viggo, is jealous of her, and it's forever soured their relationship. The last thing I want is for that to happen between Stefan and me.

We start the match again, and Stefan isn't going easy this time. It catches me off guard, and with two swipes of his foil, he breaks my stance and scores a point.

He won.

I pull my mask off as Mum and Elise stand up and applaud. Stefan offers his hand to me.

"Good game," he says.

"I'll get you next time."

"We'll see about that."

"That was so exciting!" says Mum. "Erik, that was the best I've ever seen from you!"

"Thanks, I almost had him."

"Maybe all that gaming you've been doing has helped," says Stefan, giving me a playful nudge on the shoulder.

I narrow my eyes at him. Telling him about *Arcane Realms* is one of the biggest mistakes I've ever made because he loves to make fun of me for it. I don't mind too much; I know he doesn't mean it. Besides, I'm not ashamed of liking the game. It's fun, and everyone needs a hobby. I might be a little too obsessed, but oh well. At least I'm not into drugs.

I go over to the storage cabinet on the side of the room and put up my foil. I hang my helmet and turn to see that Mum has made her way to me. Everyone says she's the spitting image of her mother, and I can see that. But Mum's hair isn't white, it's a light shade of blond, and she wears it longer than Gran, so it goes past her shoulders. She also doesn't have Gran's fondness for jewelry, as the only piece she wears is her simple gold wedding ring.

"Nicely done," she says. "Could we talk?"

"Of course," I say. "Now?"

"It won't take long. Let's walk."

Something tells me this won't be good.

CHAPTER NINE

JAMIE

"Good luck!"

Max throws her arms around me and grips me tight.

I still can't believe that I'm here. I'm at the airport, about to go through the gate. Alexander did offer to pay for our flights, but Mom insisted she pay herself, so coach it is. People are bustling all around us, not giving us any attention.

I wonder if that would still be the case if people knew who I am.

Internally, I'm still freaking out. Like, massively. But I also decided it would be best to go along with things, at least for now. Otherwise, I'll completely spiral, and it feels like a good call not to do that right now.

I keep thinking about what Erik told me. It's perfectly okay that I am having a difficult time adjusting to this. I also need to remember that even though nothing feels stable at the moment, that feeling won't last forever. I need to be kind to myself, and I'll adjust when I'm ready.

The rest of my friends have all shown up to the airport to send me off. I probably would be struggling with this a lot more if I didn't have them as a safety net. I spent a good hour talking with Max last night, reviewing how I felt, trying to put it all into perspective.

"You're going to crush it over there," she says. "Don't forget, you were literally born for this."

I give Max another hug.

"This is a boarding call for flight one-eight-nine-oh-two to Castillon. All travelers, please make your way to gate fifty-two."

Max squeezes me tight. Packing this morning took longer than we thought, and even though we've checked our bags, we still need to get through security. Simply put, we really need to go.

"Seriously," she says. "You've got this."

We break apart, and I try to believe her. Mom, Mike, and I enter the line for security, which is nearly full. By the time I put my bag onto the conveyor belt, I look back up, searching for my friends.

They're gone.

This is happening.

Everything feels like it's in slow motion, because in a lot of ways, everything that's happened over the past few days has been leading up to this. My entire life has been leading up to this. Mom's reveal, the flight here, which actually wasn't that bad. All of it was to get me here.

We've arrived in Mitanor.

And it's freaking hot.

Even in the airport I can feel the humidity. It's so different from anything I've felt back at home. Big screens around the airport show advertisements for things I've never heard of. Most of them are in Mitanorian.

Mom, Mike, and I wait by the baggage carousel. On the other side of the terminal I find a sign that says WELCOME TO MITANOR. I go over and take a picture with it, and send it to the group chat. I chew my lip, then decide to send it to Erik as well. We were messaging a little on the flight, and he asked me to tell him when we land.

We collect our bags and go out the front, where there's a man with a sign that reads: JAMIE JOHNSON. It's a little weird to me that the sign has my name, not Mom's or Mike's, but I'm not mad at it.

I check my phone as we follow him outside.

Amara is the only one of my friends who has replied, with the mouth-open shocked emoji.

Erik has also replied: **Good luck!**

It warms my chest.

The driver leads us to a limo, and opens the door for me.

"Where are we going?" asks Mike.

"Cristalia Palace," says the driver. "The king is expecting you."

Yup, that's a palace.

I'm not sure what I was expecting. Like, yeah, I knew I would be staying in a palace when I visited my father. Now that it's right in front of me, it's an entirely different story, and I'm having difficulty comprehending what I'm looking at.

It's a *palace*. It's an enormous, grand building, set on a sprawling estate in the northern Palmar region of Mitanor that the Mortenallo family, *my* family, has owned for hundreds of years. This region of the country, which I saw on the drive here, is gobsmackingly gorgeous, with rolling hills and green fields and a spectacular view of the mountains in the distance.

The palace almost feels like it's in its own world, separate from everything else. It's called Cristalia Palace, one of four summer palaces Alexander and his family own. Immaculately kept gardens surround the main structure. The cream-colored building itself is pleasingly symmetrical, a stunning piece of architecture, maybe the coolest-looking building I've ever seen.

Actually, there's no contest. This wins.

Cristalia Palace was about a half-hour drive from the airport, and I've spent the time it took to travel here trying to cram as much as I could about my father and his family's history.

Some of it sounded like a real-life version of *Game of Thrones,* with backstabbing, betrayals, and executions. But after Isabella Mortenallo outlived her jealous, unfaithful husband and took the throne nearly two hundred years ago, the family has remained a strong and steady presence in the country, one seemingly beloved by the populace, especially after they took a step back from politics around fifty years ago.

I've also done a lot of reading about Emilia's family. The Alcaron family has a history that's closely tied to the Mortenallo family. They come from old, old money. A few members, including Emilia's parents, are still alive. I hope I'll get to meet them.

A man in a maroon uniform pulls the limo door open for me, and I look up at the looming palace. It's at least three stories high, with towers reaching into the sky. Above the entrance is a metallic coat of arms, one of a roaring phoenix holding a blade and a book. I know from my research it's the symbol representing the royal family of Mitanor. The same can be found on the top left of the country's flag.

I realize who is waiting for me inside this grand building. My father. I'm about to meet him. And honestly, I am not feeling great about my looks right now, not after an eight-hour flight and this humidity.

I'm sure that's the nerves talking, though.

"What do you think?" asks Mom.

"It'll do," I say.

She laughs as we go up the steps and head inside. And again, wow. The floor of the entrance foyer is black-and-white marble in a mosaic pattern, and hanging from the ceiling is a chandelier so grand I simply have to take a picture of it with my phone, even if it does make me feel like a massive tourist. Detailed statues, one of a past king and one of a queen, stand at the sides of the room. Red columns made of polished stone hold up the second level, where a balcony looks down on us. I glance at Mom and Mike; they seem just as amazed as I am.

This is *majestic*.

I know this is a significant life change, and I'm not sure I've fully adjusted to it. But this is also pretty freaking cool. If you had told me two weeks ago that soon I would be inside a palace, about to meet a king, I never would've believed you. Yet, here I am. I don't want to let any uncertainty or negative thoughts ruin that.

Plus, I did want to push myself out of my comfort zone this summer. What's more out of my comfort zone than this?

"This way," says the driver. "His Majesty King Alexander, Her Majesty Queen Maria, and His Royal Highness Prince Tomas are meeting you in the Green Room."

"Say that three times fast," whispers Mike.

The driver leads us through the palace, and it takes all my willpower not to slow down so that I can take it all in. This is easily the nicest building I've ever been in. Every inch of it is well-thought-out and gorgeous to look at. And we get to stay here?

We reach the end of a long hallway with portraits hanging on the walls, and the driver opens a door for us. It's a magnificent stateroom with green walls adorned with golden embellishments. To one side is a towering portrait of a medieval queen, her expression mischievous, as if she's amused by everything before her.

Standing near the back of the room is a trio of people. It's Alexander, his wife, Maria, and my half brother, Tomas.

Alexander looks like the pictures I've seen of him online. He's tall, dressed in a dark suit, with his hair neatly combed back and his cheeks lined with clearly maintained salt-and-pepper stubble.

How do I talk to him? Should I bow? I am still trying to figure out what to do. And what will he think of me? I'm not ready for this. I need some time to prepare, maybe shower and clean myself up, then I can meet him. I know what Max would tell me. That I'm enough, and I can do this. It gives me a boost of confidence. I can do this; all I need to be is myself. That's enough.

Alexander glances across and sees me for the first time.

The first thing he does is smile warmly at me. I smile back and start walking toward him.

I hope Alexander doesn't judge me too harshly, seeing as I'm not at my best. I wish I had a chance to make a stronger first impression.

As I reach him I see there are tears welling in his eyes. My palms have started to sweat, so I wipe them on the back of my jeans.

I bow, in the way I read online was customary. "Your Majesty," I say.

He returns the bow. I know from reading online that as king, he doesn't have to, and I should take it as a sign of utmost respect that he did.

"Jamie," he says. "My son."

And then he's hugging me, and all my stresses go out the window. This is my father, and he is hugging me. That's all that really matters. I hug him back. We end the hug, and I find myself teary as well. I wipe at my eye with the back of my hand. I'm only realizing now how much I've wanted a hug like that. It's as if I've been waiting for it my whole life.

"I'm glad to see you're emotional, like I am," he says, as he wipes away a tear. He has a thick, musical accent and speaks as if English is his second language, which I'm assuming it must be. "How was the flight?"

"Long," I say.

"Next time, you'll have to take the jet. It's much more comfortable."

"I bet."

Behind him, Maria clears her throat.

"Ah, excuse me," says Alexander. "Jamie, I would like you to meet my wife, Maria, and my son Tomas. We are all so excited to meet you."

I shake Maria's hand. She looks every bit as regal as Alexander. Her hair is long and jet black, and her dark red designer suit is effortlessly stylish.

"I've heard so much about you," she says. "And I'm sure this is a lot for you to process, but you must know how excited we all are to get to know you."

"I'm excited about that, too."

Tomas has shaggy black hair, and his suit hangs off his lean frame, but he holds himself with the exceptional poise and posture fitting of a prince. Like Alexander, he looks like me, only his face is a little thinner and he clearly works out more than I do.

"I've always wanted a brother," he says. "May we hug?"

I nod, and he hugs me tightly.

"I'm already jealous you're taller than me," he says. "And your teeth, they're so white."

"I use whitening strips," I say. "And I'm jealous of your posture."

"I work on it," he says, grinning.

Behind us, Mike clears his throat.

"Oh, sorry!" I say. "Everyone, this is my mom, Rebecca, and my stepdad, Mike."

I wonder if Alexander is upset with Mom at all for her decision to follow through with Emilia's request. If I were in his position, I probably would be.

"Thank you for inviting us here," says Mom.

"Of course. As much as I would love to speak with each of you, I'm sure you're weary from your travels. I have set aside the prime minister's apartment for the three of you, if you would like me to take you there?"

They all look to me for an answer. A shower beckons. As much as I want to get to know all three of them, I would love to do it when I'm more refreshed.

"Sounds good to me," I say.

Alexander places his hand on my shoulder. "It must be said, I am overjoyed to meet you, my son."

Something snags in my chest. I don't think he's saying this to be polite, or for any other reason that I can think of. I think he truly means it.

"I'm overjoyed to meet you, too," I say.

He gives me another shoulder squeeze. "You're very polite, that's good. Follow me."

We leave the stateroom, and start walking down a hallway. I pass by a suit of medieval armor, the metal so polished it's reflective.

"While you're here," Alexander continues, "the entire palace is open to you. Cristalia is a private residence, which means no members of the public are allowed here, so you may travel wherever you would like. On your floor, you'll find a gym, a pool, and a movie theater, which you may use at any time. Please, make yourself at home."

The floors are covered in crimson carpet and the walls are the color of cream. We reach the central atrium and go up the grand polished marble staircase, then take the hall to the left. The place is airy and still, and everything from the gilded gold picture frames to crystals on the chandelier is faultless. Each room seems more wondrous than the last.

This feels like it's going reasonably well. I have met Alexander, and Maria and Tomas. And they seem nice. I think maybe a part of me was worried they'd look down on me: they'd judge my clothes or my shoes. It dawns on me that I met a king wearing a pair of Converse.

I remember Alexander tearing up, and what he called me. *My son.*

I thought that was a title I needed to earn. One he would only use when he knew I was deserving of it. To find out that it's not, that it's something he's willing to call me even without knowing much about me, is actually extremely nice. I am his son. It's who I am. I keep glancing around, taking it all in. I can't believe anyone actually lives here.

Alexander stops in front of a closed door.

"I'll let you do the honors," he says, as he hands me a key card. I take it, and tap the key against the panel. The door opens with a click.

Inside it's like a private version of the stateroom we were in earlier. The walls are a mixture of whites and golds, with intricate details around the edges. There's even a pearlescent white piano in the corner by a window that looks out at the palace lawns.

"What do you think?" asks Maria.

"I love it," I say. I'm not even sure that does it justice. Never in my life, not even once, did I think I would get to stay in a place this nice. I did think, and still do, that Max will make it big, but I've always known that was really her path, not mine. I would just be there for the ride. She could reach heights like this, but I always thought my life would be a lot more, well, normal.

"That's great. Now, there is one last thing you should know. My birthday ball is this weekend," Alexander says. "You are of course invited, but I understand if you would prefer to not attend."

I feel my mouth drop open as I envision it. I was invited to a royal ball. Slightly terrifying, yes, but also . . .

"Is that safe?" asks Mom. "Nobody knows who he is."

"And you two do look alike," says Mike.

"The decision is yours," says Alexander. "If you are worried, we could arrange a table near the back of the ballroom. I'm sure it will be fine. I understand the risks, but I must say, nothing would make me happier than if you decide to attend."

He looks to me.

"Sounds great," I say.

"Excellent," he says.

A problem crosses my mind. I did pack, but I didn't think to bring the one suit I own, the one I wore to last year's homecoming.

"I don't have an outfit, though," I say.

His eyes sparkle. "Don't worry, I'll have some suits sent to you. We should have some in your size. If not, we can have them tailored. I won't have any son of mine not looking his best. All right. I'll leave you all to it. Enjoy your rest, and I'll see you soon."

"Nice to meet you," says Maria. "Rest well."

As soon as they're gone, I realize what I just did. I said yes. To attend a royal ball.

"He seems nice," says Mike. "Not as big of a snobby asshole as I was expecting."

Mom swats at him. Then she turns to me.

"How are you feeling?" she asks.

"Good, I think," I say. "I mean, it's still so much for me to process. But they all seem really nice."

"You don't think going to a ball is a little sudden?" she asks.

I shake my head. "I want to get to know him. This is his world, and I want to see what it's like."

"I'm proud of you," says Mom. "You're handling this all so well."

"You really are," says Mike. "You know, kid, we'd understand if you are struggling with this. It is a *lot*."

"I'm fine," I say. "I'm just tired. I really want a shower, and to call Max and tell her everything."

"All right," says Mom. "I think we've been through enough for one day, so let's get some rest."

She lingers for a moment. I know what she wants, and it's for me to tell her I've forgiven her for keeping this secret from me. I want to do that, too, but I'm not sure I'm ready to yet, and I don't want to say anything before I truly feel it. That wouldn't be fair to either of us.

I go into the second bedroom instead. A large four-poster bed sits in the middle of the room, surrounded by old-fashioned fur-niture embellished with reds and golds. My suitcase has been left in the corner of the room, by a wooden writing desk that's facing a window. Honestly, it looks exactly how I'd imagine a palace bedroom. The only thing out of place here is me. I take out my phone and message the group chat.

> I just met Alexander, Tomas, and
> Maria. It went well! They seem really
> nice. Oh, and he invited me to a ball!
> I'm not even joking—what is my life??

I hit *send* and go into the bathroom. The tiles are a soft golden color. I strip off my clothes and step into the shower. The water heats up instantly, and the water pressure is glorious. I tilt my head down and let the water run over my face. I start to smile.

This has been, without a doubt, the strangest day of my life. It's been so wild that it doesn't feel real. But this *is* real, and it's happening. My biological father is the king of Mitanor. I'm here to get to know him. I'm not the ordinary guy I thought I was.

Even if it doesn't feel like it yet, I was wrong before when I thought about being out of place.

I belong here.

Chapter Ten

ERIK

Mum and I reach the palace gardens.

This is one of my favorite places in the world. Various small trees and lawns form a pattern surrounding a pond, with a stone statue of Queen Kristina, the first queen of Sunstad, in the middle. From above, it creates a spectacular pattern. It's as if every inch of this garden has been meticulously designed. Nothing is out of place, everything is exactly where it should be.

I'm still not sure what Mum wants to talk to me about. I'm sure it's nothing bad, but it does make me anxious.

"I heard about your talk with Gran," says Mum. "I wanted to know how you feel about it."

I chew my lip. I can be honest with Mum, but it's always a fine thread to weave. I know she is a part of this system as much as I am, and we both know how it works. When Gran tells you to do something, you do it. No questions asked.

Still, I know I can at least be honest with Mum about how I feel. It's no secret that, even with all our power and privilege, our lives can be complicated, and that we need to deal with things that nonroyals don't. We all know we are incredibly fortunate, as we never have to struggle for money like so many do, but we also know that having wealth and power doesn't mean life will always be smooth sailing. Very few people represent the country they live in on a global scale. We do. I keep that in mind every time I speak, every time I do anything. It's a lot of pressure, and it can easily break people.

How do I feel about it? She told me it's time for me to get a boyfriend. I saw Stefan go through something similar, but there was a part of me that thought I would be less controlled.

"I was surprised," I say.

"How so?"

"I didn't think people cared about who I date."

"Why is that?"

"I thought being the spare, or being queer, made me different." She laughs. "In that order?"

"Yes."

She smiles at that. "Unfortunately not. Second-borns are far from spares, and nobody at the palace has ever had problems with you being who you are."

She means it. Sunstad was one of the first countries to legalize same-sex marriage, and the public has always been very open and supportive. Of course, some are against it, but they're generally considered extreme. For most people in Sunstad, being LGBTQ+ is normal.

Even so, I am the first person in the centuries-long history of my family to come out. I'm sure I'm not the only one; there's no way I'm the first in my family who identifies as anything other than cis and straight. But the royal rules of the time meant my ancestors weren't allowed to discuss it. I'm lucky times have changed.

"I know," I say. "I wish I could pick my partner. It feels old-fashioned that she wants to pick someone for me."

"I felt the same way when I was your age when I first understood that my choice of partner wasn't as easy as simply finding someone I liked. As royals we don't have that luxury."

Mum and Dad met after Gran and her late husband arranged a date. I think they do work together. Still, to me, there's always been something a little off about their relationship. It's only subtle, and I do think they love each other. It's just they're not a perfect fit, at least in my eyes. I've long felt the missing component was that they didn't choose each other: that decision was made for them, and they made it work.

I think it's that they don't really seem like friends. Their interests rarely line up, and they generally don't spend much time together. When they do, it's usually because they're working on a project together. I appreciate that it works for them, but I have never wanted a relationship like that. Maybe it's asking for too much, but I want my partner to feel like my best friend.

"If everyone feels bad about the way things are," I say, "why don't we change it?"

She pulls a leaf from a small peach tree as we pass it. "Because the alternative is worse. I'm sure you've seen stories from abroad, of the way some royals are treated when the public doesn't approve of their partners. They can be vicious."

She's right, I have seen that. The thought of the same thing happening to me makes me shiver.

"You must remember that Gran is only trying to protect you," she continues. "You know she has a soft spot for you."

"What do you think I should do?" I ask. "I'm not sure I could ever fall for someone if I'm forced to."

"Nobody is forcing you," she says. "It's a suggestion coming from someone who knows how this world works. If you want my advice, I think you should try it out. I hear one boy has been invited to the ball in Mitanor. I say you meet him, and see how it goes."

"What if I don't like him?"

"Then you don't like him. I would remember that you're young, and we've been doing this for a long time, and only have your best interests at heart. All you can do is try," she says. "That's all we ask."

I'm not so sure that's true. Even if she says I'm not being forced, I can still feel the pressure. That's how it works in my family.

We walk back into the palace and go to our apartment. It's split over two levels, and is big enough to be a house. Kevin, our golden dachshund, comes up and greets me. I give him a few scratches on his head and he rolls over, waiting for belly rubs. I scratch the spot he likes, but then he gets up and sprints to the kitchen where Mum has just opened the fridge. He's clearly hoping she'll give him a little piece of whatever she's making. Kevin clearly loves us all, but I don't think he loves anything as much as he loves food. Which is fair enough.

The apartment is quiet, which I assume means Dad is out of the house. Dad goes through hobbies rather quickly, and right now his obsession is carriage racing. I would be willing to bet he's down in the shed, restoring an antique carriage he bought a few weeks ago. I've visited him a few times, and the progress he and his team have made is incredible. He's given it a new coat of paint and a fresh set of wheels, and the carriage, which was on its last legs when he bought it, is now in good enough shape to race.

When I get to my bedroom, I drop backward onto my bed. I'm sweaty and should probably shower, but I can't be bothered now. The palace tends to trap air, and it's incredibly hot and stuffy in here. It's made worse by the lack of any fans.

I think about Sebastian. Maybe Mum is right. I should at least try. I roll onto my stomach, grab my phone, and go to Instagram to look him up.

He's got pitch-black hair and clear skin and a nice smile. He's actually really handsome, the kind of guy I would do a double take at if I saw him on the street. That, combined with his excellent fashion sense, combined with skill at taking photos of himself, has netted him twenty-five thousand Instagram followers. A quick Google search reveals he's the grandson of the mayor of

Solheim: Paul Kragh. That makes sense why Gran would think he's an appropriate choice. I'm sure he's been trained as to how to live in the public eye as thoroughly as I have.

There are definitely worse things I can think of than being forced to be in a relationship with a guy like Sebastian Kragh. I tap on a picture of him posing in front of a waterfall. The caption reads: **take a photo of me or I'm going to lose my shit.**

It's clearly a joke, and it makes me smile.

Maybe this isn't a bad thing.

I might actually enjoy this.

Chapter Eleven

JAMIE

"Jamie!" calls Mom through my door. "What are you doing in there?"

"Nothing," I shout back.

Given the big royal reveal that took place, the past couple of days have been somewhat relaxed. I haven't spent much time with Alexander, or Maria or Tomas. They've all been busy preparing for the ball, and I think Alexander has wanted to give us some space to adjust to palace life.

Still, I've had dinner with them once, and it was nice. Yes, it was a little tense and slightly awkward, as it was clear we were all on our best behavior, but at least we were all trying. I'm sure it will feel more natural soon.

Right now I'm in my bedroom with the door closed, getting ready for the ball. Luckily one of the suits Alexander has sent to our apartment fit me perfectly, and I'm wearing it now. It's made of soft black material, and I'm wearing it over a white shirt. The plan is for me to complete the outfit with a black tie with a faint floral pattern that matches the embellishments on the sleeves of the suit, but there's one problem. I can't figure out how to put it on.

For what must be the twentieth time, I try to tie my tie, and fail.

"We need to go," calls Mom.

I know that already. The ball has started.

I leave the room with my tie hanging loosely around my neck.

"Need some help?" asks Mom.

"Yes, please."

She ties the tie for me, and then I push it up against my neck. On the kitchen table is a packet of Corellos, a chocolate cookie that is apparently Mitanor's pride and joy. Seeing as every time I have one I have to fight the urge to finish the packet, it's easy to see why. I grab another and shove it in my mouth.

"How do I look?" I ask, giving them a little spin.

"You're so handsome," says Mom.

"Aw, thanks," I say. "You look amazing, too."

She really does; she maybe looks the best I've ever seen her. Her navy dress wouldn't look out of place on a red carpet. Also, she's had her hair done by a stylist from the palace, so it's now in a tower of dark brown curls above her head.

"What about me?" asks Mike, putting on a fake scowl.

"You're stunning," I say. He pretends to flick his hair like he's in a shampoo commercial, which obviously doesn't work as he's nearly completely bald.

"Shall we?"

"One second," I say. I duck into the bathroom and try to fix my hair. It's undeniable that I'm having a bad day, and no matter what I try, I can't get my hair to sit right. It's still way too long, and I fear no amount of product will be enough to get it to sit straight.

"We need to go," calls Mom.

"Fine!" I shout back. I give up on my hair and leave the bathroom. "Let's go."

With that, we leave our apartment.

As we pass by a portrait of a glaring queen, my phone buzzes. It's a message from Max, in response to a selfie I sent earlier when I first tried on the suit.

You're so ridiculously hot I can't handle it.

I respond with a heart. I've missed her so much these past few days. We have kept messaging, but it's not the same as it is back home. Usually, she responds to my messages within a few seconds. Now, hours pass. I know it's just the time zones, but I miss feeling like I could rely on a near-instant response from her.

I look up from my phone, and found we've reached the ballroom. Even from this hall, I can hear the sounds coming from inside, through a grand set of doors. There must be hundreds of people in there.

Plus, Erik will be here. He messaged saying he'd be going.

Before I can chicken out, two royal aides open the doors.

My breath catches. What stretches out before me is one of the most magnificent things I have ever seen. People dressed in shimmering pastel ball gowns or ink-black suits fill the enormous space, having what appears to be the time of their lives. Bowls overflowing with red flowers hang from the ceiling, and golden light comes from a vast chandelier that covers a gleaming marble dance floor.

Even though the ballroom is huge, there are so many people here that it seems like there isn't much space to move. Waiters in tuxedos duck in and out of the party, carrying silver trays. I feel more aligned with them than I do with any of the guests. Those are my people.

Like, seriously. There is a couple currently on the dance floor who it seems nobody can take their eyes off. He is tall and blond and handsome, and she is maybe the most gorgeous woman I've ever seen. She wears her hair in long braids, and is wearing a brilliant emerald-green dress that sparkles every time she moves. Wait, I think I know them. That's Stefan and Elise: Erik's older brother and his fiancée.

Does that mean he's here already?

I spot an elderly couple watching me from the back of the ballroom. Why are they looking at me? I thought nobody knew who I am. Still, neither one of them is taking their eyes off of me. It seems as if the woman is on the verge of tears.

"What's wrong?" asks Mike.

The man beckons me. "I think those two know who I am," I say.

"Should we find out?" asks Mike. "We're with you, bud."

I approach their table. Nobody else pays us any attention, or even gives us a second look. I get it. Even though I love how I look in this suit, everyone here is exceptionally well dressed. Even looking the best I ever have, I blend in. There has to be a reason they've noticed me.

We approach the table.

"Hi," I say.

"You look just like her," says the woman, her voice thick with emotion. "My Emilia."

It dawns on me. These two are my grandparents.

I'm not exactly sure how to process that. At dinner last night Alexander did say there was going to be a surprise for me at the ball. Is this what he meant? Looking at the two of them, I'm sure of it.

This is a lot to handle, and I don't feel prepared.

"Alexander told us you'd be here," she says. "Did he not tell you?"

"I think he wanted it to be a surprise," I say.

And it is. It's a good one, too. I just don't feel ready. In fact, I don't feel ready for any of this. At this point I'm so far away from my comfort zone that it's just a speck on the horizon.

"I'm sorry," she says. "I hate to have startled you."

"You haven't, it's fine."

"Would you like to sit?" she asks. "I'd love to talk to you about your mother."

This is all extremely overwhelming, but I sit down.

"We'll give you two some space," says Mom, and she and Mike link arms and go toward the dance floor.

"It's wonderful to meet you," says the woman. "My name is Ruth, and this is Octavio. We're Emilia's parents."

Everything catches up to me and I start to feel lightheaded. I'm in a ballroom, and my grandparents are right in front of me. This is all too much. I'm starting to freak out. I think I might be on the verge of a panic attack. I don't want to meet them like this. I want to make a good first impression. I just wasn't expecting this, and it's bringing up emotions I'm in no way ready to deal with. I take a breath, and try to think what Max would tell me to do in this moment. She would say I should ask to be excused, so I can get my bearings, and return when I'm ready.

"I'm sorry," I say. "I'd love to talk to you, I really would, but may I be excused for a moment? I don't feel good."

"Oh, of course, honey," she says, smiling kindly. "We'll be here when you're ready."

"I'm really sorry."

"Don't be, I'm sure this is all very overwhelming. Please, take your time, we aren't going anywhere."

It makes me feel a little better about leaving them. But I know this is the right thing to do. I need my emotions to settle, and then I can properly meet them.

On the other side of the ballroom is an open door. I walk as fast as I can toward it, and go outside. There are dozens of orange trees out here, spaced amongst flawless gardens. Still, there are too many people. I keep my head down, and follow a stone path that leads away from the palace.

Up ahead, there's a white gazebo. It's empty.

Perfect.

Chapter Twelve

Erik

We've just arrived, and the ballroom is already crowded.

Even though I've been to countless royal balls, this is an undeniably impressive spectacle.

The tables spaced around the ballroom are all beautifully decorated, and there is a sense that the Mortenallos have pulled out all the stops. They've gone for a traditional Mitanorian theme, so the color scheme is red and gold and applies to everything: from the floral centerpieces on the tables to the long, flowing banners hanging from the walls.

There's even a large ice sculpture near the back of the room in the shape of a roaring phoenix, its wings outstretched. It's guarded by not one but two red-clad guards. During a ball a few years ago, an actor who was attending drunk-crashed into an ice sculpture, and they haven't been invited to a ball in any country since.

People in ball gowns and dark suits are spinning around on the dance floor to the music from the band located on a stage near the back. Waiters and waitresses in black move around the edges of the party, holding trays with hors d'oeuvres and flutes of champagne.

I stand up straighter and unbutton my jacket, keeping an eye out for either Jamie or Sebastian. As fun as these are, I can't truly relax tonight. The way people behave at balls like this is often talked about for years afterward. This community reminds me a lot of high school, and often feels less mature, if you could believe. If someone makes a fool of themselves by doing something, it will become what defines them.

Mum turns around. It's just Mum, Dad, and me, as Stefan and Elise arrived earlier.

"Remember," she says. "Best behavior tonight."

"I'll try my best not to set anyone on fire," I say, grinning. "But I make no promises."

We move forward. The palace ballroom is split over two levels, with an upper level leading to a balcony. The space is already nearly filled.

"Welcome," says a man in a black tuxedo who has been slowly letting people onto the dance floor. He's holding a tray with flutes of champagne housed in delicate glasses. Both Mum and Dad take one. I don't drink, I don't like the thought of giving up control, but now I wish I could. I am strangely nervous about meeting both Sebastian and Jamie. The former because he might become my first official boyfriend, and the latter because I don't want to let him down as a mentor.

"Follow me," says the man. "Your table is upstairs."

As a group, we follow him across the dance floor. There's a curved staircase on the side of the ballroom. As we climb it, Stefan falls into step with me.

"Excited to meet Sebastian?" he asks.

"I am, actually," I say.

"Don't screw it up," he says, giving me a light nudge.

"Thanks for the vote of confidence."

He winks. "You're very welcome."

We reach our table, which is right near the stage. On it is a full orchestra currently playing a slow classical song. It's undeniably impressive, but this type of music has never really been my thing.

I take the seat with my name on it, and I feel someone watching me. I turn around, and there he is.

Sebastian.

He's sitting at a round table on the other side of the ballroom. His eyes lock onto mine, and his lips curve into a small smile. He tilts his head toward the balcony. I nod, and he gets up from his chair.

All right. That means this is happening right now.

"May I be excused?" I ask Mum. "I'm going to introduce myself to Sebastian."

"You may," says Mum. "Though don't be too long."

"I won't," I say.

"Good luck," says Stefan.

I stand and head toward the balcony. I wonder where Jamie is, and why I haven't seen him yet. I hope I get to. I've enjoyed his messages, and I really do think we could be friends. I've also enjoyed giving him advice, and would be more than happy to keep doing that. If he wanted, of course.

From here, there's a truly grand view of the palace greens and the mountains in the distance. The sun is just setting, so the sky is a spectacular display of oranges and yellows.

Leaning against the railing is Sebastian. He's wearing a black suit tailored to perfection, and his dark hair has been swept back instead of pushed forward as it is in most of his pictures online. It accentuates his cheekbones and brings out the intensity of his eyes. He pushes off the railing and gives me another smile. My stomach does a little flip. He looks just like he did in his Instagram photos. Better, maybe.

"Hi," he says. "You look great."

"So do you."

He's wearing a silver ring on his index finger. A fashion statement, but it suits him. It's hard to imagine anything that wouldn't, though.

"Having fun so far?" I ask.

"So much," he says darkly. "If I'm being honest, I hate these things. All the posturing and the pretense is a little exhausting, don't you think?"

I'm taken aback. Yes, most of his captions on his posts have a sardonic wit to them, but I took them as jokes. There doesn't seem to be any wink of humor here, as I was expecting. He seems to genuinely hate being here.

"It can be, sure."

"Listen, Erik," he says. "You seem like a nice enough guy. So, I want to be honest with you. Or for us to be honest with each other."

"What do you mean?"

"I know this date wasn't your choice," he says, putting air quotes around the word "date." "It wasn't mine, either."

"I know, but that doesn't mean we can't get to know each other, does it?"

"Right," he says. "But the thing is, I went down this road last year. My parents picked someone for me, and I think it hurt us that we weren't honest about the reason we were dating."

"And that was?"

"To boost our profiles," he says. "I want to be prime minister one day, and if my grandfather has taught me anything, it's that every moment counts. Every relationship counts."

"Romantic," I say.

"Please, love is for children. We're both adults, are we not? This is how the world works for people like us."

I don't know what to say. I do know that relationships often are used by people in the public eye for a variety of reasons. I don't agree that love is for children. I don't agree that this is how the world works. For some, yes. And it might work really well for them. But I have never wanted that.

"Aw, you're a romantic," he says. "That's sweet. But listen, I need to be honest with you. Apparently, us dating will not only be great for me, but it'll also be fantastic for dear old Grandfather's reelection campaign. And you must be getting something out of it. Or your family is. Doesn't matter, really."

"Right," I say.

"All I ask is that we treat this as what it is. I'm doing you a favor, and you're doing one for me. I see no reason we should pretend it's anything other than that right from the start."

My face falls.

"Come on, Erik," he says. "Do you really think you could fall for someone your grandmother chose for you?"

I blink for a moment, stunned. I'm not enjoying this, and I wish I could end the conversation and just leave. But his words have reminded me that he's right, Gran did pick him for me. And that holds weight in this family. I know the expectation will be to date him.

So that's what I'm going to do.

Gran has said she wants me to have a partner by the time of Stefan and Elise's wedding. Which means if I turn down Sebastian, they will make me try again, and keep trying until I accept someone. As much as I disagree with Sebastian, at least he's being clear with me about what this is.

"Okay," I say. "You're right." I swallow hard. It feels like I'm forcing down everything I feel so I am able to contain it. I need to get this to a level that I can at least tolerate.

I can't see any other choice. Gran will be disappointed if she finds out I have rejected Sebastian.

"Thank you for being honest with me," I say. "You're right, we should be honest with each other."

He taps his knuckles against the railing. "Great. Boyfriends?"

"Boyfriends."

"Excellent. Our grandparents are going to be so pleased. I'll send you an email later with all the details. Sound good?" He claps me on the shoulder before heading back inside.

I decide to stay outside for a while, to try to process. I now have my first-ever boyfriend. And it doesn't feel anything like I hoped it would. There are no butterflies or sparks or much of anything other than cold uncertainty. But I know I'm making the right choice. It's what we do in my family. We do what we're told, even if it costs us personally. I've seen my parents do it. Now it's my turn. I might not like it very much, but it's simply the way things are done.

I start to accept that, and go inside, making sure my expression is stoic and unreadable.

I walk past my family. I don't want to talk to them right now. I go back down the stairs and then out the side doors. A few people have gathered on the steps leading into this section of the palace gardens, which have been lit by golden lights. In the far distance, I see a gazebo, which seems empty.

When I get there, I pause. Someone else has had the same idea I did. It's a guy, with messy light brown hair, wearing a dark suit. He's holding his head in his hands as if he is in the middle of a panic attack or some serious thought, so I can't quite make out his face.

Then he lowers his hands, and I see it's Jamie.

I can't believe he's here, and I'm meeting him like this. He looks up, and his eyes widen at the sight of me. Clearly, he was deep in thought when I interrupted him. I'd never be allowed to sit like he is, with his legs splayed. Actually, he is breaking almost every etiquette rule. His hair is also, quite frankly, a mess. He could've used a haircut weeks ago, as it's clearly been left to grow.

It suits him, though.

He sits up, and his eyebrows furrow. "Erik?"

"Hi," I say. I step up into the gazebo. He glances at me warily, and I'm worried for a moment that I've overstepped. Yes, we've been talking online and on the phone, but it's not like we know each other all that well.

"What are you doing here?" he asks.

"I needed some air," I say.

He frowns. "I thought this was, like, your scene."

"Not always."

He holds my stare for a moment, seemingly puzzled by me.

"Want to join?" he asks.

He pats the empty bench space beside him. I walk over and sit down.

"Is everything okay?" he asks. "You look like you're going through something."

"It's a long story. And besides, you've got enough on your plate."

He smiles. "I've got time. Come on, tell me. You've helped me so much, it's the least I can do."

I don't know what it is, but I feel safe.

I decide to tell him everything.

CHAPTER THIRTEEN

JAMIE

"Damn," I say. "Sorry, is it okay to curse in front of you?"

Erik has just finished talking, telling me how his grandma, the queen, knows about his hooking up and told him he needs to date someone. His story ended with his disastrous arranged date with Sebastian, who he apparently agreed to be with even after everything he said.

Now I totally understand why Erik looked so distressed when he first stepped up into the gazebo. He said a few times that he knows his grandma only wants the best for him, that he knows how lucky he is, but still. I can tell from the way his expression changes as he speaks, he's struggling. It's as if he's saying what he thinks he should, not how he genuinely feels. I'm not sure he's aware he's doing it.

"But enough about me," he says, his tone brightening. "What about you? What are *you* doing out here?"

Erik has been totally open with me. I should return the favor and answer honestly.

"I met my grandparents," I say. "I wasn't expecting to see them and I started having a panic attack so I left."

"A panic attack? Are you okay?"

"I'm better now," I say. "I think it all caught up to me. I thought I was doing well but guess not."

"Sorry, now I feel like I talked too much."

I laugh. "You did say it was a long story."

"I did. Still, I'm sorry."

"There's something else I'd like some advice on," I say, wanting to change the subject.

"Go ahead."

"It's about coming out. I haven't told Alexander yet, and I'm weirdly nervous about it."

"Ah, I get that."

"You don't think he'll have any issues with that or anything, will he?"

He shakes his head. "He sent me a nice message when I came out."

"So he's not a secret homophobe?"

"Not to my knowledge."

"Phew," I say. "I thought I was done with the whole coming-out thing, but then this happens."

He laughs. "Yeah, I bet you never considered coming out to your royal father."

"Actually I have, but I prepared for him to be the king of England, not Mitanor, so."

I shrug.

"If it makes you feel any better," he says, "I think Alexander already knows."

"I'm that obvious?"

"No, I mean, I think the reason he gave you my number is because I'm gay as well."

That does make sense. Plus, Mom has been filling him in on my life. She probably would've included me coming out.

"How was coming out for you?" I ask.

I realize how deep a question I've asked of someone who, up until a short while ago, was a stranger. I might feel comfort and familiarity around him, but that doesn't mean he feels the same way.

He leans back against the railing of the gazebo. "It was fine. I was terrified, but I'm still glad I did it. My family has been nothing but supportive. I was scared because it was so new, you know? Like, I thought they would be supportive but I didn't know for sure."

"Totally. I felt the same once and my mom is, like, the most liberal person ever. She always makes sure she includes as many queer books in her lesson plans as she can."

"Your mom's a teacher?"

"College professor. I'd ask what your mom does but I'm pretty sure I know."

He smiles. He has a really nice smile. Erik has sharp features, and he can look kind of stern when his face is relaxed, but when he smiles he looks way softer.

He stretches out. "I think we should probably head back inside. If I'm out here too long people will come looking."

"Oh, okay, yeah."

We go back inside. I find my grandparents sitting at the edge of the ballroom. My nerves flare once again, but it's not as bad as last time.

"I'm sorry," I say when I reach them. "I needed a moment. May I join you?"

I do, and they tell me about their lives. They tell me about how devastated they were when Emilia ran away. She left them a note, telling them she was okay but needed to live elsewhere. She filled them in occasionally, and asked that they let my mom raise me if anything happened to her, which they obliged. They told me waiting for me to turn seventeen was one of the hardest things they'd ever done, but they're glad they followed Emilia's wishes. They told me they're looking forward to spending time with me once I've adjusted to my new life. They told me the door is always open should I want to get to know them more.

They also tell me about my bio-mom. I learned so much about her—she was an adventurous child and a rule breaker. I can see why she and Mom became friends, because they both clearly have an adventurous and rebellious side.

"I think you've entertained the two of us for long enough," says Ruth, after talking for almost an hour. "It's your first royal ball. Go, have fun."

"Are you sure?"

"Yes," she says. "Enjoy yourself; nothing would make us happier."

"Okay, we'll talk soon."

I leave the two of them and explore the ballroom. Amongst the crowd, I notice Alexander and Maria, both dancing. Their movements are perfectly in time with the music. Tomas is dancing with a dark-haired girl around his age. Everyone on the dance floor seems to know what they're doing, their movements all seemingly in sync. Alexander looks up and notices me.

He beckons me over with a big smile. Nope. My feet practically turn to cement blocks. There's no way I'm dancing. No way at all.

Erik is on the dance floor, dancing with a boy I'm guessing is Sebastian. I do see why his grandma wanted them to be together— they look perfect as a couple. The song ends, and Erik and Sebastian break apart. Erik notices me, and starts approaching.

He offers me his hand. I leave him hanging for a moment.

I'm fully aware that a real-life prince just asked me to dance. That is a once-in-a-lifetime thing. Hell, it's got to be rarer than that. How many people can say that's something that's happened to them? Especially gay boys from Providence who, until a short while ago, didn't know they had any connection to royalty?

Erik is still waiting for my response. I should say yes. The big problem is that I have no freaking clue how to dance. Even at school functions, where the dancing is jumping up and down to the beat, I felt uncomfortable.

"I don't know how," I say.

"Follow me. It's easy, I promise."

Across the dance floor, I spot Mom and Mike. They both nod encouragingly. They've been dancing for most of the night even though they've never had lessons, and nobody has threatened to kick them out. At least not that I've heard of.

Okay, screw it.

I put my hand on his. I have an out-of-body moment. Erik pulls us onto the dance floor and starts to move along to the music. I stumble a few times, let go, and let Erik guide me. His hand is strong and steady, and I find myself starting to enjoy it. He lifts his hand, and I spin under it, then return to him.

"You're good at this," he says. His hand moves down to my waist, and he holds me there.

The breath whooshes out of my lungs like I've been winded.

"You're a good teacher."

I've never been held like this by a guy. And I like it a ridiculous amount. I like it more than anything. It makes me think that everything that has happened was worth it, so that I could experience this. And yes, Erik is good-looking and very much my type, but I don't think that's what this is. He's just being friendly.

He smiles. "We have to spin."

"What?"

He lifts a hand, and I spin under it, but then I realize what is happening. We're supposed to change partners. I move on to the next person, a woman in her forties who wears a black dress covered in sparkling jewels that reminds me of the night sky. I try to mimic the moves I did with Erik, and I think I'm partially successful.

"Nice to meet you," she says. Her accent is British, and—wait. I think I've seen her on TV before. She's not part of the royal family from England, but she's somehow close to it.

"Are you having fun?" she asks.

"I am," I say. "Are you?"

"A blast. You must be a Mortenallo, you look just like Alexander."

My heart skips a beat. "I'm a cousin. Distant."

That seems to dull any curiosity, and the conversation comes to a halt.

I start to enjoy myself. I might not be the best dancer on the planet, but that hardly matters. I notice a few people watching me, but I figure if they're going to judge me for not knowing the proper steps, that's on them, not me.

After a while, I've run out of energy, so I leave the dance floor. I spot Erik standing near the bar, talking to Stefan. Looking at Erik, I feel the same nerves I did back at Anchor Bros, with the hot boy who looked at me. I'm not going to make that mistake this time. I'm going to go and talk to the cute boy.

"Jamie," says Erik when I reach him. "This is my brother, Stefan."

I'm unsure if I should, but deciding to be safe, I bow to him.

"Nice to meet you," he says. "Although I think your father would like to have a word."

I turn around and notice Alexander approaching us.

"Jamie, Erik. I saw you dance, and an idea crossed my mind. Would the two of you mind joining me in my office?"

Did I do something wrong? Was dancing with him crossing some line I didn't know about?

"Of course," says Erik.

"Fantastic. Let's go."

I glance at Erik but can't get a read on what's going on from his expression. Something is happening, but I have no idea what.

I guess I'll have to wait to find out.

Chapter Fourteen

Erik

If I've learned anything in my time being a prince, it's that if a king asks you to do something, you better do it.

Not that I wouldn't want to otherwise. I've always liked Alexander, even if my interactions with him have been brief. I'm more than happy to go along with whatever it is he wants from me.

"It's this way," says Alexander, taking us down a hallway. As we walk, I notice that Jamie keeps looking around, taking in all the decorations and paintings on the wall.

After a short walk, we reach Alexander's office. Two curved armchairs sit in front of a wooden desk. When I'm older, I will have an office like this one, and I should take note of the design. There is a large model of a ship in the corner of the room, housed in a glass cabinet. I don't need one, but everything else is very nice. I especially love the number of books Alexander has on display, and they're not just old classics: he has an entire shelf of what seems to be modern thrillers with authors whose names I recognize. Who would've thought that Alexander likes the same pulpy stories as Gran?

Also, why am I here? I know that Alexander invited me, but I have no idea what for.

"Take a seat, please," says Alexander. "I'm sure you're both wondering why you are here, so I'll cut right to the chase. Erik, I have a proposition for you. I know you and Jamie have been messaging, and it seems like the two of you have been getting along."

"We have," says Jamie.

"With that in mind, I had an idea. Would you like to stay with us for a few days? Having someone his age close by, who has gone through something similar, could help. We have a lot of lost time to make up for, and I would love it if you could teach Jamie everything you know about being a prince."

I think it over. At first thought, it doesn't sound like a bad idea. I like Jamie, and I'd be happy to help him.

"What about Tomas?" asks Jamie.

"He's unfortunately going to be spending the summer in Florence, and it was decided it would be best to follow through with his commitment. So, Erik, what do you say?"

Jamie is keeping his focus away from me. I'm not sure what he wants. Would he like it if I stayed? Is him asking about his brother his way of saying he doesn't want me to stay?

If the whole point of me spending some time in the country is to help him, that will only work if he wants that. I think of some of the royal tutors I've had. Some, like my first etiquette teacher, were amazing. Others, like the stuffy, pretentious man who taught me to dance, made my lessons hellish. I don't want Jamie to think of me that way.

"What kinds of things do you want me to teach him?" I ask.

"Being a royal of Mitanor is something most of us are trained our entire lives for. It would be good to learn etiquette and how to present himself in public. This is, of course, if you are willing to learn, Jamie."

"Sounds good," he says. His eyes are a little wider than normal, and clearly he's thinking hard about this. "I'd like that."

What else does he need? How can I turn this American boy into a prince? For one thing, I need to work on his posture. Even sitting, his shoulders are hunched. I'm sure he's not aware of it, but the way he's sitting on the chair is almost comically incorrect.

"And don't worry, Erik," says Alexander. "I've spoken about this with your family, and they've already given their blessing."

I know what that means. They want me to do it. If they didn't, they would've come up with some reason why I can't. Something clicks, and I realize this isn't Alexander asking me to stay here, even though it looks like it is. This is him telling me what is happening. I'm sure I could fight against it if I wanted to, but I would certainly be in trouble with Gran, and it's not worth the effort.

"Okay," I say. "I'm in."

"Excellent!" says Alexander. "I won't forget this, Erik. If I can ever do something to repay the favor, all you have to do is ask."

"That's very kind. There's one problem, though. I don't have any clothes here."

"That can be taken care of. I'll send for a suitcase to be delivered from Sunstad tomorrow, and in the meantime, I can arrange for whatever you need."

That's it, then. I'm staying.

PART
TWO

I know it's a cliché, but the thing about love is, it happens to you when you stop looking for it. I'd given up on finding someone, and then I walked into that dive bar and saw her. Nothing has been the same ever since.

—PRINCE STEFAN

CHAPTER FIFTEEN

JAMIE

"So," asks Max. "How was the ball?"

It's the morning after, and I'm still buzzing. When I think about last night, I think about meeting Erik the most. I keep going back to the moment he first stepped into the gazebo, the moment our eyes locked.

I don't know. It's like I felt the ground shift underneath me.

I'm trying to stop myself from getting too carried away. But I mean, come on. Last night I danced with a prince at a royal ball. That's like something out of a freaking movie, so it makes sense that it felt as magical as it did. The problem is this isn't a movie, and Erik was dancing with me to be friendly. He got a boyfriend the day we properly met. I doubt he has given our dance even a second thought.

I can't stop thinking about it, though. Us, together. The way he made it seem so effortless.

I'm in bed with my laptop on my lap, on a call with the rest of the group. Each of them is in their little windows on my computer screen. It's still late at night there, and it shows. Ren is dressed like he's about to go out, and Amara is wearing a fluffy robe with hearts on it, which means she will go to bed soon. Max is sharing her screen with her golden retriever, Ollie.

"It was kind of amazing," I say.

"Go on," says Amara.

"Were there any cute boys?" asks Ren. Amara glares at him, and I can feel it through the screen.

"Some, yeah."

"Was that prince you're messaging there?"

I've only been talking to them for about five minutes, so it's not that strange that I haven't brought up dancing with Erik. Still, I'm unsure why it wasn't the first thing I told them. Usually when I meet a guy, like a cute boy browsing for video games or Pokémon cards, or at a coffee shop and I overhear him talking about a movie he loves, I tell them all about it the second I can.

With Erik, something has held me back.

It helps that, for the first part of our conversation, all of them were gushing over the "Ashes" video. Spencer sent me the finished, edited video, and I'm obsessed. Ren went so far as to say it's the best music video of all time.

"Um, yeah, he was," I say. I look down, and I know I've given myself away. I've always been bad at keeping secrets. Whenever my friends and I play a board game that requires deception, I always give myself away at the first question.

"So he was there," says Ren. "Come on, spill."

"Was he?" asks Max. Her voice cracks. I get why, I haven't told her, either. Which is very much new for me.

"He was," I say. "But it's not like that. It's a friends thing."

"Wait," says Ren. "The prince's name is Erik, right?"

"Yup," I say.

"Wasn't Eric from *The Little Mermaid* your gay awakening?"

I told Ren that once, and he's never let me, or anyone, forget it.

"Yeah, but Erik's is with a *K*."

"Still," says Ren, lifting both his eyebrows in a way that makes me think us being together is like cosmic fate or something.

"He's actually going to stay here for a few days to help me adjust to everything," I say. "Just so you all know that's, like, happening."

"Oh my God," says Ren. "I give you two days before he's teaching you all sorts of things."

"You're so gross!" cries Amara. "That sounds good, Jamie. I mean, who better to help you adjust than an actual prince."

Max is being strangely quiet. I assume it's because I didn't tell her about meeting Erik right away. I thought it was fine because of the time difference, but I guess not.

"It's done," says Spencer. He hasn't really been listening to the conversation, as he has been working on the real reason for this call: to celebrate the upload of the "Ashes" video to the internet. I do feel a little bad that so much of the conversation has been about me when this is supposed to be Max's day, but I'm doing everything I can. Every chance I get I redirect the conversation back toward her.

Everyone on the call goes quiet.

"You should do the honors, Max," says Spencer. "Tell me when and I'll hit *publish*."

"On the count of three. One. Two. Three."

I refresh my screen, and there it is. The video is online.

I feel I'll think back on this in a few years and remember this moment. The moment Max took her first step toward the limelight.

It has zero views at the moment, but I'm sure that won't take long to change. Soon, I'm sure it will have hundreds of thousands, and Max will be a household name. And it is all starting right now.

I feel a pang of not exactly sadness, but maybe longing. I am enjoying my life here, I truly am, but there's a part of me that thinks I should be with Max and the rest of my friends right now. I'm sure they're all going to go to Anchor Bros after this call ends, because it's what we always do whenever we have something major to celebrate.

"I should go," I say. I heard Mom and Mike get up earlier,

and I want to talk to them before we start whatever Alexander and Maria have in mind for us. And Erik, I guess. Will his lessons start today? "I love you all, and congratulations, Max."

"Oh," she says. "Thanks, Jamie. Love you, too."

I end the call. I get out of bed, go to the window, and pull apart the blinds. I flinch away from the brightness like I'm a vampire. It's still reasonably early, and the sun is rising over the palace lawn.

My eyes adjust, and the sight stretching above me is almost comically majestic. A few workers are out on the long stretch of grass, keeping them pristine, and it's looking like it's going to be another warm, sunny day in Mitanor. In the far distance is a shimmering lake. Even though I haven't been here that long, I'm starting to wonder if it's even possible for this country to have anything other than picture-perfect weather. I begin to smile.

Last night, I danced with a prince.

I think of Mom, and it's like a splinter through the heart. Everything is going well, but one thing still needs fixing.

A knock sounds on my door, and a split second later the door starts to open. Seems like I can't expect much privacy here.

A flawlessly groomed royal aide pushing a trolley comes inside. The trolley is covered in silver cloches. And coffee. Oh my god, the smell of it is heaven: rich, dark, and strong. Given how strong my physical reaction to it is right now, I think it's more than slightly possible that I'm addicted to the stuff.

"King Alexander and Queen Maria send their regards," says the aide. "They hope you can join them for a late lunch this afternoon."

He's still, waiting for a response.

"Sounds great," I say. "Can't wait."

The aide starts lifting the lids, revealing the dishes. "They've chosen a selection of national favorites for your breakfast this morning. Would you like me to go through them for you?"

"Yes, please."

"Mitanorian coffee, Danish and pastries, and a selection of seasonal fruits. Last is *desayuno dorado,* our national breakfast, which is baked eggs with smoked chorizo and olives. Alexander in particular hopes to know what you think of that, as it is his favorite. I hope you enjoy."

"I will, thank you."

The aide bows and leaves the room. I lift the first of the silver cloches, and my mouth instantly starts watering. It's clearly the *desayuno dorado,* served in a small ramekin and covered in melted cheese, paired with two thick slices of oil-and-herb-drizzled flat-bread.

My eyelids flutter as I take my first bite. I love an American breakfast: bacon and waffles is my favorite food of all time. This deserves a spot on that list, too. It's absurdly delicious.

I lift the other lids and find each of the offerings just as incred-ible: plates of buttered bread with a dark orange jam, a plate of sliced fresh fruit including some I've never seen before, tea and coffee, and a few pastries. Many pastries seem to be made with oranges or pears rather than the usual berries or peaches. There is even a bunch of pears on the fruit plate. Oranges makes sense, given they are the national fruit of Mitanor, but why pears? Weird.

I take a pear Danish and leave my room in search of Mom and Mike. They're both in bed, each eating from their trolley. I thought this was for the three of us to share, but did we each get one of these?

This might be heaven.

"You know," says Mike, taking a big bite of toast covered in jam, "I could get used to this."

"Me too," I say.

"How did you sleep?" asks Mom. She's wearing a faded T-shirt with the logo of the bookstore she used to work at.

"Fine, but I was wondering if we could talk."

"About what?" she asks.

"About you keeping the secret."

"I'll give you two some space," says Mike. He loads up a plate with pastries, creating a precarious tower, then leaves the room, quietly closing the door behind him. Mom tucks a strand of hair behind her ear, a nervous tic of hers.

"I want you to know I forgive you," I say. "I'm sorry it took me a while to bring this up, but I didn't want to say anything before I truly felt it."

She's quiet, listening.

"I think it's hard to understand why you didn't tell me," I continue. "But I trust you, and I feel like you only did it because you had my best interests at heart."

Tears well up in her eyes. "Jamie, I'm so sorry. All I can tell you is that I have thought about this and now realize how wrong I was. I lost my best friend and thought I was doing the right thing by her."

"I get that, I really do."

"But you're right, I should've told you, and I'm sorry."

"Apology accepted," I say.

She smiles as tears fill her eyes. "Thank you. You're handling this all so well. It's truly remarkable."

I wave a hand. "Stop."

"I want you to know that if you're struggling, you can always talk to me."

"I know," I say. "I'm good, but there's something you should know. Alexander invited Prince Erik to stay here for a few days to help me navigate this royal thing. I guess he's going to give me some crash course in being princely or something."

Mom sits up. "Is Erik the boy you danced with?"

"Maybe."

"The same one you've been messaging?"

"Yup."

"Oh, okay."

"It's not like that!" I say. "We're just friends. Or we're not even really friends. But it's not, like, a thing. He's not staying here because we danced. It's a favor, that's it."

"If you say so," she says. "I think that's a good idea. The more help you get, the better. Thank you for telling me."

"No problem."

"Can we hug it out?"

I hug her, and I can practically feel the weirdness between us lifting. Life is too short and unpredictable to hold grudges, especially with family. She's my mom, and I love her. That's enough for me.

"You done in there?" calls Mike through the door. "I'm nearly out of pastries."

"We're done," I call, not letting go of Mom.

Mike comes back in and spots the two of us hugging.

I wave him over. "I think we need a family hug."

"If I *have* to."

Mike pretends to drag his feet, but then he joins in. I can't recall the last time we did a family hug like this. We should do it more often.

Because right now, all feels right with the world.

Chapter Sixteen

ERIK

Hey, Jamie. I was wondering if you wanted to go for a walk in the gardens? I'm free this morning.

I stare at the message I have drafted on my phone. It seems innocent enough, and my intentions are only good. I want to try to figure out if Jamie truly wants me here or not, and I thought I could figure that out if I get some time alone with him before we start the lessons I've been planning.

I already have a few ideas, some of which I'm excited about. I've never been a teacher before, and I've never been given this much responsibility.

It's daunting, yes, but also exciting.

I am trying to temper my expectations. It won't matter if Jamie isn't interested in learning from me. I must remember that I'm here for his benefit, not mine. Plus, this wasn't his idea; it was Alexander's. I also shouldn't forget that.

For some reason, I can't get myself to send the message. I've edited it a few times, changing the words a little, trying to make it perfect.

The truth is I'm stalling.

It might be because I'm scared of finding out the truth. I want to spend time in Mitanor, and I like the thought of being able to help Jamie adjust to his new life. I also like that Alexander asked for me personally. It's the biggest task that's ever been asked of me, and will set the standard for the rest of my life. If I do this well, I will probably be given other important tasks in the future, not shoved off to the side to be mostly forgotten like some royal siblings are.

It's also possible I'm nervous because of the dance. There's no denying that Jamie is incredibly cute, and speaking with him I felt an ease like I don't think I have ever felt with anyone. It was like I could truly be myself around him. I doubt he's thinking about that, though. His whole world has just changed, and I'm sure he's thinking about that more than he is about dancing with me.

My phone starts to ring. It's a call from Mum.

I swipe and accept.

"Hello," she says. "How are you?"

"I'm good. Have you left yet?"

After the ball, the rest of my family went to a hotel, while I stayed in the apartment that Alexander set up for me.

"Getting ready to go now. I wanted to see how you are."

"I'm fine," I say. "Alexander's put me in a pretty nice apartment, so no complaints."

"Has he told you what, exactly, you are supposed to do while you're there?"

"I'm supposed to be there for Jamie if he has any questions. And give him lessons on etiquette and stuff."

"So you're, what, his tutor?"

"I guess so."

"Well, if you're fine with it, that's all that matters. I'm quite jealous, honestly. I wouldn't mind a holiday in Mitanor. But Erik, I've heard from Gran, and she has some concerns about your stay there."

"What kind of concerns?"

"She is worried that you and Jamie are going to hit it off a little too well."

"What does she mean?"

"Well, she has decided that you and Sebastian would be an ideal match. You two got along, didn't you?"

I think about telling Mum the truth, that Sebastian and I didn't really click. But I can feel the pressure, and expectation to do what Gran wants me to do.

"We did," I say.

"That's great."

"Two gay guys can just be friends, Mum."

"I know that, I'm only passing on the message. Gran is worried you spending time with Jamie might distract you from your relationship with Sebastian."

I breathe out. It's as if they somehow know exactly how much I enjoyed dancing with Jamie.

"Thanks for letting me know."

"You're welcome."

The call ends. On my phone is the message that I haven't yet sent to Jamie. I need to stop being afraid and message him. Either he will say yes, or he won't, and I won't find out unless I try.

What Mum said lingers in the back of my mind. But helping Jamie is different. I'm getting to know him. It's fine. I was never told that I can't be friends with Jamie. In fact, it was actively encouraged. I can't date him, because I'm with Sebastian, the guy they approve of.

I hit *send*.

I watch as the message appears in a new window, creating a chat thread. I brace myself for a long delay. He might not be near his phone, or be in the shower or something. There could be many reasons why he doesn't reply right away. He has a lot on his plate right now, and probably won't have the mental bandwidth to respond to me, or anyone, quickly.

My phone buzzes.

Yeah, that sounds fun! Now?

Sounds good. Meet you by the
entrance in five.

All right! See you then. 😊

He likes my message, making a little cartoon heart appear beside it.

Jamie is early.

He's leaning against the wall, looking like an actor from a movie. He hasn't styled his hair, but the messiness suits him. His brown curls fall slightly over his forehead.

It might be what Mum said, and because I know I can't notice him in this way, but I can't help it.

He's charming. And good-looking.

"Hey," he says, pushing off the wall. "Nice suit."

I need to stop myself from thinking about him this way. I can't notice his arms or the little dimple in his cheek when he smiles. Or the way his T-shirt fits him, giving just the hint of the outline of his chest.

I wish Mum hadn't said anything. I might not be thinking this if Jamie weren't wrapped in red tape.

"Thanks," I say.

"Shall we?" he asks, tilting his head toward the entrance to the garden.

I forgot how much I like his accent. It's faint, not as strong as some American accents I've heard, but unmissable. I like it. All right, that's the last time I will think anything like that about the American prince.

"Yes, but first, I'd like to teach you something."

I offer him my hand.

He frowns and crosses his arms, tucking his hands under his arms. I get why he's reacting this way; it's not like it's the first time we've met. Going for a handshake right now is certainly weird.

"This is your first lesson," I say. "I thought shaking hands would be a good place to start because it was the first thing I was ever taught. My dad told me that how you shake someone's hand tells them all they need to know about you."

"Okay, let's do this."

He reaches out and shakes my hand. He has a good grip, firm enough to convey strength but not crushing. This is one thing I won't have to work too hard for him to perfect. My teacher spent a solid week teaching me the correct way to shake hands, making me practice repeatedly until I got it just right. After that, Dad would often test me on it.

I try to ignore the electricity racing up my arm.

"How was that?" he asks.

"Nearly perfect," I say. "But you looked down. Eye contact is important; it's a sign of respect. Do you want to try again?"

"Sure."

This time, he looks into my eyes as we shake hands. His eyes are brown, but they're a light, pretty shade. They remind me of autumn: falling leaves and cozy weather.

"So?" he asks. "Was that better?"

"It was perfect," I say.

And there it is. Our first lesson is done.

It went well, which is good. I'm here to teach Jamie everything I can about being a royal, and that's it. Jamie seems both eager to learn and intelligent, both of which are good things. *Great* things.

I can work with this.

Chapter Seventeen

Jamie

"Do you come here often?" I ask, as Erik and I step down off the front step and into the palace garden.

It's completely magnificent. Sunlight filters through ancient orange trees, and the air smells fresh and earthy, accentuated with floral notes from the flowers. There are thousands of them, the large flowers in reds, whites, pinks, and lavenders, each one in separate segments, which all piece together to make a pattern. A white stone path cuts through the lawns, looping around rose bushes and stone water fountains.

I'm still wrapping my head around what is going on right now. I'm on a walk through a palace garden with Erik. He's right beside me, all six-foot-something of him. He truly does seem like a fairy-tale prince come to life.

Actually, he's better than that. I don't think there have been any gay fairy-tale princes. Not in canon, at least.

We start walking down a white gravel pathway. I breathe in, enjoying the sweet, fresh air.

"Only once, a few years ago," he says. He might have missed my joking tone, or maybe he's rolling with it.

"What was the occasion?"

"I stayed here with my family as part of a diplomatic visit."

All right, something is indeed up. It's subtle, but this Erik seems different from the one I spoke to at the ball yesterday. His walls were down back then, but right now, they're way up.

What's changed?

Maybe I'm overthinking it. That's another thing I'm known to do when it comes to attractive guys.

"Oh, that's cool."

"What do you think of the garden?" he asks.

I look around. "I love it."

"Me too."

We walk in silence for a moment. It's not uncomfortable, weirdly. It feels totally fine to walk with him without the need to fill every spare second with conversation.

He clears his throat. "I must confess, I did bring you out here for a reason. I wanted to know if you want me here or not."

Wait, what? I'm confused; I don't know what I did that could make him think that.

"What makes you think I don't?"

"Nothing," he says. "I just wanted to make sure. The last thing I want would be for you to feel forced into doing this."

"I don't," I say. "I appreciate it so much."

He's quiet for a moment. "Is there anything in particular you'd like to focus on?"

I think it over. "I'll let you take the lead on that—um, I mean, I guess it would be good to know how I should act. Like, etiquette and stuff."

"I can teach you that. Anything else?"

"I just want to show everyone that I'm taking this seriously. I know Americans have a bad reputation overseas, and I don't want anyone to think I'm obnoxious or whatever."

"I don't think anyone would think that about you."

"Thank you. I'm glad. I want to know how to act in a way that won't upset anyone. Is that too much?"

"I wouldn't say so."

"Noted," I say. "When did you start learning about this stuff?"

"When I was five. But I'm sure I can cover many of the basics. Besides, you're very polite already. Your mum did an excellent job raising you."

I told her I've forgiven her, and I have. But still, the mention of her stings. In the past, I would've wholeheartedly agreed. The first thought that comes to mind when thinking of her is that she didn't tell me the truth when she could've.

I catch Erik studying me.

"Sorry," I say. "Mom's a touchy subject right now."

"That's fair; I won't ask about her."

I feel myself close up. I've forgiven her, so this should be in the past. I should be able to talk freely to Erik about this.

"I did forgive her," I say. "For keeping the secret from me. Just in case you were, like, wondering about that."

"That must've been hard," he says.

I'm so relieved he said that. I think a part of me worried that being upset with Mom makes me a bad person, but that might not be the case.

"It was," I say. "She told me her reasons, and I do genuinely believe them. But it's still, like, I don't know."

"What reasons did she give you? If you're okay talking about this."

"Yeah, no, it's fine. She said Emilia made her promise to keep it a secret. She wanted me to grow up to be whatever I wanted to be. Do you think she was right?"

"Growing up in the palace, I do see where she's coming from. When I was younger, I often wished I could be from a regular family so I could do whatever I wanted."

That sinks in. If an actual prince is telling me that Mom did the right thing, then there's a solid case to be made that she did.

"I think that's normal, though," I say. "It's human nature to want what you can't have."

"That's true."

"It's complicated. I forgive her, love her, and don't want us to fight or anything. But she had so many chances to tell me, and she didn't."

"It'll take time," he says. "But your heart is in the right place, and it's hard to go wrong when that's the case."

We reach a fountain of what appears to be a mermaid and a sailor staring longingly at each other. He's holding a spear and seems poised to strike, but the expression on his face can only be described as lovestruck agony. In front of the fountain is a dark green wooden bench, faded from years out in the sun. Erik sits down, and I join him, ensuring a comfortable amount of space between us.

I'm aware I'm overthinking this, but I can't stop myself.

"Thank you, by the way," I say.

"For what?"

"For staying here. I'm sure you had things you would prefer to be doing."

He shakes his head. "I'm happy to. It's a nice break from the wedding preparations, in any case. I'm sure it's all they're talking about back home."

"Are you excited about it?"

"Mostly. I will be walking down the aisle with Stefan, so a lot of eyes will be on me. It's a lot of pressure."

My phone buzzes. I hesitate. I don't need etiquette lessons to know that checking your phone mid-conversation is rude. Plus, I like talking to Erik.

"It's fine," says Erik. "You can look."

I pull my phone from my pocket. It's from Max.

Just broke 100 baby!!!!

She's included a screenshot of the "Ashes" video. One hundred views may not be setting the internet on fire or anything, but still. It's a start. I return a string of confetti emojis, then slide my phone back into my pocket. As I do, I think of something. I usually talk to my friends using the chat on Instagram; we hardly ever actually text. The one I got from Erik might be the first real text I've received from anyone my age in quite a while.

"Do you use social media?" I ask. "I tried looking for you but couldn't find anything."

He shakes his head. "Technically, I'm not allowed. Though if you promise not to tell anyone, I have an alt."

"Scandalous." I hand him my phone.

"Only if you promise not to share it with anyone," he says, his tone serious. "I would get in trouble if anyone found out about this."

"Don't worry, your secret's safe with me."

He takes my phone and taps a few times, then hands it back.

I'm now following an account called e_theangel_07.

His profile doesn't include many pictures of himself. It's primarily landscapes. The few images of him are mirror selfies where his phone blocks his face. I try not to notice the one where he's only wearing a pair of swimming trunks. Seems anonymity is the key for him. He only has 247 followers. I'm sure if the public knew who was behind this account, he would have way more.

"'E the angel'?" I ask. "What does that mean?"

"It's nothing," he says, too quickly. It's something, but he doesn't want to share it with me. That's fine; I don't want to pry. I hope at some point we can become good enough friends that he can share the truth with me. If that takes time, that's fine with me.

For the first time, I notice how Erik is sitting. His back is straight, and one of his legs is crossed over the other. I've never seen a guy sit like him. It's not bad, though. It seems refined. Graceful, even.

"What was that text about?" he asks. "It seemed important."

"It was from my best friend, Max. She's a singer, and she just put out her first video. I know she's going to be famous in a few years."

"Can I see this video?"

I load the video and show him. He watches it quietly. The song starts, and Max's perfect voice comes through his phone.

I'll leave you as ashes.

Erik starts to smile. We watch the whole thing. As the screen goes black, he lifts his head.

"What did you think?" I ask. "I worked on the video. Max deserves all the credit, but I helped film it. I was supposed to edit it, too, but then all this happened."

"I loved it. It's so professional, how did you learn to film like that?"

"Using YouTube."

"Wow. I love the song, too. It's so catchy. Is it online anywhere?"

"It should be everywhere."

He takes out his phone and unlocks it. He goes to his music app and searches for it, then adds it to his playlist.

"So you really like the song?" I ask.

"It's great. Your friend is very talented. And so are you, if you filmed that video."

"Can I tell her? She'll freak out."

"Sure. Maybe don't mention that my brother once called my music tastes 'tragically uncool.'"

I smile at his joke. "I'd never. And please, everyone thinks their taste in music is better than everyone else's."

"You're not wrong."

My heart swells. I don't think he's putting on an act at all. I think he really liked the song and was genuinely impressed by the video. He's not humoring me.

"Fine," he says. "I'll tell you what my username means."

The way he is hesitating right now is fascinating to me. It's as if his username is some deep, closely guarded secret. Which, hey, it might be, it's not like I'm an expert on princes.

"I play this online game called *Arcane Realms*," he says. I'd guess from the fear in his eyes he wishes he could take what he said back. "And I play as an angelic warrior. I named myself after that."

That's his big secret? That he's a nerd? I know about the game. It's only for the most extreme fantasy fans. It's complicated and difficult to get into and for sure niche.

"*You* play *Arcane Realms*?"

When I picture a typical *Arcane Realms* player, I don't envision a six-foot-something blond prince who, given the way his shirts fit him, probably has abs.

"I do, yes."

"That's awesome! I've always wanted to play but worried I'd get too addicted."

"Seriously, don't start. It'll take over your life." He starts spinning one of his silver rings around his finger. "I don't normally tell people I play it."

How earnest he is right now is painfully endearing.

"Don't worry, your secret's safe with me," I say.

In the distance, an aide appears around the corner. They're frowning, and their quick pace makes me anxious. What's going on?

They reach us. They're sweating and breathing heavily, as if they've run the entire way here.

"Jamie, Prince Erik," they say. "You need to come back inside. Something has happened."

"What is it?" I ask.

"The news about your identity is out," they say. "You've gone viral."

Chapter Eighteen

ERIK

Jamie's secret is out.

The news story was first published by a tabloid called *Royals Daily,* but it didn't take long for the information to circulate everywhere. The hashtag #americanroyal is trending on Twitter, and news sites worldwide have covered it.

Jamie's yearbook picture is *everywhere.*

I've been invited to a meeting room in the palace with Jamie and both sides of his family. Joining us is a group of royal advisors whose jobs are to manage situations like this. I've seen similar people back at home clean up huge messes.

This room is on the top level of the palace, and it's remarkably simple. It's a long room with a bare table in the middle, surrounded by office chairs. If it weren't for the view out of the windows, this room could be in any office in the country.

"Jamie should put all his social media accounts on private," suggests one woman. "For the time being, until we can get this situation under control."

"Are you sure about that?" asks Alexander. "We don't want it to seem like he's hiding anything. What do you think, Jamie?"

"I guess I'll just go through and delete anything that I don't want everyone seeing?"

"Good idea," says Alexander.

"I have a suggestion," says Tomas. I heard he has delayed his flight to Florence to attend this meeting. "Jamie should do a press conference."

The entire table is quiet.

"What do you mean?" asks Jamie.

"The press are all interested in speaking to you. Unless you want them digging through your past, or worse, making things up, you should give them what they want on your own terms."

"And that is?" asks Jamie.

"Well, you. Or access to you."

The table goes quiet again. I think Jamie is incredible, and he's handled what has happened to him with, frankly, an astonishing amount of resilience. But the press are a whole other matter. Some of them are good and can be trusted. Others can be ruthless, and I don't want to open Jamie up to that kind of danger.

"Sorry to interrupt," says Jamie's mum, Rebecca. "But shouldn't we be trying to figure out how this got out?"

"The story originates from Rhode Island," says Alexander. "Someone named Grady White sold it to *Royals Daily*."

Everyone looks to Jamie.

"I've never heard that name in my life."

"Did you tell anyone?" asks Maria.

"I told my friends, but they wouldn't tell anyone else."

He pulls his phone out of his pocket, and his mouth drops open.

"What is it?" asks Rebecca.

"It was Ren," he says. "He said he was flirting with this guy who works at Anchor Bros, and he told him about me. That guy told his dad, and his dad sold it."

I feel for Jamie. It must hurt to be let down by one of his friends like this.

"It was a mistake," says Jamie. "It's not his fault."

"We need to figure out what we're going to do," says Tomas. "The public knows about him now. If you don't show them what he's like, everyone will think the worst. They're going to think he's an obnoxious American who thinks he's better than everyone here. No offense, Jamie."

"None taken," he says.

"I'm offended," says Mike, I assume jokingly. Rebecca pats him on the hand, telling him to be quiet.

"Tomas is right," says Maria. "This could be a way of getting in front of the threat, of stopping this from getting out of hand."

"He hasn't been trained," says Alexander. "You know what the press is like. They'll tear him apart."

"I think you're underestimating Jamie," says Rebecca. "He's one of the smartest, kindest people I know. If you're worried about the public thinking of him as an obnoxious American, all you need to do is put him in front of them, and they'll see that he's not."

"The problem is he represents the crown," says Alexander. "One mistake, one wrong word, and people could vilify him."

"Why would they do that?" asks Jamie.

"They could see you as an outsider. Mitanorian law states anyone with royal blood has a claim to the throne. Some locals may hate the idea of an American being this close to such an important part of their culture."

"They'll do that anyway," says Tomas. "At least this way, he has a chance."

"Can I say something?" asks Jamie.

The room goes quiet.

"What if we do a press conference in a week," he suggests. "That's enough time for me to prepare as much as possible, but not so long that they make up stories. Would that work?"

"That's too long," says Tomas. "If you're going to act, you must do it now."

"I agree," says the advisor who spoke before. "A week would be far too long."

"How long do you think we could get away with?" asks Jamie.

"Three nights," says one of the advisors. "And that's only if we put out an official statement today about the press conference."

"That could work," says Alexander. "If you are willing to do it so soon?"

"What do you think, Erik?" asks Jamie.

"It's risky," I say. "But I think you could do it."

"You don't have to," says Rebecca. "It's up to you."

"I don't want to be a villain," he says. "And I'm a fast learner. So okay. Let's do the press conference in three days."

"It's settled," says Alexander. "I'll arrange for a teacher to help you prepare."

"What about Erik?" asks Jamie. "He can teach me, right? That was the plan."

Everyone in the room turns to me. I could try my best, but I'm not an expert. If I mess this up, Jamie might become one of the most hated people in the country. I could ruin his entire life.

"The choice is yours, Jamie," says Alexander. "If Erik is okay with taking on this responsibility."

"I can," I say. "If Jamie is sure."

"I want you to teach me," says Jamie. "I have a good feeling about it."

Alexander places his hands down on the table. "I'll arrange a press conference. Jamie, Erik, prepare as much as you can. And if you need any help, make sure you reach out."

With that, the meeting comes to an end.

Everyone files out of the room until it's just me and Jamie.

"Are you sure this is what you want?" I ask. "I'm not an expert."

"Yes, you are," he says. "You've been doing this kind of thing your entire life."

"I have, but Alexander could get you the best tutors in the country."

"I feel like anyone else will want to change me. I don't want that. I want some advice, but if I'm going to do this, I want to do it as myself."

"Okay, then," I say. "Do you want to meet me in the library in an hour? I can teach you everything I know."

"Sounds great," he says.

I know he trusts me wholeheartedly. And I understand his reasoning about wanting to stay the same. If he lets one instructor guide him to follow the royal way of behaving, soon many people will come out of the woodwork, wanting to shape Jamie until he's like everyone else.

Still, it's a lot of pressure. He's putting all of his faith in me.

I hope I don't let him down.

Jamie is smiling as he enters the library.

Like he generally does when he visits somewhere new in the palace, he's looking at it with a sense of wide-eyed wonder. I can see why. This library is a book lover's paradise, timber shelves filled with countless books.

I had a quick browse when I first got here and found their collection not only includes nonfiction on many different topics, but also keeps up with new fiction releases. I spoke a little to the librarian. She told me the royal family and many people who work at the palace are avid readers, so she wants to keep the collection current for them.

I'm sitting at a table near the back, where I've been for the past hour. I have my laptop in front of me, and I've been doing a lot of research, trying to figure out some easy-to-teach public speaking techniques that can help Jamie improve as quickly as possible.

"Hey," he says as he sits down opposite me. He seems to be in great spirits for someone with a tremendous amount of pressure on him. "You should see this."

He hands me his phone. On it is his Instagram profile. I may have taken a short break while preparing the lesson to review it. Jamie has a lot of skill behind the camera, and each of his pictures is artistic. It's also clear that he genuinely loves his friends, as the same people appear frequently on his page.

It takes me a moment to see what he's pointing at. Then I see it—his follower count.

He has fifty thousand followers.

"How many did you have before?" I ask.

"I think it was around two hundred," he says. "And it was just people from school. Look at the comments, too. They're all so nice."

He scrolls the comments of a selfie of him taken at a coffee shop, and the comments *are* all nice.

SLAY KING
👑

This is so cute

Beautiful
😍 😍 😍

"I know, I know," he says. "Don't read the comments. But seriously, I haven't seen a single bad one yet."

"Be careful," I say. "Don't let it go to your head. One of my cousins was once the public's favorite. All it took were a few negative articles, and he was despised by the same people that used to idolize him. It was awful, it destroyed him."

"Oh," says Jamie, his face falling. I hate to rain on his parade, but I know how fickle the public can be. Hinging any of your self-worth on what they think is a losing game. "Okay, so, the lesson. What have you got for me?"

"First of all, these."

I slide a stack of books waiting for him across the table. They're all history books with titles like *Mitanor Through the Ages: From Founding to Modernity, Mitanor's Renaissance: Art, Science, and Culture,* and *Voices of the People: Oral Histories from Mitanor's Villages.*

"I don't expect you to read all of these by the press conference," I say. "But the more you can learn about Mitanor, the better. People will expect you to know everything, as you now represent their country, whether you know it or not."

"This is a great idea. Thank you."

"I think these in particular will greatly interest you."

The first is titled *Mitanor's Noble Families,* and the other is called *The Mortenallo Dynasty.*

"I'm sure you want to know more about your birth parents," I say.

"Thank you so much," he says. "Have you read books like this? About Sunstad, I mean."

"I have. Knowing your country's history is important. It must be said I didn't come up with this list on my own. Maria gave me advice for some of the most essential reading. Her list had twenty books, but I thought it would be best to start with these."

"Cool," he says. "I'll start reading them tonight."

"I thought the first thing we should focus on right now would be your body language. I'm unsure if you've noticed, but you tend to"—I curl my shoulders forward—"hunch."

"I know, it's because I'm on a computer so much. How can I fix it?"

"Concentrate on standing up a little straighter. I've also noticed you habitually keep your focus down, which can make you look nervous."

"What if I *am* nervous?"

"Try it out."

He pushes his shoulders back and lifts his gaze. For such a

quick fix, it makes a huge difference. He looks about a million times more confident.

"This feels uncomfortable," he says, wincing and moving his shoulders around. "I don't look weird?"

"You don't look weird, you look great. Truly."

Two dots of red appear on his cheeks. He coughs to clear his throat, and the confidence he seems to have just seconds ago vanishes. I guess we've got to work on that.

"What now?" he asks.

"Next, I want you to come up with three key points you would like to discuss during the press conference. If you have three topics in mind, you'll always be able to get back to them when it comes time to answer."

I hand him a notebook and a pen.

It's time to get to work.

Chapter Nineteen

JAMIE

My blaring alarm wakes me.

I groan and reach out until I find my phone and slap at the screen to shut it the hell up. I roll over and peer out the windows. The sun has barely even risen. I groan again, louder this time.

As part of Erik's lessons, he's asked me to join him on a run early this morning. For what, exactly, I'm not sure, but I'm going to try my best. Even if early mornings and exercise sound like a combination of two of my least favorite things. It's like the opposite of peanut butter and chocolate.

On my phone is a new message from Ren. We had a long talk yesterday, and he apologized for telling the cute Anchor Bros guy, whose name is apparently Blake, my secret. I forgave him, because I know there's no way that Ren would've told my secret maliciously. Ren Takahashi is many things, but he's not a villain. He just loves to talk.

> Seriously dude, I'm so sorry. If
> there's anything I can do to make
> it up to you, let me know.

I start typing a response.

> It's totally okay, I forgive you. Don't
> worry about it, okay? I'm seriously not

upset or anything, I know you didn't
mean it.

I pull my body out of bed and stagger to the bathroom to splash water onto my face. In the reflection, I look as tired as I feel. My secret is out, even though it's not a secret I've even known about for that long.

Everyone knows I'm royal now. Everyone. They all know something I'm not fully sure I've come to accept yet. Amara's been keeping me posted, and apparently I've caused a huge online discourse worldwide. In Mitanor reactions to me have been well and truly mixed, with some excited that I exist, while others are furious about me, mostly because I'm American.

I splash another handful of water on my face, then go through my suitcase until I find a gym T-shirt, a gift from Mom last Christmas I've worn maybe three times, and a pair of shorts. I'm thinking about canceling Erik's lesson, but that wouldn't be a good look. Plus, then I'd just stay indoors all day obsessing about things I can't change. So I put my clothes and running sneakers on and head out.

Erik is waiting for me out in front of the palace, stretching his arms. His workout gear is all brand-name, and seems new. I find myself gazing at how it fits him before I come to my senses. He's one hell of a distraction, which is just what I need right now. He swings his arms to stretch and then drops down to effortlessly touch his toes. As I advance, he straightens, putting his hands on his hips.

Despite my earlier objections, there's something nice about being outside so early. Thick fog covers the hills in the distance, and it's still a little cold. Plus, the way the sun is only just peeking out over the clouds makes the sky a beautiful shade of light blue.

I'm here, in the real world. I'm not going to worry about what people on the internet think of me.

"Morning," he says. "You look rested."

His dry tone on the word "rested" makes me narrow my eyes.

I swing my arms and start stretching, copying the stretch I saw Erik do before. "What does exercising have to do with being a prince?"

"It's about positive habits," he says. "And discipline."

"My favorite things," I say.

"Ready?" he asks, clearly intentionally ignoring me. "Good, let's go."

He doesn't wait for me to answer. He sets off at a slow jog, following the path toward the wrought-iron gates in the distance. He spins around as I plug my headphones in.

"Coming?" he asks.

I hit *play* on my running playlist, one I made last night. The first song is by the Killers, the title track from *Battle Born,* which I have to say might be their most underrated album. This song is easily one of my favorites of all time and it never fails to hype me up.

I increase my pace until I catch up to Erik. As I run, I find my thoughts getting quieter and quieter until they're barely noticeable.

I never thought I'd feel this way this early in the morning, but I'm enjoying myself.

"This lesson," says Erik, "will be about how and when to bow."

For the past hour, Ren has been sending me a steady string of messages, all screenshots of strangers talking about how cute I am. It's pretty wild that my appearance is now a thing people feel they can freely talk about, but I have to say it is a pretty big confidence boost.

Erik clears his throat, pulling me from my thoughts. The two of us are in what I'm guessing is a palace ballet studio, with timber floors and a wall covered in mirrors on one side. After the run, I showered, had breakfast with the rest of my family, and met Erik here.

My first thought when I got to this room was that Erik would teach me how to dance, and I'm a little disappointed that isn't the case.

"I'm pretty sure I know how to bow," I say. I try it out, bending down into a bow. It earns me a glare.

"Not quite," he says. "Watch me."

He bows. It seems graceful and effortless.

"I do want to remind you," I say. "I have a press conference coming up. Shouldn't I be, I don't know, learning how to talk in public without making a giant ass out of myself?"

"If you can't speak in public without making an ass of yourself, I don't think any number of lessons can help you."

I cross my arms. "Very funny."

"Bowing is a vital skill for a prince," he says. "It's simple, but you have to do this right. Now, stand up straight."

I correct my posture. He comes up to me and does a small circle around me.

"Straighter," he says.

"I wasn't born that way."

He glares at me. Fine, no more time for jokes. I stand as straight as I can.

"Good," he says. "Hold that, and hands at your sides."

I press my hands to my sides.

"Now, bend at the waist."

I try it. I'm horrifically inflexible. My hamstrings strain.

"Hold for two seconds," he says. "Now stand up straight."

I return to the starting position.

"You need to practice," he says. "It shouldn't look like it's hurting you. Try again."

I put my hands on my sides and bend at the waist. This time, it comes together in a way that feels better.

Erik watches on quietly, clearly unimpressed.

"Again," he says.

CHAPTER TWENTY

ERIK

Jamie is late.

I'm waiting for him in the dining hall, which seems almost comically empty—it's me sitting at one end of a table that could seat dozens. I check the time. He's three minutes late. Long enough to be noticeable but not so long that I should get up and leave. Lateness isn't accepted in royal circles. It's seen as a mark of disrespect. It seems that's another lesson he needs to learn.

Up until now, I'd say he's been doing very well. He's clearly trying his hardest, and while it's going to take a long time to fully shake off his upbringing and learn every single royal custom, he is picking up things at an exceptional pace. Even with learning to bow, there was a huge difference in his skills after just one lesson.

My phone chimes. I check it, expecting it to be Jamie. It's not, it's from Stefan.

How's Mitanor?

It's going well, I think.

Come on, give me more than that!
How's Jamie?

I picture how he joked with me when I taught him how to bow. It makes me smile.

> He's got a lot to learn, but he seems willing to put the work in, which is good.

Do you think you'll be friends?

> It's too early to say. But I hope so.

Me too.

I swipe through to my emails and find the one sent from Sebastian. I still can't fully process that he is my boyfriend. The email he sent is so cold, it almost feels as if he is setting up a business meeting. Honestly, I wouldn't be shocked if someone on his team wrote it instead of him. My reply was just as clinical, agreeing to all of his terms. In a way I'm lucky, as my time in Mitanor has given me some time before I'm going to have to go on staged public dates with him.

I glance up as the doors open and Jamie steps inside. He appears to have sprinted here, as he's out of breath and his face is sweaty.

"I'm so sorry," he says as he reaches me. "I got lost. I know being late's rude, but I promise it wasn't my fault."

"Don't worry about it."

He sits down.

"Although you could have messaged me," I say.

"I forgot my phone. This afternoon has been a lot, trust me. Anyway, what are we learning today?"

"Dining etiquette."

His face drops. "Like, forks and shit?"

Jamie is lucky I'm teaching him this and not my etiquette teacher. He was a stuffy old Englishman who smelled like tobacco and was fond of barking at me if I ever got something wrong. He would probably have a heart attack if he heard the casual way that Jamie swore.

"You may want to dial back the swearing," I say. "When the time calls for it, a well-placed curse word can be very effective." I nearly smile thinking of the few times I've heard Gran swear. She always did it knowing both that she was only with family and how shocking it was, and she did it with wicked glee. "But that is only when you are around people you trust with your life."

Set out in front of us is a complete dining set. Four forks, three knives, and three spoons, as well as three plates stacked on top of each other as well as one to the side, covered partially by a folded napkin. I had to get some help to set this up, and I asked for the table setting to replicate the environment at the ball.

A few moments later, two aides enter the room, each holding plates covered in silver cloches. One is placed in front of each of us at the same time and then is lifted to reveal a chocolate and raspberry tart.

"Watch me," I say.

I take my napkin, unfold it, flick it out, and lay it smoothly on my lap. Jamie observes, obviously trying to make sure he retains it all.

"Now you try."

He picks his napkin up and tries to mirror what I did. He does a little flick of the wrist, and the napkin snaps outward, knocking over his cup of water.

"I'm sorry!" he says, leaping up to turn the glass back upright. The damage has already been done, and there's now a large water mark on the tablecloth. His cheeks turn bright red.

"Don't worry about it," I say. "Mistakes happen. Plus, I was much worse than you when I first started my lessons."

"Yeah, but how old were you?"

"Five. But I've always been mature for my age."

"That makes me feel so much better."

"Don't worry about your mistakes; you'll never get anywhere if you get fixated on them. Let's get back to it. Napkin, lap."

He puts the napkin on his lap. His cheeks have faded to a light pink.

"Very good," I say. "A general rule of thumb is to work from the outside in. Seeing as this is a dessert, use the spoon on the right."

"Makes sense."

"Now, here's where it can get a little tricky. Most of the grace comes not from the utensils themselves but how you use them. Why don't you eat as you normally would, and I will correct as needed."

He stabs into the tart with the spoon, breaking it apart. I have to hold in a wince. At first, I think he's doing it poorly on purpose to make fun of this whole thing, but then it clicks that he's not. He's thinking about every action and trying his hardest.

"How was that?" he asks.

"It's a start."

"Oh damn," he says. "That bad, huh?"

"I've seen worse. Again, mind your language."

"Sorry."

"Watch me," I say.

Using my utensils, I slice off a small piece of tart. "First of all, you need to go slower. And second, never stab your food with your spoon. I mean it, never. First, you cut a piece, slide it onto your spoon, then bring it to your mouth. Like so."

I slide a piece of tart onto my spoon, directing it with the end of my knife. I make sure not to hit the plate or to make any noise.

It's a little tricky, and requires more thought than simply stabbing and devouring as Jamie did, but I think the effort is well worth it. I've never been able to stand the way some people eat.

"Now you try," I say.

He tries to copy me, but ends up banging his knife against his plate, making a loud scratching noise. Still, it was better than before, and a slight improvement at this point is a victory.

His cheeks light up, turning bright red again.

I must admit, it's endearing.

"It's fine, keep going. Try again."

He does. This time, he manages not to scratch the plate. He successfully cuts off a piece of tart, then slides it onto his spoon, then brings it to his lips. At least the way he eats doesn't need any correcting. It's not like he chews with his mouth open or anything like that. It might be a small victory, but I'll take it.

"How was that?" he asks.

"Not perfect, but better. You'll get this, don't worry. It just takes practice. When you're ready, try again."

He puts down his utensils, waits a second, then picks them back up.

It's a start, but it's a good one.

With time, he will get this.

Chapter Twenty-One

JAMIE

For the first time in a while, I have some free time.

It's night here, and I've just returned from dinner with my family and Erik. Tomas interrupted my lesson with Erik to say goodbye before he leaves for Florence, and I'm a little upset that he won't be here for the rest of the summer. He told me we have plenty of time to get to know each other in the future.

I'm already looking forward to it.

Ren and Amara have continued to keep me updated on what's going on online about me. Apparently, the discourse hasn't slowed down at all, and I'm still one of the most talked-about people online. There have been memes made about me and I now have multiple fan pages and accounts.

Amara thinks all the attention is because I'm living something out of a fairy tale, but in real life. I'm truly not sure why I've struck such a chord. The biggest moment was when an American late-night talk show host made a joke about me.

I've spent the night in my new bedroom, reading one of the books Erik got me about Mitanorian nobility, trying not to think too much about how famous I now am. This book includes a few chapters about Emilia's family, the Alcarons. Their history is nearly as long and bloody as the Mortenallos'.

I close the book. I'm finding it hard to concentrate at the moment.

My old life is gone. Actually, it's completely obliterated. There's no going back to it, even if I wanted to.

I've taken Erik's advice and haven't been reading the comments I keep getting tagged in. I don't think they've taken a dramatic dive into hate or anything, but he's right. It's better to be safe than potentially expose myself to the views of people on the internet.

Anyway, I'm in the middle of the storm right now. I'm sure it will pass. And what then? Will I go back to America? Even if I do that, I can't see it being the same as it was. I think it's safe to say I flew mostly under the radar at school before. There's no way that would happen now.

I load my Instagram and check my direct messages. My follower count has crossed the two-hundred-thousand mark, even though I haven't posted anything since the news went live. My inbox is fuller than ever, with many messages from classmates and other people from my life back home. I even have one from Mr. Shan, my gym teacher, which is very strange, because I thought he hated me.

I haven't heard from Max in a while. She's online, so I call her. She answers on the third ring. "Hey."

"Hi."

I might be reading too much into it, but she doesn't sound as friendly as normal.

"What are you up to?" she asks.

"Not much," I say as I lean back against my chair. "Just the news broke, and everyone knows who I am now."

"How are you holding up?"

"Well enough, I think. I mean, it doesn't feel real. Did you see how many Instagram followers I have now?"

"Last I checked it was like two hundred thousand."

I notice something in Max's voice like she's feeling a little weird about it. I get it, this was never part of the plan. She was the one who was supposed to become famous, not me. I don't think she's jealous, but I feel like I should tread carefully at the moment. The last thing I want is to hurt her.

"It's weird, right?" I ask. "Why are so many people following me?"

"Probably because this sort of thing doesn't happen, like, ever."

"Anyway, I wanted your advice on something." Changing the subject is deliberate, as I can tell she's not feeling great about me getting this much attention. I can't blame her—this wasn't supposed to happen. "I kind of want to hang out with Erik. Do you think it would be weird if I asked him if he wanted to do something?"

"Why would that be weird?"

"I don't know."

"Jamie."

"I don't want him to think I'm flirting or whatever."

"But you think he's cute, right?"

I go quiet for a moment, then remember that I'm speaking to my best friend. I can tell her anything. I never told her I think he's cute, but she's seen pictures of him and must know he's my type. Plus, Erik is one of those people who's undeniably good-looking. He has great hair and nice skin, and he's tall and athletic. He's undeniably cute.

"Yes."

"Then what's the problem?"

I sit on the edge of my bed so hard the frame makes a groaning noise. I'm not sure exactly how to put this into words for her. I'm worried about many things, but I think the biggest is Erik finding out I'm thinking about him in that way and then him having to let me down. He'll be here for a while, and if that happens, it could become incredibly awkward. Having him here to talk to has already helped so much, and I don't want to risk that.

"He has a boyfriend," I say. "It's a fake relationship for the press, but still."

"Then nothing can happen. Just invite him over to hang out, I know you want to. You'll regret it if you don't."

She's right, like she usually is. I will regret it if I chicken out.

"Enough about me," I say. "How does it feel having the 'Ashes' video out?"

She sighs. "It's okay, I guess. We've got nearly two hundred views, but they could be from me refreshing so much. We all worked so hard on it, and I'm thinking what now, you know?"

"Totally," I say. "But give it time. I told you Erik loved it, didn't I?"

"Yes, you did. Speaking of, you should go hang out with the prince, I'm kinda tired. Love you."

"Love you, too."

She ends the call.

I open up a text to Erik, and I start typing.

> Hey, do you want to do something?
> I have Mario Kart if you like that.

My phone vibrates.

> I love Mario Kart! Now?

I go to the living room and find Mike sitting on the couch, watching some action movie on Netflix.

On the screen, a guy is pushed away from an explosion, which is not how it would work in real life. He'd be burnt to a crisp, and his eardrums would've burst at the least. Mike has a notebook and pen on his lap, meaning he must be taking notes for an online movie review.

"Oh hey, buddy," says Mike, pausing the movie. "What are you up to?"

"Not much, what are you watching?"

"Some movie called *The Feed*. It's pretty good. It's about these scientists who find an alien spore on a meteorite and decide to make a weapon using it. Want to join me? You haven't missed much."

"I'm okay, thanks. I was wondering if it would be cool for me to use the living room tonight?"

He frowns. "What for?"

"I invited Erik over to play *Mario Kart*."

"You can have it, but you'll owe me."

"Deal."

He pauses the movie then gets off of the couch. He winks and goes past me, and he seems to be smiling to himself. I don't even know why I am so anxious. It's not like this is a date. Still, I feel jittery, almost beside myself with nerves and excitement.

I reply to Erik's message.

Yup 😊

Okay, see you soon 😊

I find myself smiling at my phone. Max was right. She usually is.

I quickly clean up the living room, putting the cushions onto the corner of the couch and straightening the art magazines left on the coffee table. Once that's done, I turn on my console and make sure the controllers are both working. They are. I'm glad I brought it from home because I know *Mario Kart* is a great icebreaker. In my experience, most people at least somewhat like it.

I recheck my phone. No new messages. That's a good sign. How long will it take for him to get from his apartment to here? It can only be a few minutes unless he had to get ready or something.

Which might totally be the case. I get the impression that Erik never goes anywhere without getting a little dressed up first.

The more time the better, as it will let me get my nerves under control.

I go back to my room. There's a large, ornate mirror in the corner. I turn to the side, inspecting my outfit. It's simple, a black T-shirt and workout shorts, but it's hardly going to impress anyone. I hurry over to my closet, and find a short-sleeved button-down and my favorite pair of jeans. I switch into them, then go over and check myself out in the mirror again. My hair is doing that annoying thing again where it sticks out in nearly all directions. I start pushing it back into place, then test my breath by breathing on my palm. It's fine, but I still grab some mints and pop them into my mouth.

A knock sounds on the door to our apartment.

Crap, I need more time. I frantically try to push my hair down, but it somehow only makes it worse. Crap crap crap. I push it down as hard as I can, and then I run across the apartment. I slide to a stop, my socks failing to get any grip on the hardwood floor, then pause for a moment to take a deep breath in. I'll be fine. I'm having an incredibly attractive, openly queer prince over to hang out. Child's play. I pull open the door before the nerves get the best of me.

As I was expecting, Erik is standing outside. What I wasn't expecting was for him to be dressed much more casually than normal. Each other time he's been in some form of formal attire, but this time he's in a heather-gray T-shirt, black jeans, and clean white sneakers. His hair is also a little messier than it usually is, in loose golden curls that fall down over his forehead. I'm a little obsessed with the entire look.

Okay, more than a little. I'm completely obsessed.

"Hey," I say. My focus drifts down, because his T-shirt fits him exceptionally well, snug around his arms.

"Hi."

As he passes, I catch the scent of his cologne. It's light and a little sweet, but distinctly masculine.

"So, you like *Mario Kart*," I ask, trying to ignore how good the cologne smells. "That doesn't seem very princely of you."

"I think everyone likes *Mario Kart*."

"Even princes?"

"Yes, even princes. You like it, don't you?"

I don't know what to say to that. But I think it's the first time he's called me a prince, and it's thrilling.

We go through to the living room. On the TV is the main menu, and the cartoony music is playing. "Um, can I get you a drink or something? I think we've got some sodas if you'd like?"

"I'll have what you're having."

I go back to the fridge and open it. I find a few different sodas, and decide to play it safe by picking two glass bottles of a Mitanorian cola brand, Solaz Cola. When I get back to the living room, Erik is already seated, and he has one arm stretched out over the backrest. Should I sit down next to him, in the crook of his arm? I know guys do that sometimes, but I don't know if I'm at that level of familiarity with Erik. I hand him the cola.

I feel more nervous around him than I have before, and I'm not exactly sure why.

"Thanks," he says, sitting forward and solving my dilemma for me.

I sit down beside him. "Cheers."

We tap our bottles against each other.

"Shall we?" he asks.

I start the game.

"I like your shirt," he says, as the game loads.

Don't blush, don't blush. I can't fight it, and I feel my cheeks grow warm. I take a sip of the cola, and it's incredible, both sweet and fizzy. I wonder if there will be any Mitanorian foods I don't like.

"Oh, um, thanks. It's from Target."

"Is Target as good as everyone on the internet says it is?"

"It's better," I say. "I'm like a soccer mom, I love Target that much. Wait, does that mean you don't have them in Sunstad?"

He shakes his head. "Now I feel like I'm missing out."

"We'll have to go there sometime," I blurt, before I realize what I've said. I don't even know how long Erik is going to be in my life, and we have an almost built-in expiry date. At some point, I will go back to America, and he will go back to Sunstad.

I grab the controller and start the game, bringing up the character selection screen. I pick my choice, Toad on a motorbike, and then he chooses his, King Boo in a monster trunk, and we start the race.

It's immediately obvious that Erik is good at this, and I will need to concentrate if I'm going to win. He did tell me he's a gamer, but I'm still surprised, as I'm not used to facing much competition. We both pull ahead of the NPC racers, so it seems like a race between the two of us. I'm in the lead, but he's right behind me. Plus, I've played enough *Mario Kart* to know that being in first place doesn't mean much. It can change at any moment; all it takes is one blue shell for your dreams to be crushed.

He overtakes me, but luckily I had a red shell prepared. I fire it, and send him tumbling.

"You bastard," he says, pushing me with his shoulder.

My skin tingles where he touched me. In the moment of distraction, I go off the cliff. Plus, he swore. I get the impression that he doesn't swear in front of many people, which makes me think I'm seeing a side of Erik he mostly keeps hidden. For maybe the first time, he seems like just a regular guy, rather than a flawless prince.

"Damn it," I say.

"Excuse you," he says. I'm shocked for a moment, but then I realize he's joking.

I give him the middle finger.

This in turn surprises him, as he goes straight into a mud patch, which slows him down.

"I see how it is," he says. "You're going down, Johnson."

"We'll see, Lindstrom."

We're neck and neck around the racecourse until we reach the final stretch. He's in the lead, and he's so far ahead that only a miracle could save me. He's so focused on the race he hasn't noticed that he's moved a little closer. His arm is right by mine, barely an inch away. I focus on the race. Even if I drive perfectly, I can't catch him.

Luckily for me, I see a miracle approaching. Seconds later, a blue shell flies past me. I swerve out of the way at the last second, leaving me unscathed.

"You've got to be kidding me," he says. There's nothing he can do.

The shell crashes into him before the finish line. I manage to overtake him, winning the race.

"That's so unfair," he says.

"That's the beauty of *Mario Kart*," I say. "No matter what, you're never out of the race."

He presses the button on his controller a few times, making the victory screen disappear. "We're doing this again, right now."

"Hope you're ready to lose again."

"We'll see."

I hit *play*.

CHAPTER TWENTY-TWO

ERIK

"What are you doing here?" asks Jamie.

I'm standing in the middle of the ballroom, and Jamie has walked in. Moonlight streams in through the arched windows. I glance around, taking it all in. It's exactly the same as it was the night of the king's ball, with one huge difference.

There's nobody else here. It's just Jamie and me. He's wearing the suit he wore to the ball, and looks as good as he did that night. His hair is still too long and all over the place, but as time goes on I'm finding I like his long hair.

Distantly, I'm aware that I'm dreaming. Still, I want to see where this goes.

"I was waiting for you," I say.

That earns a trademark Jamie Johnson smile. Big, warm, slightly lopsided. I step closer.

"Hey," he says.

"Hi."

He leans in close to kiss me.

My eyes snap open. The ballroom vanishes. I'm in my room in the palace. I was right, it was just a dream.

Still, it lingers. I close my eyes again, and I'm back on the dance floor, with Jamie right in front of me. I remember the feeling of wanting to kiss him. I huff and scrub a hand through my hair.

Of course I go and have a dream like that. I've received the explicit instruction to keep things platonic between us, and this is where my brain goes. Technically, I have a boyfriend, even if we don't talk. I let out a groan.

Sunlight is streaming in through the open blinds. This bed is extremely comfortable, and I wish I could stay in here all day. It feels far less risky than going out there, where I could make a mistake that impacts not only me, but my family and my country.

What was that dream? I don't like Jamie, do I? I mean yes, he's very cute, and I like his personality. But I didn't think I thought of him as anything other than a friend.

I remember the dream and find myself filling with want. Now I'm so curious about what it would be like to kiss him.

The thoughts surprise me, but they're just that. Thoughts. I can't control them and they don't mean anything.

I roll over, reach out and check my phone. I can't recall the last time I had a dream that vivid. It felt so real, like I really was there.

As fun as it could be, it's a bad idea, and I should be especially careful going forward. Making out with him would make things complicated for the two of us. And it would mean going against an explicit order from Gran. And what about Sebastian? Our relationship might not be based on real feelings, but he is still my boyfriend.

I unlock my phone. Jamie has sent me a meme of a dog spinning around in a circle. I laugh, and scroll through my social media until I find one good enough to send back to him. The one I find is of a respectable-looking elderly woman sliding down a staircase on a mattress.

He sends back a heart reaction, and it makes hundreds of pink love hearts fill my screen. It makes my stomach flutter.

A part of me thinks this is what a relationship should be. Sending each other jokes, making each other feel good.

I send the video to Sebastian. He replies with the thumbs-up emoji, and that's it. Message received.

My lesson with Jamie isn't for another hour now. I have some time. Today is the day of Jamie's press conference. Anxiety builds at the thought. We've made progress, but is he really ready to face the press?

I get out of bed, grab all my swimming stuff and a towel, then leave my room. I need to be as clearheaded as possible, and I've found exercise is one of the best ways to get myself to calm down when I feel there is too much on my plate.

I cross the quiet palace until I reach the pool. Unfortunately, it is being used. The pool is decent in size, but I hate sharing a pool with someone else. It's awkward and not worth it. I'll work out in the gym instead, and try swimming later. I turn, and go back toward the exit.

"Erik, wait!"

I stop, and find that the guy in the pool has stopped swimming. It's Alexander. He pushes himself out of the pool and makes his way over. He grabs a towel and wraps it around his waist, then pulls on a shirt.

"I didn't know you swam," he says.

"Yeah, it clears my head."

"Mine, too. Before you swim, mind if we have a word?"

"Of course."

He rolls his shoulders. I haven't spent much time around Alexander, but I like him. He seems like an incredibly kind man, who is clearly trying his best with Jamie, and has been nothing but nice to me. Being around him does make me nervous, as he is a king, and if I were to say anything out of line, word would surely get back to my parents.

"How do you think Jamie is coping?" he asks.

Jamie hasn't given me any indication that he's struggling in a way that is more than is to be expected, given the huge life change he's gone through, but then again, surely he must be. His whole world has been completely upended. It would only be human to have a difficult time coming to terms with that.

"I think he's doing well, everything considered," I say. "Why do you ask?"

"I'm his father, I worry about him. You don't think the press conference is a little too soon?"

"If he says he's ready, then I think he is. I wouldn't underestimate him."

"Good point. Thank you, Erik. I trust your judgment. Are you planning on doing any more lessons with Jamie today?"

"We're going to do another one this morning, after breakfast."

"Ah, good. You're his teacher, so it is up to you, but I was wondering if the two of you would like to go for a horse ride with me this morning? I want Jamie to relax, to have fun here, as well. I've found over-preparation can be as dangerous as under-preparation."

I imagine what he's suggesting. A horse ride through the countryside with Jamie sounds both incredibly fun and incredibly risky given the dream I had last night and these annoyingly persistent thoughts. Still, refusing this request doesn't feel like an option, mainly because I don't want to be the reason Jamie misses out on doing something fun with his father.

"I think he'd love that."

"Great. We will go after breakfast. That should give you enough time to do one more lesson before the press conference."

He claps me on the shoulder, then leaves the pool room. I go still for a moment, thinking it over. Jamie isn't the most outdoorsy type of guy, but I have a feeling he will love horse riding. The area around the palace is gorgeous, and I can't think of a better way to explore it than on horseback.

Once he's gone, I drop my bag and strip down to my swimming trunks, then grab my goggles.

I dive into the water. I swim under the surface until my lungs start to hurt, and then I surface, taking in a big breath. Then I swim as hard as I can toward the other end of the pool.

I think about the dream I had. It lingers in my mind.

The truth is, things with Jamie feel right. Things with Sebastian don't, and I can't see that changing.

The thoughts intertwine with what my instructions were. I can think these things, but I cannot act on them.

I swim until all I can think about is how much my body hurts.

"Hey, girl," says Jamie. "Easy."

He lifts a hand and pets the horse on the side of her face. She's a brown horse called Daisy, and according to the stable worker who has been helping us get ready for our ride, she's Maria's favorite. I can see why, she's clearly incredibly friendly. Jamie laughs as she nuzzles his hand.

"I love her," he says.

I look up at the sky. There's heavy cloud cover, like it could rain at any moment. I look back as Jamie scratches the white diamond in the middle of Daisy's forehead. She seems to love it, and him.

"All right, Erik," says Alexander. "Your horse is called Apollo."

I freeze. The horse in the stable next to Daisy's is large and jet-black. He's staring me down at the moment with cold, unblinking eyes, as if he knows what is going to happen and he isn't at all pleased about it. I don't even want to try to pet him; he seems too dignified for that.

"He only looks mean," says Alexander. He's already saddled on his horse, a dark brown male called Pony, apparently named by Tomas when he was a kid.

Apollo stares at me. I'm not sure what Alexander said is true.

A stable worker, a woman with curly, bright red hair, helps Jamie onto Daisy. Both Daisy and Apollo already have saddles, I guess put on by the worker before we got here.

"Whoa," says Jamie. "It's way higher off the ground than I thought."

"Are you all right?" I ask.

"Yeah, I think. Are you sure this is okay? I don't want to hurt her."

"You won't," says the stable worker. "Be gentle, you'll be fine."

I get onto Apollo. He snorts as I sit back on the saddle. Now that each of us is on our horse, Alexander sets off, following a path away from the stables. In the distance, standing out amongst the large stretches of green, is the palace.

"Come on, girl," says Jamie, lifting the reins up a little and then down. I am sure it's not going to work, but then Daisy starts to move. Jamie laughs.

"Follow me," says Alexander.

He sets off. Jamie and Daisy follow him.

I try to get Apollo to move, but he's completely still.

"Come on, boy," I say. "Let's go."

I get it. I would hate to be chilling, only to get forced out of my home to carry around a complete stranger.

The stable worker gives Apollo a piece of carrot, and that's apparently enough to get him to move. I catch up with Jamie and Alexander.

The three of us form a line as we follow the well-worn trail through the fields.

"Look!" calls Jamie.

I see where he's pointing, and he's noticed a baby lamb nibbling on some grass. Another sheep, I'm guessing the mother, is standing a few feet away from the lamb, keeping a close eye on everything. There's an entire herd of them, and they seem blissfully happy. My guess is that they're wool sheep, as some are incredibly fluffy, while others have clearly been recently shaved.

"Adorable," I call back.

We follow the trail around a corner, into a small thicket of woodland. It gets a few degrees cooler in here, and it's nice. We're still within the gated area, so it's secure, but out here it's much easier to feel less confined than it is back at the palace. It feels like we could go anywhere we wanted to. I get Apollo to speed up, so I'm keeping pace with Jamie and Daisy. Like most other things, he seems to have picked this up quickly. He actually seems right at home.

Apollo suddenly stops walking, and decides to eat some grass that's growing on the side of the trail. Alexander turns around, and rides up beside me.

"Horse trouble?" he asks.

Jamie does the same, easily managing to get Daisy to turn around.

"Try asking him nicely," suggests Jamie.

I put my hand on Apollo's side. I'm not sure it'll work, because it really does seem as if Apollo has already made up his mind, but I figure it's worth a shot. "Hey, Apollo. I know this isn't fun for you, but I respect you, okay? And I would really appreciate it if you would move."

Apollo lifts his head, then returns to eating.

"Keep going," says Jamie. "He's listening."

"Come on, boy. Let's go, then we can get you back home, all right? The sooner this ride is over, the sooner you can get me off your back."

He snorts, then lifts his head and starts walking again.

"Seems like Jamie could teach us a thing or two, eh, Erik?" says Alexander.

Jamie beams. It makes my chest feel strange.

We ride for about an hour, going through the farmland that surrounds the forest, which is broken up by dense patches of forest. We ride past small creeks and over cobblestone bridges. By the time the stables are back within view, rain has started to sprinkle down. It's clearly just a start, though. At any moment, the heavens are going to open.

"We should go a little faster," suggests Alexander.

Jamie must have some sort of psychic connection to Daisy, as a light nudge is all she needs to increase her pace.

"Come on, Apollo, let's go."

It might be the rain, or him sensing that we're nearly home, but Apollo listens, picking up his pace to keep up with the other two. We race down the path back to the stables, but not fast enough: the rain starts, and all of a sudden, it's pouring. I'm soaked instantly, my clothes sticking to my skin. Jamie and Alexander are similarly drenched. Jamie's hair is pressed down over his forehead, and his white shirt is clinging to his skin. I try not to notice it.

"I'll bring the car around," says Alexander. "Wait here."

I get off Apollo as quickly as I can, jumping down to the ground so hard I nearly slip on the mud.

I don't, though, thank goodness. I want to rush to the safety of the stables, but Jamie is still on Daisy. I offer him my hand to help him get down. He hesitates for a second, then grabs my hand and holds on for dear life as he drops to the earth. When he lands, his foot slips out from under him, and he crashes into my chest.

The world stops. I hold him, and he looks up into my eyes. He's breathless and clearly a little frightened from the fall, as he's clinging to me. His mouth opens a little, and I can't help but admire how soft his lips look. I think about kissing him again, and an intense surge of desire fills me.

He clears his throat, moving his hand up to my shoulder to hold himself steady.

"Thanks," he says, keeping his eyes anywhere but mine.

"No problem."

He starts to blush. I know it's something he does quite a lot, and I know I shouldn't read anything into it. Still, a small part of me, a part I can't control, hopes that maybe it means something.

Is he feeling anything like what I am? Or is this all in my head?

I remember the dream again. It's like it flicked a switch within me. Now I can't stop noticing Jamie in that way, even if I'm trying my best to stop. It doesn't help that his wet shirt is stuck to his lean frame, and it's gone almost see-through. He looks down, notices, and folds his arms over his chest.

"Sorry," he says.

"No need to apologize."

He grins. "Usually I charge for this."

Together, we hurry into the stables to get out of the rain. It smells earthy and warm. Jamie has his arms crossed, and I can tell he's looking at me. He chews his bottom lip.

"That was fun," he says. His back is pressed against the stable wall.

"Yeah," I say.

The tension between us feels palpable. I try to read him, and I get the impression he is thinking about the same thing I am. Or maybe I just hope he is, because all I want right now is to close the distance, press him up against the wall, and kiss him. But I know that's a bad idea. Alexander will be back at any time, and I've been forbidden from seeing Jamie in that way.

To test the waters, I take a small step closer. It's not enough to fully enter his personal space, but closer than I need to be.

I lift my stare, but his eyes dart away. He moves to the side, breaking the spell as he puts some distance between us. It's as clear a signal as can be.

He's not interested.

Chapter Twenty-Three

Jamie

I know I should be nervous about the press conference.

It's huge and terrifying. My entire future might be decided by it. Even though it is scary, I am freaked out by something else even more.

While we were in the stables, I thought Erik might kiss me. He didn't say anything, but he looked at me in a way that I thought maybe, just maybe, he was thinking about making a move.

I wanted him to. Honestly, ever since I left the stables, I've been thinking about how amazing it would've been if he did. Mentally, I'm stuck there, in the stables, smelling the rain and the grassy air, hoping he'll kiss me.

It would've been the perfect place. I mean, in the rain, after horse riding? Come on. I can't think of a place to have a first kiss that would be better than that.

But I freaked out and moved away. Who knows if I am even going to get the chance again? I probably won't. The tension broke when I did that, and now I'm worried he took the wrong message. Me freaking out doesn't mean I don't want to kiss him. It means I freaked out because it's what I do.

Also, I'm not sure how Sebastian figures into all this. I don't want to be the type to kiss someone with a boyfriend, even if it is a fake relationship.

This morning we had another lesson, where we went over

some pre-scripted answers for questions we decided they might ask during the press conference. Every time I answered a question, I felt my responses getting stronger. As much as I do want to kiss Erik, I pushed all of that aside to focus on my lesson. It was a good call, I think.

I wouldn't call what I'm feeling for Erik a crush, not yet. But I am certainly interested in him in a more-than-friends way. It freaks me out because it's so complicated. I know the best move would be to get these feelings under control, but I'm not sure I can.

Currently I'm walking back to our apartment, where apparently a surprise is waiting for me. I unlock the door and find Mom and Mike aren't alone in the apartment. Standing with them is an entire team of people. As I walk in, the room goes quiet.

Uh-oh. What is this?

Beside Mom is an entire rack of clothes. They've also set up what seems to be a little hairdressing station, with a mirror and a swivel chair.

"Jamie!" says one of the unfamiliar faces, a handsome man wearing a brown jumpsuit covered in zippers and chunky white sneakers. A pair of oversized sunglasses sits on the top of his head, above his long jet-black hair. Everyone else in the room is styled in a similar way: over the top but in a fashionable way. It makes them look like they're from a completely different world than Mom, Mike, and me.

The man in the jumpsuit offers me his hand. I remember Erik's lesson and shake his hand, applying only a little pressure and looking into his eyes, the way Erik taught me.

"Good handshake," he says. "My name's Simon."

"Nice to meet you," I say.

I glance at Mom and Mike. Both of them are stifling smiles. Seriously, what is this?

"They're here to get you ready for the press conference," says Mom.

"If you want," says Simon. "Alexander made it very clear that we are only to work our magic if you want us to."

It clicks.

This is a makeover.

"So," says Simon. "What do you say?"

"Let's do this," I say.

It's time for the big reveal.

Simon and the team have been working on me for the better part of the past hour. I've had a face treatment, including a mask that smelled like green tea. Then I got a haircut, in which Simon fussed over me much more than the usual barber I go to.

Then I was given my pick of new clothes. I ended up picking a white button-down, black slacks that have a dark red floral stripe down the sides, and shiny black boots. It's not the showiest of outfits, although I did try on a few more avant-garde pieces Simon said I could wear when I have a film premiere to attend. I hadn't realized that is something that might be in the cards for me, and the way he said it so confidently, like it is inevitable, has me hyped up.

I wish I could say it was enough to completely take my mind off Erik. Truly, though, the whole time I was thinking about what he'd think of my makeover.

Mom has pulled a large mirror from my bedroom. I go up to it, and for a split second, I don't recognize the guy in front of me.

I do a double take.

I look good. Like, really freaking good. My hair is shorter than I usually wear it, but Simon has kept some length on the top and shaped it so it only slightly falls over my forehead. For the first time in my life, I have a haircut I think is legitimately cool. I do a spin. The clothes fit me perfectly. They make me look older, in a good way. I look like I've stepped off a runway.

Now I get why they did this. It's a pure shot of confidence.

"I take it that means you're pleased?" asks Simon.

"I love it. I need to text my friends, they're going to freak out about this."

I take a selfie in the mirror, and send it to the group chat. The picture is mind-blowing—it barely even looks like me. I didn't even know it was possible for me to look like this. Dare I say it, I'm kind of hot.

I get an idea. I am going to the press conference. I may as well post to my social media as well. I have nearly three hundred thousand followers now, even though I still haven't posted anything new. I've been waiting for the right time, and this clearly is it. I post the photo, as well as the caption: **About to do my first press conference. Wish me luck!**

"We're running a little late," says Mom. "People are waiting."

Comments and likes start flooding in.

That's really exciting, but I can't focus on it too much, as I actually need to do the press conference now. I breathe in, hold my breath for a few seconds, then exhale. This will be fine. I need to remember my lessons with Erik. I felt confident during those. The worst thing I can do right now is let my anxiety take over.

As we get closer to the press conference hall, I realize that I was talking a much bigger game than I actually feel. I start to hear the sounds of a crowd assembled and waiting. Alexander and Maria greet me in the stateroom. Erik is missing. My stomach plummets and my heart starts fluttering. Where did he go? Does he think I'm going to bomb so hard that he can't witness it?

"Jamie," says Alexander. "You look incredible."

"Thank you," I say. "Simon's amazing."

"So are you," he says. "I know this must make you nervous, and I am so proud of you for following through with it anyway."

"I'll try my best," I say.

"That's all you need to do. I don't want to distract you from the conference, but there's something I want to give you tonight. I will have it sent to your room."

"Okay," I say. "By the way, where's Erik?"

"He ducked out for a moment to take a call. Ah, here he is now."

Erik rounds the corner, his focus on his phone. He lifts his gaze, and stops in his tracks when he sees me. He looks stunned. I couldn't have asked for a more perfect reaction. I take it that means he likes it.

"What do you think?" I ask.

"You, it's, um. You look great, Jamie." He clears his throat, as if he surprised himself by giving such an earnest answer.

"Any last-minute advice?"

"Just be yourself out there, and everyone is going to love you."

There's this look in Erik's eyes. It's soft and affectionate. I've never had anyone look at me like this. I don't want to leave this moment. I could live my whole life here, with him looking at me like this. Like I'm something wonderful.

"Jamie," says Alexander, breaking the spell. "It's time."

"See you soon," I say, to Erik. "Wish me luck."

"You don't need it. You've got this."

Alexander and I enter the conference room. Cameras start flashing as we make our way to the front, where a table with two chairs and two microphones has been set up. Erik's words mean the world to me. He believes in me, so I should believe in myself.

The room is almost completely full, and they are all here for me. Up at the front of the room is a large table, but there are only two seats. I look around for Mom and Mike, and spot them as they take a seat in the back, among a bunch of reporters. A hush falls over the crowd as I sit down. I pull the microphone closer to me and it makes a loud screeching noise. The room goes completely silent.

"Sorry," I say.

Alexander sits down beside me. At the back of the room, Erik joins Mom and Mike. A little farther in front of them are my grandparents on my bio-mom's side.

"Let's get started, shall we?" asks Alexander. "I'm sure you all have a lot of questions for Jamie, but I thought it would be best for him to introduce himself in his own words. Take it away, Jamie."

There are so many people here. My eyes settle on Erik. He gives me an encouraging smile, and something kind of miraculous happens. My nerves settle, just a little. They don't feel out of control anymore. We've prepared for this. We've even gone over this question a few times. All I need to say are the answers we have prepared, and I'll be fine.

"First of all, hi, everyone," I say. "Thank you all for coming out today, I appreciate it. And thank you for giving me the time to process everything."

The crowd is quiet. They don't seem against me or anything, it's more they are giving me the space to speak.

"I'm sure most of you know the story by now, but for those of you who don't, I think I'll say it again."

I recount the story of Mom telling me the truth. As I do, I notice the feeling in the room starts to change. A few people let out *aww*s when I tell them about me forgiving Mom, and I find any sense of hostility that was once there is now totally gone. I wrap up the story, and become aware that everyone has been listening intensely. It's actually really cool.

"Does anyone have any questions?" I ask.

Almost everyone in the room raises their hand.

"Um, you," I say, tilting my head toward a serious-looking reporter wearing a beige blazer.

She stands up. "Hi, Jamie, thank you for taking the time to

talk to us. I was wondering how your classmates back home re-acted to this news?"

"They've been cool, actually. I've gotten a few messages from them, and they've all been really supportive."

She sits, and another reporter stands, taking her place.

"How exactly did you feel when you found out your father is a king?"

"I was shocked. It's not really something I was expecting, you know. But I think I rolled with it pretty well."

That earns another round of chuckles from the crowd. An-other reporter stands up. "Have you truly forgiven your mother for keeping the secret?"

A hush sweeps over the entire room. I see Mom in the back row, and she's hanging on every word.

"I have," I say. "She's my mom, and I love and trust her. It's as simple as that."

"It must've hurt your feelings?"

"It did," I say. "But I understand why she didn't tell me. She was trying to do the best thing by my bio-mom. It's hard to be mad at her for that."

The reporter finally sits down. Alexander gives me a pat on the shoulder.

"I'm sure you've seen, but there's been a lot of speciation on-line about your love life," he says. "Everyone is curious: Is there a girl back home waiting for you?"

"No, there's no girl, but I'm gay, so if there were someone in the picture they'd be a guy."

That causes another shift in the room. If anything, people are even more curious now.

A different reporter stands. "Are you dating anyone?"

"Nope," I say, feeling the blush on my cheeks fire up again. I accidentally glance at Erik. "Let me say how weird it is to be asked that question in front of an entire room of people and my parents."

A bunch of people in the crowd laugh, and the atmosphere changes. I can feel it. People relax, and I do as well. This might be a little scary, but they don't seem to be hell-bent on destroying my reputation or anything. The next reporter stands.

I look at Erik again. We haven't really spoken about guys, other than me coming out to him. I try to read into his reaction, to see if there's any obvious response to me saying that. I can't tell anything from it.

"Do you think you'll stay in Mitanor long?" asks a different reporter.

"Um, I'm not sure. We haven't talked about that, but I'm having a really good time getting to know Alexander and his family."

"Jamie is welcome to stay for as long as he likes," says Alexander.

Wait, really?

That's awesome.

I answer questions for the next half hour, but I keep thinking about Alexander's invite. I settle into a comfortable groove. I even crack a few jokes which all land, and make the audience laugh. I must say, that's a pretty good feeling.

"We've got time for one last question," says Alexander. "Make it a good one."

It's a male reporter who stands up.

"Have you decided where you'll go to school, if you decide to stay in Mitanor after the summer?"

I frown. I'm actually not sure the answer to that one.

"As I said before, we haven't discussed that far ahead yet," says Alexander. "As with most things, the decision is Jamie's to make. We're out of time now, thank you all for coming."

"It was nice meeting you all," I say.

Reporters continue to shout out questions, but Alexander gets up and walks off the stage. I follow him, and then go through to a stateroom. Mom and Mike appear a few moments later, with Erik trailing close behind.

"You were amazing," says Mom, giving me a hug.

"You really were," says Mike. "They all loved you."

"Could you tell I was blushing?" I ask.

"A little, but it was endearing."

Erik joins us. He's smiling sheepishly. God, he's cute. It seems like he's doing that thing where people put on a fake upset look before delivering good news so the moment lands harder.

"How was I?" I ask.

"You were *incredible,*" he says. "You couldn't have done it better if you'd tried. Did you feel that?"

"Feel what?"

"The crowd, they *loved* you. I've never seen anything like it."

"Really?"

"I've gotten word from the communications office," says Maria, who is looking at her phone. "We've gotten a dozen offers for an exclusive interview already."

"What does that mean?"

"It means they love you," says Alexander. "That's my boy!"

My boy?

It does seem a little early for him to call me that, but I actually don't mind. If I'm being honest, I love that he said that. I'm not ready to call him Dad, or anything along those lines. But Alexander, at least so far, has been everything I could hope for in a father.

I find myself smiling.

I look at the four of them. Mom, Mike, Alexander, and Maria. It might be a little unusual for a family configuration, but right now?

I wouldn't change it for the world.

Chapter Twenty-Four

Erik

> Hey, are you free tonight? Want to
> do something?

I look at the message he sent. This whole day, I've been wondering if Jamie would ask me to do something with him. The hours passed in our usual routine: run, breakfast, lesson. Today I taught him about public speaking, as well as the various greetings required for different members of a royal family.

I spent the rest of my time this afternoon in my apartment, playing *Arcane Realms,* trying to decide if I wanted to invite Jamie over or not.

I decided not to, because I have to fight this. From now on, if Jamie asks me over, I will stay away. I need to resist his pull.

I should only spend time with him when I have to. If I do that from now on, hopefully that will be enough to get this back on track.

I message him.

> Hey, I'm feeling pretty tired and might
> have an early night. Raincheck?

It might be a lie, but I don't think I need to bother Jamie with the truth. It might hurt him. What I'll do is retreat, and hope the rest of my time here passes quickly. I envision myself as nothing more than one of the countless stuffy tutors I had while growing up. That's what I need to be to Jamie. Pompous, boring, and a stickler for the rules. Distinctly not someone fun for him to spend time with.

The typing bubble appears, then vanishes.

I can't take my eyes off my screen. Even though I know it's for the best, a part of me aches at the thought that I could be spending time with him, but I'm choosing not to. Even with all the swirling doubts, being around him feels so easy. So much about my life has always felt like work: carefully analyzing every interaction, making sure I'm presenting an appropriate version of myself, one that represents myself, my country, and the crown, with the appropriate amount of reverence.

With Jamie, I don't feel that way. My walls are down in a way they've never been before, and spending time with him is simply easy. It just works, in a way that feels special.

My phone vibrates. I take a moment to brace myself, then read the message.

> Oh, okay! I had a thing planned
> but that's all good. ☺

He had a thing planned? And now I'm missing out? It claws at me from under my skin. Knowing him, it was something great. This is good, though. It's the right thing to do. It is difficult, but that doesn't mean it's not the right move. An entire life spent as a prince has trained me for this very thing.

Sometimes, one simply can't have everything they desire.

I focus on the game. Maybe killing Ashondra's legion or the demon queen herself will be enough for me. It's what I need right now. A night in a fantasy world, where my only concerns are the bloodthirsty demons that are trying to murder me. I'm not sure it's a good thing that I would prefer to face a horde than my own life, but there's not much I can do about that.

I put my phone down beside my computer. A second later I check the screen. Nothing. I find myself wishing Jamie would gently push me and ask me to spend the night with him again. I already know if he asked again, I wouldn't have the strength to say no.

Seriously, what did he have planned for us?

I fast-travel back to my home base, a location I have spent countless hours decorating and organizing. My character, also named Erik, is dressed in a simple tunic. His wings are tucked in up against his back. It's not good enough for battle, though, so I switch into my current armor. It's one of the highest-level pieces available in the game, and it shows. It's made of intricate plates of silver and gold. Detailed runes have been etched into the metal. My character stretches out his wings and unsheathes his golden sword. Now that I'm ready to face my demonic enemies, I fast-travel to the wastelands, where Ashondra and her armies reside.

I start exploring, and quickly kill a group of demonic enemies, but I know my heart isn't in it. I grab my phone and text Jamie.

What was your plan?

Haha. I'll see you soon. 😊

I exit out of the game, and head to my room. I'm in a tank and sweats, and my hair is a mess. I'm completely and utterly unpresentable. As I reach the closet, I stop. Mum and Dad would hate it if I were to be seen wearing something like this, but they aren't here. Plus, Jamie has only ever seen me when I'm looking my best. A part of me wants to see what he thinks of me without all of that. As with most guys, I'm curious if he is interested in me, or the fact that I'm a prince.

I shut my closet.

A few minutes later, a loud knock sounds on my door. I jog across the apartment and open it.

Jamie is standing outside, holding a whole bundle of things. He's brought his laptop, as well as a bottle of champagne. From the looks of things, it isn't a non-alcoholic version; it's the real thing. He glances down, and his eyes widen for a split second before he catches himself.

I caught him checking me out.

"Hey," he says. "I know you're tired, but I thought maybe we could make it quick?"

I grip the door. A war goes on in my mind.

"All right," I say, opening the door the rest of the way to let him in.

"I feel overdressed," he says.

"I'll go get changed."

"You don't have to, it's fine," he blurts. "I mean, it's a good look. Forget I said anything."

"Thank you," I say. "I feel like I look like a mess, so I appreciate that."

"Anytime. Cool apartment, by the way."

I retreat to my bedroom. What is going on with me? I should've fought him again, and told him I'm too tired to hang out. It would've taken all my willpower to do so, but it was still the right move, I know that without a single doubt.

Still, I have an attractive guy in an apartment that is all my own. This moment is one I have dreamed of ever since I first realized I liked guys.

He puts the champagne and the two glasses on the coffee table, next to each other.

"How did you get that?" I ask.

"Alexander gave it to me as a celebratory thing, to congratu-late me for doing well at the press conference. I thought we could try it?"

That sounds fun.

It also sounds extremely dangerous. My family aren't any-thing like the Mortenallos. The legal drinking age in Sunstad is also eighteen, but if I were caught drinking with Jamie I could be in more trouble than I have ever been in my life, even if Alexan-der did give it to him as a gift. It checks out, the legal drinking age in Mitanor is eighteen, and alcohol is treated very differently here. Wine is often served with dinner, and it isn't considered too big of a deal for someone underage to drink it.

Jamie is looking at me in such an open, friendly way. He wants to do this with me.

"One glass can't hurt," I say.

"Totally okay if you don't want to, I'm not going to pressure you. You know that, right?"

"I do. I'm okay with one."

Jamie pauses.

"Is something wrong?"

He laughs. "So, I actually don't know how to open this."

He offers me the bottle. It's got a cork, and that's the problem. I've seen people pop corks before, but I've personally never done it.

"I'll try," I say.

I take the bottle, and take off the metal wire that surrounds the cork. Carefully, I pull on the cork, but it doesn't budge. I pull harder, and it opens with a surprising amount of force.

"Nice," says Jamie.

I pour each of us a glass.

"Cheers," he says, and we tap our glasses. We each take a sip. I don't mind it, but Jamie pulls a face that's pretty close to revolted. "*That's* what it tastes like?"

"You're not a fan?"

"Actually," he says, taking another, more cautious sip. "I don't mind it. I thought it would be sweeter. What do you think?"

I try another sip. "It's good. I don't have much of a sweet tooth. How was the rest of your afternoon, by the way?"

He puts his glass down. "It was good. Alexander gave me something."

"Oh?"

"He gave me some letters. Apparently he wrote them to me over the years, filling me in on his life. They're, like, things he wishes he could've sent to me, you know?"

It's clear these mean the world to him.

"How does that make you feel?" I ask.

"Good," he says. "I feel like I know him a lot better now."

"Well, that's good."

"Yeah," he says. "Anyway, I had an idea for what we could do tonight."

"I'm all ears."

"I thought I could make an *Arcane Realms* character?"

He's already got the game downloaded on his computer. A part of me can't believe he suggested this. I haven't told many people about how much I love this game. I still remember Stefan making fun of me for it. But not Jamie. He found out, and wants to try it.

"It might not be for you," I say.

"I think it will be." He clicks on the game, launching it. "I love nerdy stuff."

"Are you calling me a nerd?"

"Hey, if the shoe fits."

I'm not sure he knows how exposing this is for me. I have invested so much time into this, which might be a little sad, but I'll be crushed if he doesn't enjoy it.

The game loads, and the theme music starts. It's orchestral and epic.

He clicks on *create character*.

I take another sip of champagne.

I've had a bit too much to drink.

Jamie and I are almost through the bottle of champagne, and it feels like it's hit me hard. We've spent the past few hours playing *Arcane Realms,* and it's been easily one of the best nights of my life. Jamie made himself a character, a druid knight, which he chose for earlier access to pets. Now he fights with a large War Wolf. His weapon of choice is a massive ax, which he hopes to use to "royally eff them up." I'm assuming that's a joke in response to my advice to tone down his swearing.

After he spent a ridiculous amount of time getting his character's appearance right, we started questing together. Jamie was actually pretty good at the game, and Jamie the druid and Erik the angel actually made a pretty great team. He dealt out a lot of damage, and I made sure his health bar didn't drop too low.

I never thought *Arcane Realms* could become more. But playing with Jamie?

It's so much better.

"Oh sh—I mean, oh sheesh," he says, grinning at the swerve he made away from cursing. "It's nearly midnight."

I check my watch. Being drunk is different from what I was expecting. I haven't completely lost control, it's that everything has gone slightly hazy, and my inhibitions feel lowered. I think it helps that I feel so safe around Jamie. We work together. I don't feel like I need to put up a front, or behave in a certain way in order to get him to either like or approve of me. I'm being honestly, truly myself, in a way that feels radical for me.

I've also laughed more tonight that any night I can remember.

He moves forward on the couch, then glances back at me. There's something almost like a question in his eyes. He's asking me if I want him to stay longer. Even though it's late, and it's probably not the best idea.

I wish I could ask him to stay, but as fun as tonight has been, and even though I'm slightly drunk, I know that there is a right move here and a wrong move. But I feel really good right now, and I don't want this night to end. I don't want to go back to what I know I have to be: nothing more than Jamie's tutor. I like this version of myself that feels genuine and fun to be around.

"I should go," he says. He chews his lip, and his eye contact lingers for a moment.

"Yeah," I say, clearing my throat. "Sorry, I lost track of time."

"Don't be, this was really fun."

He closes the lid of his laptop, and leans against the back of the couch. I sign out of my game, then lean back, too. We're only a few inches apart.

I smile. "You're not leaving."

"I need a moment. The alcohol."

Right.

The room feels supercharged, like something momentous is about to happen. I would like it if it did. If anything, the alcohol has made Jamie seem even cuter, and the thought of making out with him right now is incredibly appealing. The desire to lean over and kiss him is so strong I'm not sure how much longer I can fight it. I want to put my hands on the sides of his face and run my hands through his hair. I want to lose myself with him for a moment.

That could risk this night, though. I don't know if he wants to make out with me, and seeing as this level of friendship isn't something I've ever experienced, I don't want to ruin it. So I keep myself totally still, but distinctly aware of the space between us. There can only be, what, a few inches of couch space between his hand and mine. It may as well be miles. I simply cannot cross that line.

I'm with Sebastian. I can't do this.

"Can I ask you something?" he asks.

"Anything."

"Do you like Sebastian?"

I blink a few times, surprised by the question. I had thought that he knew what the deal with Sebastian is, and the agreement that we have.

"No," I say. "We've barely spoken."

"Then why are you with him?"

I suck in some air. "It's for my family. Our families, really. Why do you ask?"

He shrugs. "He's your boyfriend."

"I know."

"Is this, like, normal for you?" he asks. "Fake dating someone?"

"I'd say it happens a lot more than the general public thinks it does. The thing is, Jamie, we are supposed to represent a fairy tale. And we did, in the past. Royal families have been rocked by so many scandals over the past few decades that the sheen has worn off, but I think everyone, like my gran, wants things to go back to the way they were."

"And fake dating someone will do that?"

"Better than people knowing the truth."

"And that is?"

"That I'm not perfect. I like hooking up with guys. And yeah, I'd like to meet a guy and find something serious, but I also like casual hookups like anyone else our age. But with me it always has to be so serious. Everything I do is."

I've never disclosed anything like this, with anyone. It makes me feel like a raw nerve.

"Sorry I asked you that, it was really nosy."

"It's okay. You can ask me anything you'd like. I like being honest with you."

"Really? Because sometimes you close yourself off."

I nod. I was wondering if he had noticed that.

"I know, I'm sorry. I'm working on it. I've never really connected with someone like this."

"I haven't, either," he says. "Especially not this quickly."

He tilts his head toward me. I look into his eyes, and for a moment, I think we might go there. That this might happen. I truly can't decide if I want it to, but in any case, guilt starts eating into me. Jamie is right, I am with Sebastian right now. He is my boyfriend, even if it is only for show, and even if it is only because our families want us to be together. And even with our agreement that we can see other people, it feels wrong to me that I am sharing a moment like this, and having all these feelings for Jamie. Plus, none of this is fair on Jamie. I'm taken, and we will never be able to take this anywhere public. The guilt starts to sober me up.

"I should go," he says again.

"Okay, I think that's a good idea. It's late, and we've got your lessons tomorrow."

He stands. "And don't worry, I won't tell anyone about this. The drinking, I mean."

"That's a good idea. I'd get in trouble if they knew."

"But I'm the one who brought the champagne. If anything, *I'm* the bad influence on you."

I shake my head. "They wouldn't see it that way."

"I feel like," he says, then he cuts himself off. "I don't want to say anything out of line."

"You can't. What were you going to say?"

"I don't know. It seems like your parents are maybe a little too controlling. I mean, you should be able to date whoever you want to, don't you think?"

I go quiet. He's right, I don't know what to say. Saying anything bad about my family goes against everything I've been taught for my entire life.

"They expect a lot from me," I say. "It's not personal."

"That must be tough, though, right?"

"I'm used to it. They only want the best for me."

"I know. But Erik?" He steps a little closer. "You're an amazing person. And you deserve to be able to make your own choices. About everything."

We cross my apartment. Jamie steps outside, then hangs out in the hallway.

"Thanks for a fun night," he says. "I'll see you tomorrow. I can't wait to find out what you're going to teach me." He grins. "God, maybe I'm the nerd. I mean, gee, maybe I'm the nerd."

"Goodnight, Jamie."

"Bye."

I shut the door and press my head against it.

I'm so screwed. I rest my head there for a moment, and an idea crosses my mind. It might be a side effect of the champagne, and a part of me already knows that I wouldn't be able to do this if I were completely sober, but I know what I have to do.

I start typing a message to Sebastian.

I can't keep doing this.

I need to break up with him.

CHAPTER TWENTY-FIVE

JAMIE

So *this* is what a hangover is like.

I have a headache even a dose of painkillers won't kill, and my body has been zapped of energy. This morning, Erik still made me go on a run with him. I didn't try to get out of it because I knew what he would say. The whole point of the daily runs is to teach me about discipline. As a prince, I won't be able to skip things simply because I'm not feeling it.

Plus, even hungover, I want to spent time with him.

At least he didn't make me run as fast as he did the first time. Again, I have felt his wall go back up. It's like there's a distinct difference between the two sides of him. One is open and honest with me, and the other keeps his distance. It might be in my head, but his walls seem especially high today.

His lesson is taking place in the ballroom, and I think I know what that means.

He's going to teach me how to dance.

He's danced with me before, so he knows that saying I have two left feet doesn't properly express my lack of ability on this particular front. I remember spotting Alexander and Maria dancing at the ball. They moved so effortlessly, looking exactly like a king and queen as they moved about the dance floor. They were confident, in control, and yeah, I'll say it: they looked regal.

I'll need to learn that.

I open the ballroom door. Erik is standing by the side, leaning on the wall beside one of the windows. It seems unfair that he hasn't been hit by the same freight train of a hangover as I was. He drank as much as I did, so it would only be fair if his skin wasn't as faultless as it usually is. It seems he's even shaved, too.

I trudge into the ballroom, my feet feeling like they have cement blocks attached to them.

"How do you do it?" I ask, when I reach him.

He tilts his head to the side. "How do I do what?"

I gesture at him. "I feel like I've been beaten with a sack full of bricks."

"That's very specific," he says.

"I have more," I say. "I feel like I've gone ten rounds with a pro boxer. I feel like I've been put through the washing machine."

He pushes off the wall. "You've been thinking about these."

"Well, yeah," I say. "What do you think?"

"They're very detailed, and I appreciate that. But that's not what you're here for. Shall we get started?"

"I guess," I say, crossing my arms. "Are you going to teach me how to dance?"

He nods. "It was Alexander's idea. Don't worry, we'll start with a simple waltz. You'll be fine."

"If you say so."

"You've got this, Jamie. It's easy."

I have doubts about that, but keep them to myself. We move to the middle of the ballroom, so we're directly under the largest chandelier. Erik—at least I am assuming it was him—has used tape to make a square on the floor. It reminds me of the night we met and danced. I remember how excited I was to dance with him then, and now that I know more about him, the prospect is even more exciting.

"Step one is your posture," he says, as he walks around me, clearly looking for any flaws. "Remember what I taught you."

I stand up straighter.

"Good. Hold that. Now we need to focus on your expression."

I lift an eyebrow.

"It's important," he says. "I'll tell you what my instructor taught me. Look at your partner like they are the most beautiful person in the world."

I try it out. I soften my expression, and let myself look at Erik in a way that's full of affection. It is actually quite easy, given how I truly feel for him. He is easily one of the most beautiful people I've ever met. Not just shallowly, although even that way, he is very good-looking. But that would make him hot, and my assignment is to look at him like he's beautiful. He's beautiful because of the way his smile is a little crooked, and the ways his eyes light up when he talks about something he's passionate about. He's beautiful because he is secretly a huge nerd with a big heart who clearly cares deeply for the people he loves. I like it way more than someone who is simply hot.

Erik was right. Maybe this is easy. Looking at Erik like he's beautiful is actually the easiest thing in the world.

"Good," he says, and he lifts a hand. His expression is soft. He looks like he did last night, when we were drunk on his couch. A few times, when the conversation lulled, I caught him looking at me with a sort of softness that I'd never seen before. He's always been friendly with me, but this felt like a step further.

As if we could be more than friends.

I think I'm reading into this way too much. He was drunk. That would explain it.

He has a boyfriend. Nothing can happen.

I take his hand in mine, and I have to fight the urge not to shy away. I wonder if he has any idea about how being this close to him feels for me, and how fast my heart is racing right now. He moves closer, putting his hand on my back. His hand is sure and steady, completely reassuring. He is taking charge, and that means I'm going to be okay.

He starts to count out loud, and we move around the square. I stumble, but he catches me, and then we fall into a rhythm, moving each time he speaks.

"See," he says. "I told you that you would get this."

He stops counting, but we keep up the same pace. I imagine us dancing in a crowded ballroom. It might seem complicated, but the movement is actually pretty simple.

We keep practicing until it becomes second nature. Erik then plays some classical music through his phone. Together, we're able to keep pace with the beat.

The next ball I go to, I'll at least be a little less out of my depth.

I owe Erik so much.

I'm so glad I met him.

Chapter Twenty-Six

ERIK

There's no way I'm surviving this.

I pull out my sword and lift it to the sky, holding it long enough that the blade turns golden. I slash down, sending a beam of light right at my opponent: Ashondra, the biggest raid boss in this area and one of the hardest in this region.

Am I playing this right now to get my mind off Jamie?

Yes.

Is it working?

It's questionable.

I've joined a battle with a bunch of strangers, and we're all fighting together in order to try to take her out. If we kill her, each of us will get a bunch of experience points, as well as a chance at some legendary weapons.

If we survive the battle, that is. And that's not a given. Ashondra is notoriously difficult, and has the ability to kill even the bulkiest of characters with only a few hits. I have to focus, to make sure all my moves are correct. Otherwise it's lights out for me.

Jamie invited me to spend some time with him tonight, and I, for some reason, said yes. Against my better judgment, I might add. My instincts were practically screaming at me to tell him no. That it's not safe for me, that I need to keep him at arm's length in order to stop myself from wanting him in a way I'm not allowed to. Ever since the horse ride, I feel myself drawn to him in a way that might be stronger than I've ever felt. Still, I know that hanging out with him outside of our lessons is a reckless and bad idea.

Plus, I haven't yet told him I ended things with Sebastian. I messaged him the night we got drunk, telling him the truth. After that, I broke the news to my family. Apparently, Gran is disappointed with me, and I'm sure I'll be in trouble for it when I get home.

I'll deal with that then, though.

As for Sebastian, he dealt with our breakup in the same businesslike manner as he did our relationship. If anything, it confirmed my reasons for ending it. I know it might get me in trouble with my family, but I'm simply not built to be in a relationship where I don't have genuine feelings.

Even though I'm now single, I was told to stay away from Jamie. I know that's what I should do.

And yet, I said yes.

I think it has to do with his eyes. He has serious puppy-dog eyes, ones that make it nearly impossible to refuse him. I should've told him that I was busy doing something. I could've lied and said that I had some sort of prince duty that required my attention. The truth is that I had planned to spend the entire night playing *Realms* and trying to squash any attraction I feel toward him so that I can make it through this trip.

Ashondra attacks me with her sword. I roll out of the way too slowly, so the hit connects, knocking my health bar to half.

I retreat, moving away from my enemy. I've only got one health potion left, and she's still got half her health bar remaining. She hasn't even changed into her second, more aggressive form yet.

That confirms it. I'm dying tonight.

But at least I can go down taking out a chunk of her health. That's why I like this game so much. I do love the world, and the NPCs are really well written. But what I like about it the most is that here, in this community, nobody knows who I am. I'm not

Prince Erik, the spare, the one who is defined by what I'm not, who is always told what to do and who to be.

In the game, I am another soldier on the battlefield, an angelic warrior who can cast light spells and heal others. I am nothing special, but together, my team and I can take down an opponent as fearsome as Ashondra. It might be cheesy, yes, but I don't think I would be able to function nearly as well if I didn't have this second, fantasy life. Escaping into a world where I can choose anything—what I look like, what I do, where I go—is one of the ways I cope when the royal life gets to be too much. I imagine in this life, this version of Erik could do whatever he wanted.

Kiss whomever he wanted.

Kissing Jamie has become something that I want to do so strongly I'm not sure I'll be able to hold myself back for much longer. He's just so adorable, and also hot, and he does this little thing where he chews his lip sometimes that makes it feel impossible for me to not notice him. I picture him now, chewing his lip. Want spreads like a fire through me.

Ashondra flies backward, sending up a wave of flames with a flap of her wings. I backstep, and take a swig of health potion. I instantly know this was a mistake. She dives toward me, her enormous, blood-red blade extended. I don't have time to dodge, and the hit strikes me in the chest, knocking me down to only a sliver of health. I'm out of potions, and Ashondra is too aggressive to try a healing spell.

I need to go on the attack.

I sprint forward. Flames appear around her blade, and I know my timing needs to be perfect. She pushes forward, and a fireball comes flying my way. I roll at the last second, just missing the flames, and then I reach my target. I start slashing, dodge-roll so I'm behind her, and continue my attack. I'm relentless.

I might be dead soon, but I can do a lot of damage before she takes me out.

She spins, her sword sending out a torrent of flames, catching me before I can do anything. My health bar vanishes, and the screen goes blank. I close the lid of my laptop.

I'm back in the real world.

I'm dead. And my plan didn't work. I can't stop thinking about him.

He is expecting me in about twenty minutes. I get up from the chair and go over to my bathroom. I take my shirt off, then check my appearance in the mirror. I shake my head. I've gotten careless. I shower, then groom myself until everything is perfect. It reminds me of who I am. I am a prince of Sunstad. I can control myself. Generations before me have done it, so I can do the same.

Once my face is clean and my hair is in place, I head to my closet. I search through the clothes. They're all nice, but most of them are more formal: dress shirts, suits, slacks. I didn't bring many casual clothes, and only have a few plain T-shirts and two pairs of jeans, one light and one dark. I can't be casual Erik right now. I am Jamie's royal tutor. I have to dress like it. I pick a white shirt and gray pants, as well as a fine pair of dress shoes.

When I get to Jamie's door, I stop. Maybe I shouldn't be here. This is a bad idea, I know it. I'm attracted to him, I can't help it. I should leave before this gets messy and complicated. I don't want to do that, though. And I can control myself. I don't have to do anything with him, even if I want to. I can keep our relationship platonic. I raise my fist and knock on the door.

I wait for a moment. I can't hear anyone inside. Did he forget? And why am I so nervous? I never felt nerves like this with Nate.

The door flies open.

Jamie is on the other side. I still haven't completely adjusted to his new look, but it does suit him. I do like how the stylist left his hair slightly long, so that it still curls down over his forehead.

"Hey," says Jamie. "Come in." He moves aside, and I brush past him.

"You look good," he says. I certainly feel overdressed now, seeing as Jamie is wearing a Paramore T-shirt and shorts.

There are noises coming from the kitchen. We make our way through, greeting Rebecca and Mike as we pass, then Jamie and I go to the living room.

"Do you want to watch a movie?"

I smile and sit on the couch. "All right."

Jamie sits down beside me.

"I owe you a thank-you," he says, seemingly out of nowhere.

"What for?"

"For your lessons. I really appreciate all of them. I hope you know that."

"It's what I'm here for."

"I know. But in case me inviting you over all the time doesn't make that obvious, I like spending time with you."

"I like spending time with you, too."

"Even if I beat you at *Mario Kart*?" he asks, clearly joking.

"Yes, even then."

Jamie laughs and moves a little closer to me. There's practically no space between us. The space feels charged with static, and I'm so aware of it. All it would take is one little movement for my arm to be against his. But that feels massive. I can't.

"What about *Mean Girls*?" he suggests. "You've seen that, right?"

"Of course," I say. "But it's so good."

"Musical or original?"

"I love both, but original."

"Good answer."

He hits *play* and puts his hand down on the couch, right in the space between us. I think it might be a sign, or a hint. If he were anyone else, I would say it for sure is. I have done this before, with Nate, and I generally know what a guy means when they ask me to come over and watch a movie with him. I'm not naïve. It's just that with Jamie, it's so complicated.

So I don't move. I leave his hand there. Still, I picture what my life could be like. I would brush my fingertips against the back of his palm, making contact. I'm single now; all that's stopping me is what Gran said. And if he moved closer then I would properly initiate. I could take that risk. I want to take that risk. Jamie clears his throat, and lifts his hand up, moving it back to his side.

"Would you like a snack or something?" he asks.

"What have you got?"

"I'll see."

He gets up, and disappears from the room. He returns a few moments later holding a packet of bright green candies I've never tried before. I feel a little queasy looking at them: food should not come in fluorescent colors.

"I've got some Jolly Ranchers. Wait, have you never had these?"

I shake my head.

"Oh man," he says. "Get ready. They're bad but they're good. I used to love them as a kid. I know you don't have a sweet tooth, but they're worth trying, trust me."

He rips open the packet and offers it to me. I'm wary. He's right, I'm not really a big candy guy at the best of times. Still, I have been trying to push Jamie out of his comfort zone with his lessons, the least I can do is the same with a piece of candy. What sort of message am I sending to him if I can't even do that?

The candy is sour, and actually maybe not as bad as I feared. Jamie is clearly awaiting my review.

"It's sour," I say.

He laughs, and pops one into his mouth. "Yeah, you get used to them. I can't believe you don't have these in Sunstad, that's wild."

"I've been missing out."

"You really have been. No Target, no Jolly Ranchers. What *do* you have?"

"The best slopes in the world. Oh, and free college and health-care."

"Touché."

He starts the movie. I remember the dream I had of Jamie. Of him kissing me. I shove it down and try to focus. Jamie grabs a pillow and holds it to his chest. After about half an hour, Rebecca enters the room and tells us that she and Mike are going to bed.

"Okay, night!" says Jamie.

Rebecca lingers for a moment, like she wants to say something else, but then she retreats out of the room. I glance at Jamie, who has started blushing, but is otherwise focused on the screen.

As soon as the movie ends, Jamie turns to me.

"What did you think?"

"Amazing as ever," I say. I check the time, and it's already well into the night. I'd guess by now that Mike and Rebecca are fast asleep, which means we have some privacy. It means I need to get out of here as fast as possible, because this is too risky.

"Are you okay?" he asks. "It seems like you've got something on your mind."

I decide to be honest with him. He deserves that. What's scary is I know where this could lead. If my instincts are right, my being with Sebastian is what's stopped us from progressing past friendship. If I tell him what I did, anything is possible.

"I broke up with Sebastian."

He sits up. "Way to bury the lede! What? When?"

"A few days ago."

"Erik, that's huge. Why?"

"I realized," I say, being extremely careful with my words, "I can't fake how I feel for him."

"I get that," he says. "You could've told me sooner."

The room becomes completely silent.

I can tell Jamie is looking at me, and I'm sure my resolve will melt away if I even so much as glance at him.

"It's late, I should get going."

"Oh, okay, yeah."

He stands up, and he walks me out to the door. While we were watching the movie, Rebecca and Mike went to bed, so it's just us. Jamie opens the door to his apartment for me, and I linger for a moment.

I wish there was some way to see the future, a chance to know that, if I were to kiss him, everything would work out okay. I wouldn't get in trouble with my family and everything would be fine. I don't have that superpower, nor do I have the sort of life where I can take that sort of risk.

I notice he has a little green speck on his cheek. It's Jolly Rancher dust.

"What?" he asks.

"You've got a little . . ."

He wipes his cheek with the back of his hand, but it's the wrong side.

"Here," I say.

I go to wipe it off for him, but stop. The space between us crackles with sparks. He scrubs it silently.

"Good night," I say.

"Night."

He closes the door. I wait there for a moment. That was the moment, my chance. I should've kissed him. I wish I had kissed him. No, that's not true. I wish my life were different. I wish I were the type of guy who can kiss anyone he wants to and not face any consequences.

I wish I weren't a prince from a family that has my entire life planned out for me. Being around Jamie makes me realize more than ever how badly I don't want that. I want to do something simply because I want to, not because it has been decided it is what I must do.

Is there anything I can do? Can I knock on the door again to get his attention? Is that something he would want?

The door opens. I turn and look back over my shoulder to see Jamie waiting just outside his apartment.

"Do you want to go for a walk?" he asks.

He chews his lip. It's painfully cute, and I feel my heart in my throat.

A walk. Late at night. Away from his parents. It means something is going to happen between us. He's not asking me if I want to just go for a walk. He's asking if I want to make out with him.

Here's my chance. I need to say no, and keep this platonic. I've received my instructions, I need to follow them. I've already let it go too far. Every instinct is telling me what I need to do.

I don't listen.

"Yeah," I say. "I'd like that."

Chapter Twenty-Seven

JAMIE

I'm honestly not sure what came over me.

I followed Erik outside. I asked him if he wanted to go on a late-night walk, and given how close we came to kissing inside, it was pretty obvious what I was really asking, which is: Do you want to make out?

His response was a yes.

At least that's how it went in my head. I close and lock the apartment door as quietly as I can. I'm half expecting someone to appear and scold us for what we're doing, but no one does.

Erik is waiting for me, and I can't get over how attractive he is to me right now. Tall, fit, and blond, he's totally a dream guy.

Am I really going to have my first kiss with a guy this perfect?

"Are you okay?" he whispers as I reach him. The empathy and compassion in his voice only make my desire to kiss him grow stronger. "You seem nervous."

What—me, nervous? Never.

"I'm fine," I say, the unmistakable quiver in my voice giving away my bald-faced lie.

"Cool," he says. "Good."

I think I detect a similar note of fear in his voice. It might be strange, but it's comforting knowing I'm not the only one freaking out. This isn't the way kisses happen in the movies. Normally people just kiss, and then the music swells and everything is wrapped up in a nice little bow. But this is complicated, and I'm still not totally sure he's feeling what I am.

One of us is going to have to make a move, and I'm not sure I have the guts.

We reach the end of the hall and start going down a flight of stairs. I can't get myself to initiate. It's way too risky. What if I'm reading this completely wrong and he isn't in fact interested in making out with me? How could I ever spend time with him if I make a move and he's like, thanks, but I'm good?

I don't want to find out.

I glance his way and catch him looking, but his focus darts to look out the window.

I imagine myself taking hold of his shirt and pulling him into an empty hallway and kissing him. That's what he's here for, right? So why can't I get myself to do what I want to so badly? Why do I have to have a stupid brain that makes me doubt everything when it comes to guys?

He clears his throat, and I wait for him to say something. But then he presses his lips together.

I'm usually not this brave. I should be proud I'm here, not in my bedroom, wishing I'd made a move. I have at least done that.

I remember the hot boy at Anchor Bros. It feels like a lifetime ago. Who'd have guessed Ren talking to him would be the reason my secret got out?

Erik stops walking. We're right by a door. Come on man, be brave! All I need to do is go in there with him.

Erik scrubs the back of his neck. "Are we going somewhere in particular, or are we just exploring?"

I'm glad it's dark in here, as I'm blushing harder than I maybe ever have. And for me, that's saying something.

"We could go to the gardens?" I suggest. Given how full and bright the moon is right now, plus the street lights, we would be able to see out there.

"I'd like that," he says.

We go through the central atrium with the grand stairwell. Up ahead is a heavy oak door, with the wood carved into the shapes of vines and flowers. Real ivy hangs from pots on either side, cascading down the sides. Through two arched windows, I can see into the gardens that surround this area of the palace.

He pushes open the door. I brace myself for an alarm, but the palace remains silent. Nice. We're on the east wing of the palace, and I haven't seen these gardens before. They're as grand as the others. In the distance is a giant hedge maze, and the lake is closer here. The dark water is almost entirely still.

I look up. I start to smile as an idea forms.

"Should we check out the maze?" I ask.

We start walking toward it. Our shoes crunch on the gravel, and that's the only sound.

I may not have known Erik for long, but I've spent enough time around him now to know a little bit about the way he acts. He seems reserved, and I don't think he's the type to initiate.

If I want this, I have to go for it. We reach the entrance of the maze and go inside. The walls are tall enough that I can no longer see the palace.

Plus, nobody can see *us*.

"Hey," I say. "Can we, um, talk?"

He stops, and turns to face me.

"I should tell you something," I say. "But I'm really scared to say it."

"Don't be scared," he says. "You can talk to me."

I take one last look at the gorgeous boy in front of me. The prince from a fairy tale made real. Not only that, he's the guy who's been so kind to me, and so gentle. He's intelligent and funny and easily one of the most wonderful people I've ever met. Telling him how I've been feeling seems incredibly risky, but I think the risk is worth it.

"Fine, I'll say it," I say. "I'm wondering what we're, like, doing here."

He lifts an eyebrow. "Doing here?"

"Tonight, I mean. Like, right now. I'm having a really hard time telling if you want to kiss me or not."

"Oh."

"Sorry," I say. "That was really demanding, I'm clearly not good at this."

"Jamie," says Erik, and he's smiling now. His expression is soft and affectionate. "Of course I want to kiss you."

Did Erik seriously say he wants to kiss me? Is this real?

He pauses for a moment. Whatever is going on in his head right now seems pretty intense.

"You want to kiss me?" I repeat.

He steps closer. "Yes. More than anything."

More than anything?

"You sure? Because—"

He rushes forward, silencing me. His hands fly up to my face, and a fraction of a second later, his lips are meeting mine. We move backward, until my back crashes into the wall of the maze. I don't care, not about anything, because he's kissing me and it feels incredible. I don't care about anything other than how good this feels.

We stop for a moment. He rubs his thumb against my cheek. I feel totally out of breath in the best possible way.

I grab his shirt, bunching up the soft material. He's pressed up against me, and I marvel at how well we fit together. We're still for a moment, looking into each other's eyes. His eyes truly are the prettiest shade of blue I've ever seen.

"What?" he asks.

"Nothing," I say. "I've wanted that for so long."

"Me too."

I can barely wrap my head around that. Erik has wanted to

kiss me for a while? I am going to need specifics, but those can wait.

"Can we do that again?" I ask.

He kisses me slower this time, and my knees get so weak I can barely stand. This night is perfect. This kiss was perfect.

I feel like I'm made of fireworks.

As I wake up, my first thought is about last night.

I start to smile as I remember what happened. I kissed Erik in the most magical, surreal way possible. That really happened. I had my first kiss with a literal prince in a moonlit hedge maze. Me. Jamie Brian Johnson had the kind of kiss that belongs on a silver screen.

It was real. This is my actual life.

I'm so freaking giddy. I smile up at the ceiling.

Like, wow. Seriously, wow.

I can remember every tiny detail. The surprise and delight on his face when I left my room, chasing after him. I was so anxious, but the way he reassured me was so comforting.

The kiss itself couldn't have been better. But there's a nagging thought that's running circles through my mind, stopping me from total happiness.

As I think it over, I remember how he acted right before kissing me. It's as if he wanted to hold himself back, but couldn't fight it. Maybe I'm overthinking it, because we ended up making out for about half an hour, and only stopped because we both decided it was risky to stay out any longer.

He walked me back to my room and gave me a kiss on the forehead before saying good night. I feel slightly giddy just remembering it.

After that, though, he looked at both sides of the hallway as if he was petrified someone had seen us.

I want to talk to him about that as soon as I can. I'm not some evil temptress or whatever, even if that does sound fun. Either he likes me or he doesn't, and the last thing I want is to be a part of some narrative where I'm pushing him out of his comfort zone or making him do something he doesn't want. That's a huge deal-breaker for me.

I touch my lips, remembering how he felt when I kissed him. I swear they're still tingling.

What happens now, though? Where do we go from here?

I do know one thing I need to do. I had my first kiss. I have to tell my friends about it.

I message my group chat.

I KISSED ERIK!!!

I get out of bed and cross the room to find Mom and Mike. They're in the kitchen, and Mom is making coffee while Mike makes pancakes. Pancakes? Just when I thought today couldn't get better.

My phone starts buzzing with messages from my friends.

GO JAMIE!

I told you!!!

Yesssssss I love this for you!

"Morning," says Mom. She leans against the kitchen counter, holding a freshly made cup of coffee in her hands. "What are you so happy about?"

"Nothing," I say, pocketing my phone. Max is the only one who hasn't replied yet, which feels typical given our new status quo. Lately she's been the last person to reply to any of my messages.

"How'd you sleep?" asks Mom.

"Really well," I say, hoping that answer will be enough to keep her from asking too many questions about last night. I've never been a good liar, especially not with Mom, and I'm sure if she asks too many questions, she'll figure out that something happened while I was hanging out with Erik.

"I think we should talk," says Mom.

I freeze. She knows. How? Did she see us? There's no way. She and Mike were in bed by the time Erik and I went for our walk, and there's no way anyone could've seen what we did in the hedge maze.

Or could they?

What should I say? Am I even in trouble? It's not like we broke any laws or anything, all we did was kiss. Still, I feel like I'm a criminal right now. I'm not sure why I'm thinking about this.

Mike pauses his TV show, and sits down opposite Mom. I brace myself. Is this the birds and the bees? It shouldn't be, I'm a little too old for that. The sex ed at school was laughably terrible, but I have access to the internet, and I taught myself everything I need to know. I don't need them to tell me about any of this.

"We know you're having a good time here," she says. "And we're so happy for you."

"We really are, bud," says Mike. "It's been so great seeing you get to know everyone."

"It feels like a 'but' is coming," I say.

"*But* it's time we started talking about our plans going forward," says Mom.

Huh. Maybe that means they don't know about Erik and me, and I'm not going to have to sit through a horrifically awkward birds-and-the-bees talk.

"What do you mean?"

"I only get three weeks off for summer break before I'm due

back," says Mom. "And it's hard for me to prepare all the materials I need to while overseas."

"And Stronghold needs me," says Mike.

I figure it out. They're talking about going home. I get it. They have jobs and lives back home. So do I. We can't stay here forever.

"We know how important this is to you," says Mom. "But at some point, we're going to need to go back to America."

"This isn't us telling you we're going home," say Mike. "We're just starting this discussion, because we want to know how you feel."

"I thought we were going to stay the whole summer," I say.

Suddenly I wish they *were* talking to me about kissing Erik. Because even though things were awkward with us at the end, I still want to keep seeing where things between us go. Can we even keep up a relationship if I'm back in America? I know we've always had an expiration date, because he will never live in Mitanor. But still, me being in America feels a step further. Sunstad is only a three-hour flight away from here, but it will take nine to get to Rhode Island from Sunstad. That's a massive difference.

"We are," says Mom. "If that's what you'd like."

"We want to make sure we're all on the same page," says Mike.

"We were invited to Stefan and Elise's wedding," says Mom. "All three of us, and we'd like to go."

The wedding. That's in about two weeks.

"We thought we would go back to America after the ceremony," says Mom.

I do the math. That's nearly two more weeks here. There was a part of me that thought she was going to tell me that we were going to have to leave, like, tomorrow.

Still, given what happened with Erik last night, it doesn't feel like enough time.

"And Jamie," says Mom. "Things don't need to go back to the

way they were before. We can always visit here during the holidays, if you want to. Your life here is important."

"To all of us," says Mike.

"I know," I say. "And all right, that makes sense. We'll go home after the wedding. Have you told Alexander?"

"Not yet," says Mom. "But I'm sure he'll understand."

I'm not so sure. He's been acting as if he thinks I'm going to be here forever, and properly step into my role as a prince of Mitanor. It might crush him if I go home.

But I still have a year left of school, and I'm not even sure that I can study here, even if I wanted to. I have a plan for my life. I want to do all the senior year things with my friends. I want Amara to help me with assignments, to console Max when the pressure of exams gets too much, for Ren to top a bunch of his classes without even trying, for Spencer to look the best out of everyone at prom. None of those things involve me being here, or me being a prince at all.

The truth is that as much as I love being here, I also love my old life.

I check the time on my phone. Crap, I'm almost late for my run with Erik already.

"I have to go," I say. "I'm late for my run."

"Who are you and what have you done with Jamie?" asks Mom.

I know she's joking. And I get it, but I feel different. The old me never would've woken up early to go for a run. He also never would've had the confidence to kiss the guy he's starting to get a crush on.

It feels like I'm living in the present, going with and appreciating everything.

And it's so much fun.

"What's Erik going to teach you today?" asks Mike.

"Not sure yet," I say, as I slide out of my seat and go back into my room. Given what happened last night, I don't want to spend any time longer than necessary around Mom. I'm sure she'll be able to tell what I did. What we did? I guess it doesn't really matter. I get ready as quickly as I can, then head to the palace front steps to meet Erik.

As I expected, he's waiting for me on the lawn. He looks as good as he always does in his workout gear, and the early-morning sun makes his hair seem especially golden. He smiles when he sees me. I wish I could kiss him right now. I want him to push me up against the palace and kiss me. Can we? No, it's way too risky.

"Morning," he says. I'm curious if he's thinking about the same things I am. Does he want me in the same way? Is kissing all he can think about when he's around me, like it is for me? "Ready?"

I pause. What is he doing? Does he want to pretend last night didn't happen? I'm not sure if that's cool with me. Actually, I know it's not.

"Can we talk about last night?"

Erik's normally pretty good at containing his emotions. But for a moment I see what I think might be fear.

"We can," he says. "After the run, okay? Otherwise people might be suspicious."

I'm totally out of my depth here. How do people manage situations like this? It's all so confusing. We kissed, which was amazing, but what does it mean for us? There are so many blanks that I need to get filled in. Does it mean he likes me? And where do we go from here? Will we kiss again? Does he want that?

There are so many questions I don't know where to start, but one thing is certain and that's that we do need to talk about this. I need answers.

"There's really no getting out of this run, is there?"

He grins. "Nice try, Johnson."

My body lights up from the inside.

"Sounds good," he says, and he taps his smartwatch, which starts a timer countdown.

I put in my headphones and hit *play* on my phone. Erik doesn't wait for me, he sets off down the path.

With my music blaring in my ears, I chase after him.

Erik is sitting at the same table in the library as he was last time.

We still haven't spoken about last night. We decided it would be best to keep to our usual beats, to make sure nobody notices anything different. That means run, shower, lesson. So that's what we've done so far today.

That's the only thing about today that feels normal. It's like my world has tilted on its axis. I'm now officially someone who has kissed someone. I will never go back to being a guy who has never been kissed. And it's not even that I got a kiss from someone who I don't even know or care about. Both Max's and Ren's first kisses were makeouts with strangers, significant more because they were their first than anything else.

Kissing Erik was kind of everything to me.

"Hey," I say as I swing into the chair next to him.

"Hi."

I drum my fingers against the table. As I prepared for this conversation, I realized I haven't told Erik about the conversation I had with Mom and Mike about going back to America. I'm sure he knows that the plan was only for me to spend the summer here. But I think I got a little lost in it all, and he needs to know that I won't be here forever. It's yet another complication, one I can't see any easy answers to. Yes, we both want to make out with each other. Our lives aren't that simple, though, and we'll need to figure out how we can make this work given everything between us.

"So, last night," I say. "We should probably talk about what it means."

He smiles. "I agree."

"It was amazing, yeah, sure. But it's complicated, right? Like, we're, I don't know."

"I should start by telling you that I, like, like you in that way," he says. "In case that wasn't obvious."

Did he really say that to me? I know there's a huge difference between kissing someone and liking them. You can kiss someone you don't like, because you think they're attractive or you're bored or countless other reasons. In a lot of ways, that confession feels even better than the kiss, because it means what I'm feeling isn't unreciprocated. He likes me as well.

"I like you in that way, too," I say.

I look into his eyes. As scary as this conversation is, I know I need to have it. Unfortunately for us, we're not just two guys who like each other. If we were, it would be much simpler. We could go on dates and see where this leads. However, I'm an American only here for a few weeks, and he's a prince of Sunstad brought here to be my tutor.

"But," I say. "I know this is complicated, but last night I felt as if, I don't know."

"You can say it," he says. "Tell me what you're thinking."

I know I have to, even if it scares me. Because otherwise this could grow into this big thing and that's the last thing I want. I want Erik to know exactly how I'm feeling about everything.

"It's that, last night, before we kissed. It seemed like you, I don't know. Like you were trying to stop yourself or something?"

The doors to the library open and the librarian enters, pushing a trolley of books. She wheels it up to us, and starts shelving right by our table. She can hear everything.

Erik tilts his head toward the door. I stand and put my bag over my shoulder.

What we need is complete and utter privacy.

If I've learned anything, it's that in a palace, that can be difficult to come by.

Chapter Twenty-Eight

ERIK

The palace is busier than I've ever seen it.

I'm not sure what is happening, but it seems that there are almost no empty rooms anywhere nearby. Jamie and I have been trying to be as subtle as possible, which is difficult when there are staff members everywhere.

I know I need to talk to Jamie, honestly and openly, about what I've been feeling. I might need to keep my feelings under control around everyone else, especially my family. But after last night, I need to tell Jamie everything.

He deserves the full and honest truth from me. The issue is I can't exactly do that if there are people nearby, people who might listen in on every word. I do trust my parents, but there's no denying that they think differently from most people. I'm sure they wouldn't consider it a breach of privacy to ask the palace staff what I've been up to in my time here.

In fact, they would think of it as entirely normal and nothing I should be bothered by. They know I ended things with Sebastian, but they don't know the real reason, which I can't deny to myself any longer.

I have started to have feelings for Jamie.

We reach a door, and I try the door handle. A security guard is standing by, but he simply nods his head toward me. I'm sure he would've stopped me if we weren't allowed in. I pull the door open, and my breath catches.

We've stumbled into the palace throne room.

The throne is a grand, golden chair, atop a set of marble stairs at the back of a long room. It towers above the entire space. Two maroon banners hang on either side of the chair, emblazoned with the golden crest of the Mitanorian royal family.

"Wow," says Jamie, clearly awestruck.

The door closes behind us. We're completely alone, which is what we wanted. Jamie seems to be almost in a trance as he brushes past me. I understand why. There are a few throne rooms in the palaces back home, but very few are as magnificent as this. Jamie crosses the entire room, only stopping right before the throne. I glance back at the entrance. We still have total privacy. I check the ceiling, and can't see any security cameras, but that doesn't mean there aren't any.

Now is the time. We should talk.

"We might not have long," I say.

"Right." He scrubs the back of his neck in a way that's utterly adorable.

I clear my throat. "You deserve to know everything, so I'm just going to tell you how I feel."

"Okay," he says. He rocks back on his heels.

"I like you," I say. "I know we haven't known each other for a long time, but I feel something for you. And I want to see where it could go."

His expression softens, as if he's relieved, or possibly bracing himself for something else. "I want that, too."

"The issue is, I was asked here to be your teacher," I say. "If anyone finds out what we've done, I'll be in a lot of trouble."

"Oh," he says. "Right."

"They take these sorts of things incredibly seriously, and I doubt they will react well to finding out I've crossed that line. Because there's something else. When I first got here, I was told to keep things between us platonic."

His brow furrows. "By who?"

"My gran."

"You mean the queen?"

I nod. "It's why I tried to keep my distance. And I'm sorry, I should've told you before we did anything. It was unfair of me. Truly, Jamie, I'm sorry. I lost control and it was unfair of me."

He laughs.

"Why is that funny?" I ask.

"Oh, just someone like me having the ability to make you lose control. It's like, yeah, right."

I step closer. "Jamie, fighting the urge to kiss you is one of the hardest things I've ever done."

"Oh wow, you're serious."

"I am."

He laughs again. "I guess I've never really seen myself as the kind of guy who has that sort of power." He unfolds his arms. "Hang on, do you know why they told you to stay platonic?"

"They wanted me to be with Sebastian."

"But you broke up with him."

"I did. I'm worried that they'll find out why I broke up with him."

"And that is?"

"Meeting you," I say. "And liking you made me realize I don't want to pretend for my entire life."

"Okay, so I think I have a pretty easy solution."

"And that is?"

"We make sure nobody finds out," he says, shrugging. "I don't think anyone noticed we made out last night. So we've done it once. We could do it again."

He gives me a mischievous grin. The urge to kiss him comes

back, stronger than ever. This boy drives me wild. Now that I've kissed him once and know how good it feels, it's even harder for me to resist. I'm not sure if I'm strong enough.

I might not have to be. I have kept hookups a secret before. Plus, there is a big difference between being an official couple and hooking up in secret. Stories like that are dotted throughout royal history. There are the people royals truly love, and then those they are with to appease the public.

"Are you sure?" I ask. "As much as I like you, we might never be able to be together officially. Is that okay with you?"

"If it means we can keep making out, then yes."

"Are you sure?"

I'm surprised, I took him for a romantic.

"Yes," he says. "Look at me, I'm fine with that. We can keep it casual."

That settles it. My heart soars. Jamie knows the full story, and he isn't backing down. It means we can keep doing this.

"We'll have to be careful," I say. "I can't stress this enough. I'll seriously get in so much trouble if anyone finds out."

He winces. "I've already told my friends. Is that a problem?"

"Did you tell Ren?"

"I did. I'm sorry, I should've thought more. I was just so excited."

"It's okay," I say. "I'm sure Ren's learned his lesson. Please ask him to keep it a secret."

"I will." He takes a small step closer so he's right on the edge of my personal space. "Out of curiosity, how long have you wanted to kiss me?"

He deserves honesty, even if it scares me.

"Since the stables," I say. "At least. I've been trying to fight it."

"Me too," he says. "I mean, I would've made out with you in the rose garden if you had wanted that. You're hot."

I laugh. Guys have said that to me before, but hearing it from

Jamie, a guy who is usually so sweet, is especially nice. I'm glad he thinks that about me, because I think that about him, too. He's cute, sure, but he's also ridiculously good-looking. "Hot" isn't a word I use very often, but Jamie is undeniably hot.

"You should know something else," he says. "If we're being honest with each other."

"Go on."

"Last night was my first kiss. Sorry I didn't, like, tell you that before."

A new worry takes hold. I had thought that he was more experienced. His being so new to this isn't a dealbreaker, but it could make things more complicated. First kisses might not always be special, but they are memorable. Ours was both. I don't want him to regret his first kiss being with me, something that might happen if I handle this situation poorly. Which it feels I might, what with my family.

"I'm honored," I say. "Truly."

"Was I bad?"

I shake my head. "You were incredible."

I try to hold myself back. I shouldn't kiss him. Talking about this has helped us reach a steady place now. Kissing him again could throw us back into danger. I don't think I'm strong enough to resist right now. His eyes are practically locked onto mine. He reaches out and his fingertips brush the back of my hand.

"This okay?" he asks.

This close, he's even more gorgeous. His brown eyes are spectacular.

I shake my head. "Not here," I say.

Even though I haven't seen any cameras, we can't be sure.

"Can we go to your apartment?" he asks. "We can pretend we're doing a lesson."

We leave the throne room, and rush across the palace to get back to my apartment. I unlock the door with shaking hands. As soon as we're inside, I do a quick search, making sure there aren't any cleaners or other members of staff inside.

"We good?" he asks.

I close the gap between us and kiss him. I lose myself in the moment, my mind going blissfully blank as his lips meet mine. It's the same rush of pure joy as last time. He ends the kiss, but we stay close by, our faces inches apart, his arms curled around my shoulders.

"Sorry," he says.

"What are you sorry for?"

"I just really needed to kiss you."

I brush his cheek with my thumb.

"We don't have long," I say. "And no kissing in public. We have to be careful, all right?"

"One more before we go?"

I give in. This time, he kisses me. I don't care that this might be the biggest mistake I've ever made.

I don't care at all.

CHAPTER TWENTY-NINE

JAMIE

I haven't been able to focus all day.

I'm sitting in the kitchen of our apartment, scrolling on my phone, searching for a distraction to make the time go faster.

The past day has passed so slowly. After Erik and I left his apartment, we went back to the library, and he taught me about the art of conversation. I did try my best to pay attention, but I kept noticing little details about him.

The guy I am now secretly hooking up with.

He has tiny freckles on his forearms, and his hair seems lighter at the ends than at the base.

After that was dinner with Mom, Mike, Maria, and Alexander, and the entire time I needed to act like I wasn't into Erik. It was difficult to do, because I feel like it's radiating off me at the moment. For one, I can hardly stop smiling. I keep thinking about him doing something cute, and it's always enough to make me feel so freaking happy. The day is passing slowly because I am hoping that Erik will come over tonight, and we'll be able to make out again.

Mike enters the kitchen, startling me.

"You're in a good mood," says Mike.

Am I that obvious? I shrug.

"I'm glad," says Mike. "Can I make you a hot chocolate?"

Mitanorian chocolate might be the best on the planet, and

Mike has started shaving it directly into heated-up milk, making what could be one of the most delicious drinks I've ever had.

"Yes, please," I say.

Mike makes one for me, then hands me the steaming cup. I bring it to my lips and take a sip. It's rich, dark, and chocolatey, and as good as the mint shakes at Anchor Bros, something I don't say lightly.

"Want to watch a movie?" asks Mike.

"No thanks," I say. Mom is sitting at the dining room table, within earshot. I have to be more worried about her than I do about Mike. I love the guy, but he can be a little oblivious. Mom, on the other hand, I need to be very careful around. If I slip up, she will see right through me.

I'm not even sure she would disapprove of Erik and me. She's always said she trusts my judgment when it comes to people, and I know Erik is a good person. He wants to keep it a secret for reasons I totally get, so I will have to try my best to stop Mom and Mike figuring it out. I've already messaged my friends and made Ren promise to keep it a secret, something he swore he would do on his life.

"Oh, by the way," I start. "Erik is coming over tonight. We'll play more *Mario Kart,* but we'll play in my room so you can have the TV."

Mom comes over. "When?"

"Anytime now," I say, sounding as casual as possible.

"All right," she says. "I'm heading to bed soon, but have fun. And Jamie?"

"Yup?"

"Just be careful, all right?"

What's that supposed to mean? She's never spoken to me about that. Am I really that obvious? Does she know about us? I think she must.

I wince and retreat into my room. I think she knows. She has always been able to see right through me, after all.

Still, my plan worked. I now have permission to hang out with Erik in my room. My anticipation is already off the charts. My phone buzzes. It's from Erik.

Hey, still on for tonight? Should I come over?

I get a surge of endorphins so strong I can barely contain them. I message him back: **of course!! And yup, see you soon.** ☺

I know I'll spiral with excitement if I don't do something, so I call Max. She picks up on the third ring.

"Hey," she says. "Good timing, I just got to the diner. Everyone is here."

I hear them all call out to me through her phone. They're all at Anchor Bros without me? I know it's to be expected given where I am, but still. My heart pangs.

"How are you?" she asks.

"Good, actually. Erik's about to come over."

"Oh yeah? Going to make out again?"

"I think so," I say, keeping my voice low, in case Mom or Mike is nearby. I'm in my room with the door closed, but I figure it's better to be overly cautious. "I want your advice. He wants to keep what we're doing a secret."

"What for?"

"It's complicated."

"Spell it out for me."

"He was supposed to date a guy his family picked for him, but he met me and likes me, so he ended things with that guy. Now he's single but his family doesn't know I'm the reason he broke up with the partner they chose."

"That is complicated," says Max. "If they want him to date someone, why can't he date you?"

"I think they want to pick for him. He was actually told by his gran to keep things with me platonic."

"Are you okay with that?" she asks. "If his family don't approve, I doubt that will change."

"It's whatever. They don't have to know, and we agreed to keep it casual."

"I don't know about this. I know you're excited and probably a little love drunk, but this seems messy to me."

I flinch. "I'm fine, Max."

"I only mean you're in that part of a new relationship where it's all you can think about. And I know how exciting that is. I just want you to be careful, because I hate to be the one to tell you, but I don't know about this."

"I'm fine, I promise. I know there are risks, but where has playing it safe ever got me? I'd rather live my life with the risk of getting my heart broken than always play it safe."

"Listen, I'm not going to tell you what to do. Just be careful, all right?"

"I will." I sit down on the end of my bed. "But anyway, why are you at Anchor Bros?"

"We're commiserating," she says. "'Ashes' only got ten views today."

Ouch. If it hurts me, I have no idea what Max must be feeling. I've talked to her at length about this very thing, and even though we both knew it was unlikely, I truly think we both thought that the song would take off. And yet, it's stopped climbing at around two hundred views.

"It flopped," she says. "I'm a flop."

"It'll take time," I say, trying to muster up some confidence I'm not sure I have. I know how seriously Max takes her music, and how much this must be crushing her.

And I'm not there, like I should be. I should be home, talking her through this. I'm her best friend, and I can't be fully there for her while she's having a tough time. It stings.

"Maybe a bad idea for me to get so excited about it," she says. "I feel like, I don't know."

"Like what?"

"Like nobody cares, I guess."

Something inside me shatters. I know Max, and I can hear the pain in her voice. This is hurting her even more than she's letting on. I have learned her tells through years of friendship, and when she's really hurt, like she was when her first boyfriend, Noah, cheated on her, or when her dad told her he doesn't believe she will ever make it as a musician, she closes up.

I have to do something for her. I have to.

"Anyway," she says, putting on a bright tone of voice I can tell is fake. "Gotta go drown my feelings in cheese fries."

"Good plan. Okay, love you."

"Love you, too. And seriously, be careful, all right? Heartbreak is no joke."

She ends the call.

What can I do? Even though I'm across the world, there must be something that I can do for her. Something that can make this at least a little bit better. I can't be there physically for her to go over her feelings, but sometimes that's not what she needs.

After she found out about Noah, I baked her favorite dessert, caramel brownies, and got her a new vinyl from one of her favorite bands, Falling for Alice. We spent the night curled on the couch watching movies. Typical best-friend-duty stuff.

I can't do that because I'm here. Then it dawns on me. I *can* do something. All this royal stuff has felt like a barrier between me and my friends. It doesn't have to be, though.

I have more than three hundred thousand followers on Instagram now.

I go through on my phone and find the "Ashes" video. I post

the link to it as a story, along with the caption: **sooo my best friend released a song, check it out!**

And, post.

The comments and likes immediately start coming in.

I hear a knock on the front door. I put my phone on mute, then jog over.

Erik is outside.

"Hi," he says.

"Hi."

He hugs me. Any worries about me being awkward melt away at his touch. We seem to fit together, and this feels completely natural.

"You look nice," he says.

"So do you," I say. "Like, really good."

"Thank you."

"Hey there," says Mike, emerging out of the kitchen.

Erik waves. He seems surprisingly sheepish, and I'm worried he's going to give our plans away.

"We're going to my room," I say.

Neither Mom nor Mike object, so I lead Erik through our apartment until we reach my room and go inside. I close and lock my door as quietly as I can.

"You should know," I say, keeping my voice down. "I think Mom suspects us."

"She does?"

"Yeah, but don't worry. She won't tell anyone."

"I trust you," he says. "As long as you know how bad it would be if anyone in my family found out."

"I know," I say.

He is standing by the foot of my bed, shifting his weight from side to side. Should I go up to him and kiss him? I sit on the end of the bed, and he joins me.

"What's going on?" he asks. "Are you okay?"

"Yup," I say. I wonder why he's asking me that. I'm not the one in any danger of getting in trouble. If Mom and Mike found out what Erik and I are doing, I'm sure they'd set some ground rules, but it's not as if I would be in any trouble.

"You seem a little nervous," he says. "Is there anything I can do?"

"I'm fine."

"It's okay to be nervous," he says. "I'm nervous, too."

"You are? But you've kissed other people, right? Sorry, that's really nosy."

He starts to smile. "I have more experience, but normally, I don't really care, or at least I don't care this much about it going well. It's something I do for fun. But with you, I'm terrified about screwing it up."

"Me too," I say. "I don't want things to be awkward with us."

"Me either."

"At least we're on the same page," I say. "I still really want to kiss you, if you want that."

"I do."

"I guess I should do that, then."

He smiles at me. I close the distance and press my lips to his. It turns out, kissing on a bed is a little more complex than kissing while standing. Or maybe I'm not used to it. I turn to kiss him. He puts his hand on my side and lets out a soft moan, which might be the hottest sound I've ever heard. I touch his chest, feeling him through his shirt.

"You're so good at that," he says. He runs his hands down my back. They keep going lower, and I wonder where he will stop with each inch. He stops above my waistband; then he moves back up.

"So are you," I say.

I stop kissing him momentarily, because I need a second to catch my breath. My heart is pounding. I think about Erik with his shirt off.

"You okay?" he asks.

"I'm so good," I say. I kiss him gentler this time. He presses his tongue against mine. It's not like what I was expecting. It's not like he's trying to force his tongue into my mouth; it's much gentler than that. I try copying him, and it's so good it's dizzying. His hand is still on my side, and it feels steady and reassuring.

For a moment, I remember this is a secret. And probably always will be.

I rest my hand on his chest and feel his heartbeat. I start kissing the side of his neck, trying to force my brain to shut up so that I can enjoy this.

"Does that feel good?" I ask.

"It does. Lie down," says Erik. "My turn."

I laugh, because this is so risky. But there's an intensity in Erik's expression, like he isn't joking, he's taking this incredibly seriously. Even with the risks, I can't get myself to call this off and play video games instead. What I want is to do this.

I lie down.

Erik kisses up my chest until he reaches my neck. And oh damn. He's outstanding at this. The kisses are just hard enough. They make my whole body feel like jelly.

"You'll have to teach me how to do that," I say.

"Sounds like a fun lesson."

We make out for a while until we tire. I don't want him to leave, so we start watching a movie on my laptop while holding hands. Mom and Mike have clearly both gone to bed, so we decided the risk was worth it.

"I was thinking about something," I say, as I play with his fingers. "I've always wondered why people in positions of power don't help more. It never made sense to me why some people hoard all the wealth and power and let everyone else struggle."

He's quiet, listening. I know it's a sudden change of topic, but given that my time in Mitanor might be running out, I want to make the most of it.

"And now I have some access to power," I continue. "And maybe wealth, but I'm not doing anything to help anyone else. I've been thinking it would be a good idea to do more. If that's even possible."

"I get what you mean," he says. "I've tried to do things back home, but every time I tried suggesting something my parents shot me down."

"Really?"

"They told me I should focus on my school because they're already doing all they can and don't need a teenager getting in their way."

The way Erik says it, like it's a matter of fact, like it's normal, rings alarm bells in my mind. It doesn't sound normal. I can't even imagine what it would feel like to be dismissed like that.

"But things might be different here," he says. "We should talk to Alexander and Maria about it tomorrow."

"I'd like that," I say, as I lean across to kiss him. "Thanks for listening."

"Anytime."

He kisses me back slowly, making the room, and the rest of the world, melt away.

Chapter Thirty

ERIK

I've been thinking a lot about my family.

When I was younger, I remember wanting to do the same thing Jamie brought up last night. To help people. I asked my parents, and they always assured me they were doing everything they could to help. They told me that they would tell me when I could be of assistance.

Still, I can recall the way they treated me when I brought up wanting to help more. I was dismissed. They told me they knew better, and that I should stick to my role.

It's one of the things Jamie is so good at. He's not as entrenched as I am, so he can do things I wouldn't be allowed to do. He hasn't internalized the rules of royalty yet, which gives him power.

I catch him looking at me, pulling me back to reality.

We're on our way to breakfast with Maria and Alexander, and we plan to tell them what Jamie and I spoke about last night. I feel a little sickly. Alexander and Maria are clearly different from my parents. Very different.

Still, I'm worried they might treat Jamie like my parents treated me. That's the last thing I want. I don't want him ever to feel as brushed aside, as small, as I did. Especially when all he wants is to help people.

Alexander and Maria are sitting near the end of the dining room table, deep in conversation. I'm happy for them, but the sight stings. I never really see my parents speaking like this. They talk, but it's always about work, and they never seem to like spending time together. Both sets of Jamie's parents look at each other like the other is the most wonderful person in the room. I wish my parents looked at each other like that.

Jamie and I sit near the two of them.

"I hope you're hungry," says Alexander. "I had the chefs prepare us something special today."

Three waiters enter the room and place plates down in front of us. Each one has waffles on it, along with a side of bacon, a scoop of ice cream, candied nuts, and a drizzle of maple syrup.

"Rebecca told me this is your favorite," says Alexander.

"It is," says Jamie. "Thank you."

"You're welcome," he says. "So, what lessons have you planned for today, Erik?"

I chew my bite of waffle and swallow. I haven't had waffles in a long time, and I regret that. I now see why these are Jamie's favorite; they're pretty much the perfect food. I watch as Jamie eats, and he shows that he paid attention in my lesson. He doesn't scrape the plate. I don't have any notes.

"There's something Jamie and I were hoping to ask you," I say.

Jamie wipes his mouth on his napkin, then rests his knife and fork to the side, as I taught him.

"I was talking to Erik yesterday," he says. His voice is clear and confident, and he's keeping his head up. "And I was wondering if there was anything I could do while I'm here that might help people."

"Help people?" asks Alexander. "In what way?"

"I'm not sure," he says. "But I feel like I've got all this attention on me, and it would be good to be able to do something positive with it."

Here we go. I brace myself for the dismissal. For them to tell Jamie something similar to what my parents told me. He's too young; he doesn't understand the way things are done. They've got it under control.

"That's a wonderful idea!" says Alexander. "You're brilliant."

"I have an idea," says Maria. "I get a lot of emails from people asking me for help. If the two of you would like, you could come to my office, and we could go over them and see if there's anything you would like to work on?"

"Sounds great," says Jamie.

Once we're finished with our waffles, we go to Maria's office. It's farther down the hall from Alexander's and is designed entirely differently. While Alexander's office is all dark wood and green, Maria's is bright, with lots of white and accents of soft gold.

Maria pulls chairs up for Jamie and me, then opens up her email inbox. There are hundreds of emails. Most of them have been marked as read, but at least a few dozen with their arrival dates within the past few weeks haven't been opened.

"I do what I can," says Maria. "But it can be hard to keep up. My team sifts through for anything pressing, but I'm always worried that someone truly in need might slip through the cracks."

Jamie clicks on the first email.

Subject: Seeking Your Grace's Guidance and Assistance

Your Majesty Queen Maria,

I hope this message finds you well. I am seeking your guidance and assistance in a matter causing me considerable distress.

My neighbor, Carlo, has three dogs who bark constantly whenever he leaves the house. I work from home and find it difficult to concentrate, given the never-ending barking of his demonic animals. Can you help me, please? I don't know who to ask, as the local council has done nothing.

Jamie clicks out of the email.

"A lot of them are like that," she says. "Sometimes people just want to vent about their problems."

Jamie clicks on another email.

Subject: Formal????

Dear Your Majesty (?),

My best friend has had a big crush on you for years, and he wanted me to ask you if you'd like to go to prom with him. I'm sure you're busy but you've got to shoot your shot, you know? So how about it? He'll get you a corsage.

I glance at Maria. She shakes her head. Jamie scrolls momentarily, then clicks on one of the emails.

Subject: Hope House

Dear Queen Maria,

I don't know if this will reach you, but if it does, I hope it finds you well. My name is Talia Kastel, and I am the director of Hope House. Funding cuts have meant we have had to close our doors, meaning there is no space for queer youth to go in Castillon. I genuinely believe this is a systematic attack launched by John Valencia and his conservative party.

We need funding to survive, and currently, queer teens facing poverty or homelessness are forced to try their luck in one of the general shelters—which are already stretched thin and are often incredibly dangerous, especially for queer teenagers. We need help, and I don't know who else to turn to.

If you can help in any way, please let me know.

Blessings,
Talia

"Can we help her?" asks Jamie.

"I'll reach out," says Maria. "Good spotting, Jamie. I'll let you know when she gets back to me, and we'll do whatever we can."

I reread the email. It only arrived this morning, and it's cosmically good timing that Jamie had this thought when he did. He has found someone with a genuine need. Plus, he hasn't been shot down like I was. It might be different here. He might be able to do things his way.

They listened to him.

I hope he never has to feel what I've felt. More than that, I hope they never try to control him like I have been controlled.

CHAPTER THIRTY-ONE

JAMIE

It didn't take long for Talia, the director of Hope House, to get back to Maria.

Now a group of us, including Erik, are in a car, traveling across the city in order to make it to the shelter.

On my phone, I load the "Ashes" video. I refresh again, making sure the number is right. It's been going up rapidly ever since I posted about it, but in the past hour it's jumped by around ten thousand views.

It's at 89,000 now. Ren has been messaging me almost non-stop. Apparently my post got enough views that it's started showing up in people's recommendation windows on YouTube, and that's enough for the views to seriously spike. They're behaving like my followers, in that they're constantly going up.

Weirdly, though, I haven't heard from Max. I've messaged her a few times, but she's ignored me each time. She hasn't even posted anything in the group chat, which has been freaking out about how popular the video is now that I gave it a boost using my new social media following.

I know I need to call her and ask, but I've been a little distracted between things between Erik and me, my lessons, and the Hope House stuff.

I put my phone back into my pocket. I want to be present right now. The only person missing is Alexander, who had some

THE RULES OF ROYALTY   217

other work that he needed to do, but he trusted that we could handle this. He did tell me how proud of me he was for coming up with this idea.

I'm not doing this so he, or anyone, is proud of me. I'm doing it because it's the right thing to do. Still, it feels nice.

We go around a corner and spot a large crowd of people. There must be a few hundred of them, all waiting out in front of a building. On the front is a sign that says HOPE HOUSE. That's the only thing that tells me we're in the right spot. The exterior is a pretty average, generic-looking building, and the boarded-up windows make it seem especially dilapidated.

A huge crowd has assembled around the entrance. Why are there so many people there?

Then it hits. They're here for me.

No, they can't be. For one thing, nobody is supposed to know that we're even here. On the other hand, it still seems ridiculous that this many people would care enough about me to come out and see me. I know I have a lot of followers now and that a lot of people are curious about the so-called American prince. The people out there are acting like I'm a movie star, though.

"What's going on?" asks Mom.

"Word must've gotten out somehow," says Maria. "I'm sorry, Jamie. We can come back later."

I remember the email that Talia sent. There are kids in this city that currently have nowhere to go. It's incredibly messed up, and if there's anything I can do to help, then I want to do it. Even though there's a crowd, I'm not giving up that easily. Too much is on the line.

"No," I say. "I want to talk to Talia. Besides, I should say hi if they want to see me."

"It might not be safe," says Maria. "We need to get security."

"I'll be fine," I say. "Look at them, they're kids."

Everyone looks out the window. I'm right. The crowd is very

218

young; there are only a few adults among them. I would guess that those are parents acting as chaperones. Plus, there is some security: a few police have arrived and set up barricades to control the crowd. I guess they also got the warning that I would be here.

The car crawls to a stop. From this angle, I notice a few news vans parked in a nearby parking lot. Standing nearby are some reporters and a few men holding large cameras—an uneasy fluttering dances in my stomach.

Is my arrival somewhere newsworthy? My nerves spike at the thought of being filmed and that footage being shown nationwide.

"I know what happened," says Erik.

He shows me his phone screen. On it is a post from Talia.

Do you want to meet #jamiejohnson?? Come to the location of the former Hope House, 43 East Street, at 1:00 today for his first-ever public appearance!

"I can't believe this," says Maria. "She sold us out."

"It's fine," I say.

"No, it's not!" says Maria. "We come to help, and this is how she thanks us? I will have words with her, Jamie, trust me."

I kind of love how much anger she's showing right now. It feels protective and nice that she cares so much.

"It's fine," I say. "Look, I'm not bothered, I promise."

"It isn't the way things are done," says Maria. "We haven't done a security sweep. We need to go back."

I glance at Erik. He tilts his head toward the door.

Is he encouraging me to break a rule? What have I done to him?

I unclip my seatbelt. Maria gives me a death stare.

I open the door and step outside as quickly as I can. I move a little too soon as I stumble forward and nearly face-plant. A hush falls over the crowd until I stand up straight and wave with one hand. I'm okay, folks—nothing to see here.

The moment passes, and the crowd starts screaming. It's not a cheer, and I'm not sure whose benefit this is for. One girl, who is probably about thirteen, starts sobbing. Oh my God. Her T-shirt has a *chibi* version of me on it, complete with a little cartoon crown. When did she find the time?

I go up to her. "I love your shirt," I say.

"Oh my God!" she says, wiping her cheeks. "You're talking to me!"

"I am!"

"I love you!"

I find myself smiling. This amount of unbridled enthusiasm is honestly ridiculously charming.

"Can you sign this?" she asks. It's a royal tabloid magazine that I'm on the cover of. The picture is my yearbook picture. Yikes. That picture is not flattering in any way.

Still, I sign it. Many people here have brought that very magazine, and I move on to the next person.

"How long are you going to stay here?" asks one of the fans, a guy I would guess is around fifteen. He has a trans pride pin stuck to his chest.

"I'm not sure yet," I say as I sign his copy of the magazine.

"I wanted to say thanks," he says. "I'm not sure if you know, but things for queer people haven't been great here for a while. You being here, being so open. It means a lot."

I think about my plan. I'm supposed to go back to America after the wedding. How will they feel when that happens?

I glance across. Erik is taking pictures with a group of girls. He is giving them a polite royal smile. He turns and smiles at me. This time, it seems more natural. It pulls all focus.

"Can I get a picture with both of you?" asks a girl, breaking the spell. "I'm a fan of yours, too, Erik."

"Sure," I say. I pull Erik over. He moves close to me, throwing his arm around my shoulder. I feel the same things I usually do when I'm this close to him, but I try to keep my composure. Erik wants what we do to be a secret, so I will do my best to make sure no one finds out.

"Thank you," she says. "Would you mind if I posted this?"

"Go ahead," says Erik.

I check on Erik again. He's currently signing a girl's phone case with a gold Sharpie she must have had on hand. I focus and take a picture with the next person in line, a guy who might be around my age or maybe a few years younger.

"We have to go," Maria says. I get a vibe she's angry, but I don't regret doing this. These people came out, hoping to see me. The least I could do was give them some attention. I think it's because I've been in their shoes once. Mike and I waited outside a film premiere, hoping to meet one of my favorite actors. But when he left the theater, he kept his head down and walked right past us and the crowd that had built up. He treated us like we were nothing. I don't want anyone to feel like that.

"Talia is waiting," says Maria.

"I'm so sorry!" I call out to the crowd. "That's all I have time for, but seriously, thank you so much. It was so nice meeting all of you."

"Jamie, wait!"

"One more picture, please!"

I take one last selfie, then follow Maria up into the shelter.

Inside, it smells musty, like a place that hasn't been used in a while.

Everything is at least a few decades old. The carpet is stained, and the couch is lumpy and ugly. There's a kitchen at the far end of the space, but it's got its roller doors down. A layer of dust covers almost everything.

Still, the bones here are good. Once upon a time, this place would've been a fun place to hang out. I can imagine people playing foosball or lounging on the bean bags and playing video games.

Those days are long gone now, and it makes my chest ache. This place would've been a lifeline to so many, and it was allowed to close. For what? To give the ultra-wealthy more tax cuts so they can buy another boat?

"There you are," says a voice, who I am guessing must be Talia. I'd guess she's in her early thirties, and has long blond hair with pink streaks at the ends and is wearing a boy band T-shirt and jeans. On her wrist is a smartwatch with a rainbow-colored band.

"Sorry we're late," says Maria.

"I'm not," she says. "I saw what you did out there, and it was amazing. And look," she says. "You're trending. This amount of exposure is priceless."

She shows us her phone screen, and she's right. The hashtag #jamiejohnson is the third-highest trending topic in the country. A few people have already uploaded the pictures they took with me, and have gotten hundreds of likes. A large number of them have also posted about Hope House, and are questioning why it is closed.

"We saw your tweet," says Mom, her voice flat.

Talia crosses her arms. "I'm sorry, but desperate times call for desperate measures, and as you can see, we're truly at that point. Jamie, I'm sorry."

"If I can do anything to help," I say, "then I want to. Tweet as much as you want."

"I'm glad to hear that. I nearly gave up, to be honest." She breathes out. "But you're here now."

"How can we help?" I ask.

"Our problem is funding. Or, lack of it, really."

"You need more money?"

"Desperately," says Talia. "We were the only queer youth shelter in the city. We provided a safe space for anyone, no matter how they identify. And with the rise of anti-queer rhetoric led by John Valencia and his party, we simply couldn't fight any longer."

John Valencia is the prime minister of Mitanor. That's who we're up against?

"Sorry," continues Talia. "I know you have to be impartial. But he's cut our funding so much it's impossible to operate. I put everything I had into this place, but it wasn't enough. We closed our doors almost a month ago."

"That's horrific," I say.

"I agree. But this sort of thing happens while we have an ultra-conservative party in power. Again, sorry, I know you have to be impartial."

"Not me," I say. "Not with this."

"I agree," says Maria. "But you must know our hands are tied. I would love to give you the money, but how we spend our budget is carefully monitored."

"It is?" I ask.

"We have an agreement with the government," she says. "We receive some of our income from them. Because of that, how we spend is heavily regulated."

"So you can't give them the money, even if you have it?"

"That's right. If we did, Valencia might see it as a slight and could restrict Talia's budget even more. He is not a kind man."

"You can say that again," says Talia, the bitterness in her tone unmissable.

I try to wrap my head around it. "What can we do?"

"You can help us raise awareness," says Talia. "You might not be able to give us palace money, but there are no laws against you helping us fundraise."

"I could post something," I suggest. I think about what I did with the "Ashes" video. If I send out a message, people listen.

"I'm sure if people knew, they'd help. If I film you, maybe you could tell everyone what's happening."

Talia shakes her head. "I've been trying to get people to listen for months. I think you should try. Put it in your words."

Maria gives me a reassuring nod. I take my phone from my pocket. As soon as I start the live, hundreds of people start watching. That number quickly climbs into the thousands.

"Hey, everyone," I say. "Sorry for the unexpected live, but I wanted to tell you something. I'm at a queer youth shelter in Castillon that has had its funding cut so badly that it hasn't been able to stay open. I don't know what the solution to this problem is, but I was wondering if we could do some crowd-funding thing? I don't know if I'm allowed to do this, but yeah. If you have any ideas about what to do about this, please let me know. Okay, bye."

I tap my screen, ending the live. "Do you think that'll help?"

"I have a good feeling about it," says Talia.

When I get back to the palace, I decide that enough is enough.

I need to call Max and find out what is going on. She still hasn't replied to any of my messages, and that's made it very clear something is going on. All my other friends saw me at the shelter, and messaged me to lend their support. But not Max. And I know how much she cares about this sort of thing. She got a lot of shit from her dad about being bi, and she'd hate the thought of a queer youth shelter being shut down due to funding cuts.

Mom, Mike, and I have reached our apartment after spending about an hour with Talia, going over plans to raise both money and awareness. We haven't come up with any ideas other than a crowdfunding campaign, which Maria is going to create and I will post about when it's ready.

I feel really good about that. Yes, this royal twist my life has taken has been a curveball, but I really like the thought of using it to do some good. I know I'm not going to be able to fix all of

Mitanor's problems or anything like that, but I can at least be a positive force.

"Are you all right?" asks Mom.

"I'm okay," I say. "I need to call Max. I feel like things are weird between us."

"Oh, how so?"

"She's not responding to my messages."

"Maybe she's busy?"

"She's always busy. She's upset with me, I don't know why."

"Try and be kind," she says. "This adjustment must be difficult for her, too."

"I don't think it's that," I say. "I think it's about her music. She was upset about the music video not getting many views, so I posted about it. Now it's doing really well, but she's annoyed with me for some reason."

Mom gives me a blank stare like the answer is obvious; I'm just missing it. "Did you ask her if you could post it?"

"Well, no," I say.

"Oh, honey. She probably feels upset that you did something so important without asking her."

I'm still for a moment. She's right.

I really should've asked her before posting it. I've had so much going on that I wasn't thinking about it. Max has always been very particular about her music, and everything has to feel right to her. She trusts her instincts, always. Now I see why she must be upset: it's not that I posted it. It's that I didn't ask first, and I changed the trajectory of her career without her permission. As her best friend, I know she hates control being taken away from her more than anything.

I should've known this. I was distracted by everything that's been happening to me lately, and it made me make a mistake. I hope she can forgive me for it.

"You're right," I say. "I'll apologize."

"Good call."

I go into my room, close the door, and call Max. It rings out, so I call her again.

This time the call connects.

"Hey, Jamie," she says, her tone blunt. "Now isn't a good time."

Knowing Max, I know this means she simply doesn't want to talk. If she were truly busy, she'd give a reason, and her tone wouldn't be so short.

"Please hear me out," I say. "I'm sorry that I posted the video without asking you. I should've checked with you first, and I'm sorry."

There's heavy silence on the other end of the line.

"Thank you for the apology," she says. "I know I've been distant. I guess I feel like that's something the old you wouldn't have done. Have you read the comments? They only like me because of you."

"I'm not sure that's true."

"I don't know if you know how big of a deal this is to me," she says. "It's great that it's doing well, it really is. But now I won't know if it's just because you're famous now. I'll always have that in my mind, and I didn't want that. I wanted to earn this myself."

"Does it matter?" I ask. "You wanted it to do well, and now it is. I don't see what the problem is."

"It matters to me!" she says. "I thought you knew that, but I guess not. Let's talk about this later."

"No, I want to talk about it now," I say. Tears well up in my eyes. "My whole life has changed, and I really need you right now. I'm sorry I messed up, I really am."

"It's fine, but I have to go," she says. "Sorry."

She hangs up.

Chapter Thirty-Two

Erik

Jamie's fundraiser has already raised nearly $20,000.

It's only a third of the target that Talia set, but that was her goal for the entire month. The fact that Jamie has earned a third of the amount they need in a single day is extraordinary.

I'm so proud of him.

It would've been so easy for him to sit back and live a life of luxury. But he's trying to make changes. He's trying to help people.

It scares me how much I like Jamie and how wonderful I think he is. Because I don't know what the future holds for us. What we're doing is fun, but I am becoming attached to him in a way I never have before.

But nothing has changed. My family still don't approve, and I can't see that changing anytime soon.

I don't know what to do.

I'm in the palace pool, swimming laps. I swim over to where I left my phone and check it. As I had hoped, there's a new message from Jamie waiting for me.

Hey, are you free?

I'm swimming some laps, want to do something after?

Or I could join you?

I think about it. Jamie in a pair of swimming trunks. There's no way I'm going to say no to that.

I'd like that. ☺

Yay! I'll be there in five

I like his message, making a little heart appear beside it.

I take off my swimming cap and goggles and rub some water through my hair. The anticipation is already killing me. I float on my back, looking up at the tiled ceiling.

After a few minutes, the door opens, and Jamie enters the pool room. His black trunks cut off above his knees. It makes my throat go dry, and any thoughts of resisting him fade away.

"This is cool," he says, glancing around the pool room.

The lighting here is soft and gold, reflecting off the pink marble walls. On one side of the walls is a tile mosaic of a mermaid. It might be the same one that's on the statue outside. In this one, she's free and swimming in what appears to be the middle of the ocean. Still, there's a ship in the far distance, seemingly chasing her, and a literal storm on the horizon. She has no idea the danger that's coming for her.

I wave my hand through the water.

"Coming in?"

He unzips the gray hoodie he was wearing, then pulls it off. I have to pull myself together after seeing him like this. He truly is gorgeous. The way the pale light dances across his skin highlights every fine line and contour. He's lean but slightly more muscular than I thought he was, with definition on both his chest and stomach. He moves around to the ladder and climbs in, then swims up to me.

"Brr," he says. "I want credit for how smoothly I just got in. That took a lot of willpower."

"I bet."

He sinks a little lower into the water. "I've been thinking a lot lately."

"About what?" I ask.

"I wish I could help Hope House more. There's the fundraiser, but surely there's more we could do. Do you have any ideas for how we could raise money for them?"

I think it over. "You could throw a garden party. People pay for tickets, and the money raised goes to a charitable cause."

"You think we'd be allowed to?"

"You'd have to ask, but I think so."

"I'll ask Maria. I want to help as much as I can, you know? It's all I can think about. I'm here, and some people don't have anything. We have to help them."

"I know," I say. "We will."

The pool room is quiet, and the water goes still. "This is going to sound kind of random," he says. "But I feel like we're similar."

"I feel that, too."

"It's like, even though we're from totally different worlds we've got so much in common."

"Oh yeah," I say, moving closer. I loop my arms around him. "Like what?"

"Well, we both like games."

"Yup."

"And we have the same taste in movies."

"Correct."

"And I feel like we, I don't know, see the things the same way. Most of the time. It's like we're always on the same page."

"I agree," I say. "And I'm so proud of you. What you've done today, it's incredible."

"You helped."

I shake my head. "You've done so much, so quickly. I'm amazed by you."

He chews his bottom lip in a way that drives me wild.

He wades closer. "There are no, like, cameras here or anything, are there?"

"There probably are."

The thought of kissing him right now is so appealing, but it could be risky. I look around the roof, searching for any cameras, and I can't see any. Sometimes old palaces have rooms without cameras. In fact, most of the time those are only in the hallways or rooms like the throne room, with precious items that need to be protected. This pool room is nice, but it might not have any cameras anywhere.

We might get away with it.

He grins at me. "Probably? What would we do if there wasn't?"

He's adorable. He comes even closer, so his chest is right against mine. I don't have the willpower to move away, even if there could be cameras we're not seeing.

I close the distance between us. My stomach does somersaults, constantly twisting and turning. I lift a hand and brush my thumb against his cheek. This is thrilling and terrifying all at once. My breath catches, and for a moment I'm worried that he's going to pull away.

Then his lips are against mine.

This boy. This wonderful boy. I don't know if he even knows how far he's pushed me. How he's made me do things I never thought I would, and how I don't regret those choices for even a second, because they mean I get to have moments like this. A boy who has adjusted to his new life so well it's almost as if this is always what he was supposed to be doing. Who he was born to be.

I pick him up, so he wraps his legs around me, and I move him to the pool wall. We crash into it and kiss furiously, not caring if anyone sees us, or any cameras. The risk is worth it.

I smell chlorine and his cologne. He tastes like mint, and I realize he must've brushed his teeth before coming here. I kiss him like the world is going up in flames and this is my last chance. I kiss him with everything I have.

He stops and rests his forehead against mine. We're both breathing heavily.

"Hey, Erik," he says.

"Yeah?"

I put him down. I search his face, but I'm already bracing myself for him to cut things off. I would understand. I can't give him what he deserves; it is probably the right decision.

"You know that I'm going back to America soon," he says. "Right?"

My stomach drops. "I know."

"I want you to know that I really like this. And I really like you."

"I really like you, too."

"What I'm saying is, I maybe don't want this to end. Even if I leave. And I know about your family, but I'm just saying how I feel. I'd get it if you want to, like, stop this, we can."

"I don't want that," I say. That's the last thing on my mind. I know how good this is, and how rare. I've had crushes before, but with Jamie it's different. I feel more for him than I've ever felt for anyone, and I'm not going to give up on that easily. "Do you?"

"No," he says. "But I don't know how it will work."

"I don't, either."

"I also know I don't want to stop," he says. "I think it would be smart to call it off, but I don't want to."

I take hold of his hands. There are so many things threatening to come between us. But right now, we're here, and we have each other.

"I feel like this is really special," he says. "Something like this has never happened to me before."

"It hasn't happened to me, either. And listen, I'm going to want to keep spending time with you, no matter where you are, or how it works."

"Me too."

I lean down and kiss him.

A scary thought crosses my mind. He's right. I don't know how this will work, which means it might end at some point.

I'm not sure I'll survive that.

Chapter Thirty-Three

Jamie

Erik offers me his hand, and our fingers link together. They fit so perfectly it's like they were made just for this. His hand is warm and his grip is strong and reassuring.

We're in my room, with the door closed. Our bodies are pressed against each other, and we're practically tangled. It feels nice and cozy and perfect. I think I'd be truly happy if I could have moments like this for the rest of my life.

This is a terrifying realization to have, considering how precarious things are.

I've completely lost control of this. Things with Erik seem like they're destined to end in disaster. We're from different countries. His family disapprove. This is well in advance, but I did some research and found that no member of Erik's family can get married without the queen's blessing. It's wholly forbidden and part of the law in Sunstad.

I don't see how this could work in the long run. Even knowing all of this, I can't get myself to stop. I should make the wise decision and go back to being platonic. Tutor and student, that's it. That way, he's not at risk of his family finding out and I'm not in danger of getting my heart broken. I can't bring myself to cut him off, even if I am pretty sure we're both strapped into a car that's hurtling toward a cliff.

I should be smart and jump out. But my heart wants me to stay in this until the gory end.

"What if the garden party doesn't work?" I ask instead.

That fear has been steadily building all day. A few days ago we brought up the garden party fundraising idea with Maria, and she loved it.

Invites have been sent out, and hundreds of people are expected to appear. It's more rushed than usual, but Maria said she wanted to get the money for Hope House as quickly as possible.

"I think it'll be okay," he says, squeezing my hand. His touch is gentle yet firm, and I find it grounds me. Yes, things might not work out. But in this moment, it feels this good, and isn't that worth something? "Maria seems excited about it."

"She does."

"What have your parents said?" he asks.

"They're looking forward to it," I say. "Mike already has his outfit planned. He got Simon to pick one out for him. I don't want it to fail."

"Hey. It won't."

He says it like he genuinely believes it, which helps more than I think he knows. If he believes in me and in this, then it will be fine. He hasn't steered me in the wrong direction at all so far, and his advice has always been sound.

"I could use a distraction," I say.

"Oh yeah?" He sits up. "What kind?"

I grip his shirt and pull him to me. We kiss for a moment, and then I stop. Like always, kissing him makes my worries seem miles away.

I get up, and slide the latch on the door across.

"What are you doing?" he asks.

I pull my shirt off and toss it across the room. Normally, I'm worried about what people will think when I take my shirt off around them.

Erik looks at me like I'm the hottest guy on Earth. Even better, he makes me feel like I am. I join him on the bed.

It's the middle of the day now. Mom and Mike are out at the moment, but could come back at any time. This is so risky.

I reach for Erik, and we start kissing. My breath catches. I know I've been around him shirtless and kissed him shirtless. Those times were great, but the context of being in a semi-clothed state around him in a bed is radically different from being in a pool with him. He puts his hands on my sides, and heat fills me. We kiss harder than we ever have. I don't think I'm ready to have sex yet, and I don't think Erik is, either. I probably will be, in the future, but for the time being I'm more than content with making out.

"I hope you don't feel any pressure to do this," he says, resting his hand on my chest. He runs it down, until he reaches my hip. Turns out I have a ton of nerve endings there, and they all ignite at his touch. "We can go as slow as you'd like. We don't even need to do this, if you don't want to."

"I know," I say. "I don't feel pressure, I want to. As long as you do."

He kisses me. We fall back onto the bed, still kissing. Erik props himself up, and then moves over, so he's sitting above my waist. I look up at him and grin. I run my hands up his chest, and then unbutton his shirt. He doesn't object. Once I'm done, I pull it off his shoulders. He does the rest, balling it up and tossing it across the room.

Wow.

I can't help noticing the definition in his muscles. His skin is smooth and flawless, and I think he knows it, as confidence is radiating from him like an aura. When I first met him I wondered if he had a six-pack. Turns out he does, and it's amazing.

I run my fingers down his bare chest. He goes still and quiet as

I touch him, my fingertips running down until I reach his navel. He feels firm, but his skin is so soft.

"God," I say. "You're so hot."

He scoops me up with surprising strength and moves us backward, so I'm lying on my back. He positions himself so he's on top of me. He smiles devilishly. He looks so charming when he smiles like that. It feels different from the usual reserved one he has while in company. This feels like a smile that belongs just to me.

"How is this?" he asks.

"What do you mean?"

"For a distraction?"

I laugh. "It's pretty good."

His mouth drops open. "Pretty good?"

"Fine, it's amazing, you're amazing. Is that what you wanted to hear?"

He starts kissing me, then pauses. This is why I haven't stopped this, and why I won't even if there's a high chance it will all fall to pieces. This, right now, is maybe the best I have ever felt in my entire life.

"Yes," he says, his voice nearly a whisper. Before I can say anything, he runs a hand through my hair and kisses me again.

The voices telling me to be careful fade away.

It's the morning of the garden party, and I've gotten dressed in the white suit Simon picked for me.

I really like how I look. I'm hoping Erik will, too. Even though we both feel this fundraiser is important, I'm hoping at some point, well, he'll get a chance to take this fine suit off me.

I can't believe I have thoughts like this, or that there's a good chance they'll come true.

Through my window I can see we've gotten lucky. It's a perfect sunny day, with no clouds in sight.

"Come on, let us see!" calls Mom through my bedroom door.

I recheck my phone. I texted a picture of my suit to the group chat, and have received responses from almost all of them telling me how much they love it.

Max ignored it, as I expected. Amara and Ren have both messaged me separately, trying to get us to stop fighting. I don't really feel like doing that right now. I've already apologized, and I'm a little annoyed at Max for making this such a big thing. I get she's upset, but I already said that I'm sorry, so I'm not sure what else I can do.

Anyway, the video now has over 150,000 views, a bunch of comments, and has nearly as many streams. For a first-time independent release, I'd say it's performed better than any of us could've hoped for. And yes, that's because I boosted it, but still. A win is a win.

Plus, it seems like the garden party is going to be a success. Maria told me almost everyone that was invited has accepted the invite, and a lot of them have made separate donations to Hope House.

The suit Simon chose is perfect: it's paired with a matching vest, brown shoes, and a patterned tie. Even though it's a lot of clothing, and it's hot out, the material is light and breathable, so it's not that bad.

I step outside. Mom is in a floral gown with a matching hat, and Mike's suit is only a shade or two darker than mine.

"What do you think?" I ask, and I do a little spin.

"Oh, Jamie," says Mom. She wraps me in a hug. "You're so handsome."

The three of us go down to the palace garden. The party sprawls out before us. Hundreds of guests, all in bright, summery clothing, are chatting either out in the sun or under a few white tents that have been built specifically for this event. On a platform, a woman in a light blue dress plays the violin, and the music fills the entire space. To the left of the party is the hedge maze. Two small children run out of it, laughing.

"Get off the grass!" shouts a woman, I'm guessing one of the children's parents.

The whole thing is picturesque. There's even a table filled with pastel-colored cupcakes, which I must try.

Maria has done an incredible job. She has made my vision come to life.

"Is it as good as you hoped?" asks Mom.

"It's better," I say.

We make our way into the party. As I walk, I recognize a few of the guests. Actually, I recognize a lot of them. I spot a bunch of famous people: actors, writers, singers. They're all busy, either playing croquet or mingling with the crowd. Their appearance here is exciting because it's cool to be at the same party as a bunch of people I'm a fan of. More than that, though, it means they paid the price for a ticket, which means for every one of them, at least a thousand dollars will be given straight to Talia and Hope House. I notice Talia standing under one of the tents, near the chocolate fondue station.

"Drink, sir?" asks a waiter. "We're serving virgin cosmopolitans and non-alcoholic champagne."

I take one of the virgin cosmopolitans, then go up to Talia. I take a sip, and really like it.

"There you are," says Talia. Standing beside her is a girl around my age.

"Jamie, this is Naomi. She stayed at Hope House before it closed, and now that we are reopening, she will work with me."

"Nice to meet you. Wait, you've made enough to reopen?"

"We have. We've received nearly two hundred thousand in donations already. That's enough to open our doors, and we have a few very wealthy people who have promised to make sure we never close again. And it's all because you got the word out."

"That's not true," I say. "If you hadn't messaged, I wouldn't have known. You did this."

Tears brim in her eyes. "You're too sweet. Mitanor is lucky to have you.

"Seems like someone would like a word," she says. I turn, and see someone who takes my breath away. Erik is watching a game of croquet, along with his older brother, and who I would guess are his parents. Erik told me they were invited, and asked me to be especially careful while they're here.

I am going to. It is difficult given how good he looks in his off-white suit, but I'll do it.

His family makes me wary. They're the reason we can't be together. I have to be careful around them. If I make a mistake and they find out about us, I doubt Erik would ever forgive me.

"Excuse me," I say. "We'll catch up later."

Stefan catches me looking, and waves me over. Erik takes a sip of his drink.

I don't need him to tell me anything to know what he's thinking: *be careful*. I will be. It isn't easy, though, because I have to clamp down on how happy the sight of Erik makes me.

"You must be Jamie," says Stefan, and he claps me on the shoulder. "Erik's told me a lot about you."

"He has?"

This seems to surprise Erik as much as it surprises me.

"No," says Stefan. "I'm joking, but Erik never tells me anything."

"That's not true," says Erik.

"It's nice to meet you," says Elise, cutting off the brothers before they can start seriously bickering. "How are you finding life at the palace?"

"I like it," I say. "Erik's helped a lot."

"That's good," she says. "For me, it was quite the transition. The more help you can get, the better."

"I agree."

"Jamie," says a voice. I turn and see it's Maria. "The prime minister would like to have a word with you."

Oh, shit.

"You've got this," says Erik. He stands up straighter. I mirror him. We've worked a lot on my posture in our lessons, and I know how important it is.

Maria guides me across the party. A lot of people stop to look at me as we pass. For a moment, I wish my friends were here so I wouldn't be the only one aside from my parents who is totally new to this world. Even though things are tense with Max right now, I would still prefer to have her here.

"What does he want to talk to me about?" I ask.

"I'm not sure. Just be careful, okay? Off the record, he can be quite the bully sometimes."

The prime minister of Mitanor, John Valencia, is sitting at a table primarily by himself, save for a brunette woman who is at least twenty years younger than him. He's manspreading, and he's got a little bit of pink cupcake frosting on his cheek.

I like to think I have a pretty good read of people, and my instincts are telling me that this guy is bad news, and not because of what Maria said. I remember how he is the reason that Hope House had its funding cut, and my feelings toward him veer dangerously close to hatred.

"There you are," he says, offering his hand but not standing up. "I've been waiting for you to introduce yourself to me."

"Sorry," I say, instantly regretting that I said it. What am I sorry for? This guy is the very reason that Hope House is in trouble in the first place. We wouldn't even need to throw a party like this if he had maintained their funding. I remember what Talia said and how much she despises him. It's easy to see why.

We shake hands, and his grip is so strong it hurts. It's as if he's trying to crush my hand.

"Take a seat," he barks.

I glance at Maria.

"What are you looking at her for?" he snaps. "Can't you make up your own mind?"

I almost apologize, but instead I sit down.

"May we have some privacy?" he asks, speaking to Maria. "I'd like to speak to the American on my own."

"I'll be at the bar," says Maria. "Come see me when you're done."

She gives me a consoling look, but then leaves, going toward one of the white stalls set up by the hedge maze that is offering drinks. My grandparents are watching from their table. Ruth gives me a wary look, I assume because she knows who I'm speaking with. I wish I was talking to her, because there's still so much I want to learn about Emilia's side of the family. And I want to tell them about Naomi, the girl who attended with Talia. I hope that would mean as much to them as it does to me.

"Now, Jamie," says John. "From all I can see, you are a bright, intelligent young man, so I am sure you must be confused as to why I'm here today."

"A little, yes."

"I came because I wanted to talk to you. Our politics may differ, yes, but I'm not a bad guy."

"You cut Hope House's funding," I say, my annoyance rising. "We wouldn't even need this event if you hadn't done that."

"That is true. But do you know *why* I did that?"

I'm stumped for a moment. His lips curve into a smile. I don't want to give him the benefit of getting one up on me.

"I assume it has something to do with homophobia."

He leans forward, smiling like he wanted me to say something like that. It unsettles me. "Do you think public money is an inexhaustible resource?"

"Well, no, but—"

"And I'm sure you know that the Kettering highway has been in desperate need of redevelopment for at least a decade. Do you know how many requests I've received to fix that?"

"No."

"It's thousands, Jamie. Do you know how many I received to restore your precious Hope House?"

He says the words like they're dirty. I shake my head as a shiver races down my spine. This guy is terrible, and in a way that feels really scary to me. He's also clearly better than me at both politics and debating.

"Less than *fifty*," he says. "Don't get me wrong, I listen to everyone, but it's my job to make sure we serve the most people, not the loudest. People like you live in a bubble, something you always seem to forget. Besides, this shindig should be more than enough to get it to reopen. No harm done."

Behind him, the woman, who I think might be his date, glances over.

"Leave him alone," she says. "He's just a kid."

"It's why he needs to learn," he says. "I am not a villain, Jamie. And I don't appreciate you spreading that message to your followers. Did you know I have received more hate mail in the past few days than I have in my entire career?"

"You think that's because of me?"

His eyes are dark. "I know it is. And trust me, you do not want me as your enemy."

"I didn't tell anyone to send you hate mail, if that's what you're suggesting."

"Listen, Jamie. I have two years left in office, and it seems like you're going to be here for a good while. I want to remind you that you were born into your position of power, but I earned mine. Keep that in mind if you want to make an enemy of me. Trust me, it will not end well for you."

I want to fight back, but then I remember I am speaking to the prime minister of the country. I can't let my emotions get the better of me.

"I'm going to go," I say.

"Suit yourself."

I get up from the chair. My heart thumps like it wants to break out of my chest. I head to the bar. I catch someone watching me. It's Erik, from across the party. His brow is furrowed, and his eyes are filled with unease.

What just happened? By the time I reach Maria I've finally caught up. He was intimidating me. And it was working. He's a bully, through and through. I met people like him when I was younger, and I always thought that treating other people that way is something that people grow out of.

Seems that's not the case. No matter how much power he has accumulated, he still wants to make me feel like I'm small.

"Are you all right?" asks Maria. "I'm sorry, I shouldn't have let him speak to you."

"Yeah, um, it's fine."

"No, it's not," says Maria. "He is a cruel man, Jamie. I'm sorry to say that there are people like him everywhere. You've done incredible work here. Do not let him ruin this."

Her focus is intense. She is right. He is a bully. I shouldn't give him even a second more of my attention.

That's easier said than done. I'm shaking, filled with both anger and fear. He just wiped the floor with me. I was bullied in elementary school, and this is the exact same feeling. I feel helpless, like there's nothing I can do.

I don't know where I'm going, all I know is I want to be somewhere quiet for a moment to collect my thoughts. I would love to tell Erik about what happened, but that seems too risky. For the time being, I'm on my own.

I see the entrance to the hedge maze. It's open, but it doesn't seem like many people have gone there yet, so I go inside. I keep walking until the party appears miles away.

I know I'm trying my hardest to be a good prince.

I'm worried it's not enough.

Chapter Thirty-Four

ERIK

I'm not sure if I should follow Jamie.

I saw him speak to the prime minister of Mitanor, John Valencia, a man I know can be cruel. It's clear from Jamie's facial expressions that the conversation didn't go well. I'm not surprised. I've heard about John, that he's an aggressive, mean man. My heart shatters a little at the thought of him being cruel to Jamie. He doesn't deserve that kind of treatment. Nobody does.

Jamie has done an incredible job. Everyone in my family commented on it, mentioning how surprised they are that Jamie is already using his public platform to help others instead of just himself.

"Is everything all right?" asks Mum. I'm with her and Dad, standing in one of the white tents.

"I'm fine," I say. Even though admitting I'm concerned about Jamie shouldn't be too risky, considering they know that I have been advising him, I've decided it would be best to be as careful as possible whilst they are here. My heart starts to race. Jamie needs me, but how can I break away from them without giving too much away? It seems like an impossible task.

"This party is quite remarkable," says Mum. She's wearing a white dress with a matching hat covered in feathers. It shouldn't work as well as it does, but it's somehow genuinely stylish in a way a lot of the outfits here today aren't. "How involved were you in the preparation?"

"I helped as much as I could," I say. "Maria did a lot of it."

"In any case, you've done an exceptional job," she says. She takes a sip of her champagne. Mum rarely drinks at events like this, so I'm sure this will be her first and only glass. I remember the night Jamie and I drank champagne in my apartment, and my heart pangs. He looked so wounded only moments ago. I need to see him, which means I need to shake off my parents, somehow.

"May we have a word?" asks Mum. "In private."

I swallow hard. Jamie is in the maze, alone. But this is a request from Mum. I simply can't turn it down. If I did, she might get even more suspicious about Jamie and me.

I hate myself for doing it, but I nod.

Dad claps me on the shoulder, and Mum leads me to a quieter part of the tent. From here, I have a great view of the entire party. Jamie has done a remarkable thing with this event. People seem to be having a great time, and so far, there's been no drama. I'm sure it will go down for many as one of the best garden parties any palace has thrown. More than that, this event actually has a purpose. Because of today, Hope House will get to reopen.

I'm so proud of Jamie I could burst. And how do I repay him? By being stuck here when he could really use me. Guilt gnaws at me from the inside as Mum sits at one of the tables.

"I wanted to talk to you about Sebastian," she says.

"What about him?" I ask.

"You never told us why, exactly, you broke up with him."

I would hardly call what we did a breakup. We met one time and agreed to be partners to keep our families off our backs.

"We weren't a match."

"Ah. Well, in that case, we should try to find a different date for you. There are still quite a few appropriate partners interested in you."

I'm sure she means partners that Gran has approved of.

I go quiet. The idea of taking someone other than Jamie to Stefan's wedding is hard for me to even imagine. But if I were to tell them that I would like to go with Jamie, then that creates a huge risk. What we have been doing now is risky enough, because I know they wanted me to keep my relationship with him platonic. If I tell them I disobeyed and they give me another instruction not to be with him, I will have no choice.

I long for freedom. A life that is something other than this. One where I can make my own choices and nobody can control me.

"Gran still thinks it would be best for you to attend the wedding with a partner. It's up to you, but would you like us to find you a date?"

I think about telling her about Jamie. That seems too soon. Given the hundreds of thousands of people that are expected to watch, it would be confirming our relationship to the world, when we haven't even defined what we are.

Plus, in order to do that, I would need to tell Mum that Jamie and I have moved past being friends, which has its own dangers. What we're doing now is one thing, but if she knew about us, and forbid it, that would mean what I am doing is explicitly against her wishes. I'm not sure I can do that.

"Would I be able attend alone?"

"A date would be preferable," she says. "But given the time constraints, I'm sure Gran will understand if you can't find a partner before the wedding. But Erik?"

"Yes?"

"Please trust us when we say we have your best interests at heart. All we want is to protect you, and Gran feels, as I do, that a steady relationship will be the best thing for you at this time. After the wedding we expect it to become your priority."

"All right," I say, even though I don't agree.

That pleases Mum, as she starts to smile. "I know it's difficult. But it's the best thing for you, I promise."

I wipe my hands on the back of my pants.

"I'm sorry, but may I be excused?" I ask.

"So I have your word?"

"Yes, you do. After the wedding I'll find a partner."

"Very good, I'm glad that's settled. If you decide you would like to try one last time before the wedding, I'm sure Gran would be thrilled. But if not, after the wedding will suffice. Now, can you give your mother a hug?"

I do as she asks. Once that's done, I go in the direction of the hedge maze.

They're not going to let me be with Jamie after the wedding. They've already said they don't approve of us. They will want me to be with someone else.

As I approach the entrance to the hedge maze, Alexander appears in my path.

"Erik!" he says. "You look fantastic, as usual. Have you seen Jamie?"

"He's in the maze, I was about to talk to him."

"Well, seeing as you're here, I might as well tell you. Tomorrow is the first day of Serena la Sol, and there's a festival happening tomorrow in Ciello. I'm going to make an appearance, and I thought that it might be fun for the three of us to go?"

A beach trip? With Jamie?

Even after what Mum just told me, I still want to go.

"That sounds great," I say.

"Do you think Jamie would enjoy that?"

"I do, yes."

"Fantastic. We'll have to stay the night as it's a long drive, so I'll book us a hotel. If you see Jamie, let him know, okay?"

"I will."

I go into the hedge maze and follow the path down, then take

a left. I reach a dead end, so I backtrack, and then take a right.
It takes me a while, but I finally get to the middle of the maze
where there is a white gazebo, one that looks nearly identical to
the place where we first met. Vines covered in pastel pink flowers
are wrapped around the wooden frame. Jamie is sitting on one
of the benches, his head in his hands. I approach slowly, and he
looks up.

"Hey," I say. "Are you all right?"

"I'm not really sure."

"Do you want me to go?"

"No," he says. "Please, stay."

I sit down beside him.

He kicks at the floor with the point of his shoe. "Does this
ever feel normal to you?"

"What do you mean?"

"I got bullied by the prime minister of Mitanor. He tried to
intimidate me. But it's like, everyone is going around acting like
all of this stuff is totally normal but it's really not. Normal was
my life before. This is completely different."

He looks down, and a strand of hair falls down over his forehead.

"You're doing so well," I say.

"Am I?"

I move closer. "Jamie, yes. This party wouldn't have happened
if it weren't for you. The shelter should be able to reopen, and
that's all because of you."

"I guess," he says. He swallows hard. "I don't want to let anyone down."

I move a little closer. "You aren't."

"You sure?"

I take his hand in mine and give him a squeeze. I wish he could
see the way I think about him. How much I respect him, and how
astonished I am by him so much of the time. How I know to my

very core that he is one of the strongest, kindest, and best people I've ever met.

"I don't have a single doubt," I say.

He lifts his focus. Finally, a smile breaks through. "I really like you."

"I really like you, too."

I should tell him what Mum said.

But he looks so crushed right now, and I can't bring myself to. I will tell him later, when he's feeling better.

"By the way," I say. "Alexander invited us to a thing on the coast tomorrow. We'll need to stay in a hotel, so it's an overnight trip. Would that be okay with you?"

He smiles, totally radiant. "I think I'll be okay with that. Do you think we could risk one kiss now?"

I can't say no. Not when he looks like he needs some sort of comfort. I put my hands on the sides of his face as he moves closer. He nuzzles his forehead against mine for a moment, and it's as enjoyable as it is terrifying. The maze may give us some seclusion, but what if it's not enough? What if someone sees us?

All of this could get taken away.

"Just one," I say.

He leans in and kisses me. I know I can only have one, because anything more than that is too risky. We're in public, and anyone could walk up and see us. Even knowing that, what I want is an entirely different story.

I want a million more.

CHAPTER THIRTY-FIVE

JAMIE

"Now, boys," says Alexander. "I know I don't need to tell the two of you this, but I need you both to be on your best behavior today."

Erik and I are in the back seat of Alexander's convertible. To get to Ciello, we had to drive for a few hours. In the front seat is a security guard, someone I've never seen before. Both Alexander and Erik seem totally fine with having a completely silent stranger in the car with us, but I've found it pretty weird, I must say.

"We will be," I say.

"Good. I know I can trust the two of you. But remember, Jamie, you represent the crown now, as well."

"I know."

With that, we get out of the car. We're not the only people from the palace—waiting outside is what can only be described as a small squadron of security. Each guard wears a dark suit, standing out among all the golden clothes of the other festivalgoers, and has a pin of the Mortenallo family crest on their chests. From what I've gleaned from conversations I've overheard, there was a significant security operation earlier, one that swept through the festival looking for any threats.

The fairground is on the outskirts of town, on a big, flat area that has been converted for the festival. Red and orange tents have been set up, and in the far distance is a performance stage, where a live band is currently playing traditional Mitanorian folk music, which is upbeat and features both Mitanorian violin and some hand cymbals. The musicians are all wearing bright red-and-gold outfits and are dancing across the stage, matching the energy of the music.

I take it all in. The air is fresh and slightly salty, and even though the sun is out, it's actually a perfect, dreamy temperature right now.

I feel so lucky. I get to go here with my father and with Erik. I don't want to take any of it for granted, because I know how fortunate I am. Alexander is still a very new addition to my life, and getting to do things like this with Erik might not last forever.

Actually, I *know* it won't last forever. At some point, he will leave. He will have to.

That's a problem I can tackle in the future. I want to enjoy this while I can.

We enter the festival through a side gate, skipping the line that's built up near the main entrance. Each of us, including the troop of security, goes through a metal detector, and then we're allowed inside.

The sights and sounds are nearly overwhelming. It all looks so incredible, and I don't know where to start.

On the drive here, Alexander told Erik and me about this festival. It's called Serena la Sol, also known as the festival of the sun, which I now know is a yearly tradition in Mitanor. Hundreds of years ago, the festival started as a celebration of the sun god. Now, it's an annual celebration on what is historically one of the hottest days of the year.

Almost everyone is wearing a shade of yellow, including Erik, Alexander, and me: Maria gave me the outfit to wear before we left. A lot of the crowd are wearing golden headdresses shaped like the rays of the sun. I take it all in. This is Mitanorian culture. Given my new position, I need to know about all of this.

"There's always a risk attending public events like this," says Alexander. "The best way to stay safe is to listen to everything I tell you, all right?"

Erik nods his head. I do as well.

"Great," says Alexander. "Now stay close, and whatever you do, don't go anywhere without security."

We go down to the beach, toward the heart of the festival. Even though I am here on royal business, I find myself more relaxed than I have been in a while. Once again, I'm reminded of how wild it is that I'm even here. My life is so different from what I thought it would be, and I'm enjoying every second of that.

"King Alexander!"

We turn and see a woman who is working a stall selling a variety of deli goods, from biscuits to cheeses and preserves. Erik and I approach, and he moves so close that my arm brushes his.

"Would you like to try one?" offers the woman, handing me a piece of bread with some cheese on it. "This is my bestseller. It's pepper and spiceberry."

I take a bite as she hands Erik a matching piece of bread. The jam is sweet, but with a peppery kick. To my left, some people start filming us with their phones. The attention is like a switch flipped, as more and more people notice us. Soon, a crowd has formed to watch us. The security keeps them from getting too close.

This crowd is made up of much older people than those who came to see me at Hope House, and they're responding very differently. Nobody is screaming at me like I'm a rock star. They're curious, but also polite and respectful.

We move on to the next stall, which sells chocolates. Erik tries a sample, and his eyelids flutter.

"Good?" I ask.

"You have to try it."

I take one of the samples, which is a salted caramel dark

chocolate. After one bite, I know I'm buying a block. I buy a few, because I'd love to give some to my friends when I go back home. The thought reminds me how little time I have here. It hurts, but I decide not to dwell on it. I want to have a good time today, and thinking about going back to America will ruin it.

"Good, right?" asks Erik.

"It's amazing."

Now that the crowd has left us mostly alone, it seems like we're entirely free to explore. I see a pair of stalls farther down, selling jewelry. I browse, and find something I need to get: a golden pendant of a pair of angel wings attached to a thin golden chain. Erik is distracted by a different stall, so I need to be fast.

"See anything you like?" asks the salesperson.

I buy the necklace. Erik notices me as I shove the necklace into my pocket.

"What did you get?" he asks.

"Nothing," I say. "Come on, let's keep going."

"I'm sorry, boys, but there's been a mix-up," says Alexander.

We're in the grand, gleaming lobby of a five-star hotel. It's the kind of place I've only ever seen in TV shows, and never thought I would get to stay in. Even with my new clothes and hair, I don't feel like I belong here. Almost all the guests are impossibly pretty, and most wear loose white linen clothing, all effortlessly stylish. A few of them glance our way. We're not exactly inconspicuous, given our security detail.

"What happened?" I ask.

I feel the weight of the necklace in my pocket. I really hope he likes it. I think that he will. My hesitation comes from him maybe thinking that it's too early for us to give each other gifts like that. I know we've said we like each other, but we're not boyfriends, and I would hate to overstep.

"They accidentally only booked us two rooms," says Alexander, lifting up two key cards. "I tried to get us another, but they're fully booked because of the festival. Would it be okay if the two of you shared a room?"

I try my best to keep a straight face. Can I share a room with Erik?

I honestly think that's a dream come true.

"We could try another hotel if it would bother you," says Alexander. I must be doing a good job containing my sheer and utter delight at the prospect of this idea. "I'm very sorry."

Alexander looks at the both of us expectantly, as if agreeing to this would be doing him a huge favor. He has no idea that what he's suggesting is actually him doing *us* a huge favor.

"It's fine with me," I say. I shrug and put my hands into my pockets. I'm going for: slightly bothered but cool with it.

"I'll survive," says Erik. He turns to me. "Do you promise not to smother me in my sleep?"

"I can't promise that."

"Good," says Alexander, ignoring our joke. He clasps his hands together and points them toward us, as if we'd bestowed upon him some miracle.

"I appreciate you being such good sports about this."

An aide comes up to us and pulls Alexander aside. Erik and I can't speak openly, as there are three security guards within earshot, but I can tell from the way his lips curve up that he's as excited as I am.

"What do you think of the coast?" asks Erik. He's put on his dignified, princely voice, assumedly because of our present company.

"It's so nice here," I say. "I love it."

I mean it, and it's not just being here at the festival, or with Erik. I love Mitanor, and I love going to things like this.

Maybe I could move here after I graduate. It's not that long until then. It would be just over a year. I could always follow my original plan of going to an American college. But now that I know about this side of my life, how can I ever go back?

I don't think I can. My future is here. I know it. It's terrifying even thinking about admitting that to anyone, because there are so many moving pieces. What if Alexander doesn't want me to stay here? What if Mom or Mike say no?

I've also never been the best at advocating for what I want. It feels so dangerous to me.

Alexander and the aide join us, stopping my brain spiral.

"Our rooms are ready," says Alexander. "Shall we?"

We ride an elevator up to the top level, where there are multiple penthouse suites. Alexander goes into one, and we have the one next door.

"I'm going to have a nap," says Alexander. "I'll see you boys at dinner?"

"Sounds good," I say.

With that, Alexander goes into his apartment. Erik and I go into ours, which is next door. It's a gleaming, modern apartment, with large windows on one side that look out at the beach and the ocean. The sight stretches out like a painting, with miles of golden sand meeting the ocean. The sky is a brilliant, cloudless canvas of bright blue. Thousands of people, tiny from here, are out enjoying the sun. As nice as it looks, there's nowhere I would rather be than in this room.

Erik closes the door behind him and it locks with a click.

"Does Alexander have a key?" I ask.

"I don't think so."

I reach into my pocket. My nerves skyrocket, but I pull out the necklace. The gold catches the sunlight so it looks like it's sparkling.

"I got you something," I say.

I show him the necklace. His features soften. His reaction is as good as I was hoping. It might even be better than that. I was worried he'd think I crossed a line, but it seems like he truly loves it.

"It's like your character," I say. "I'm not sure it's exactly the same, but—"

"It's perfect," he says. "Jamie, thank you."

He turns around, and I clip it on around his neck.

"What do you think?" he asks.

He takes hold of my shirt and pulls me to the bedroom.

"So you like it?" I ask, laughing as we frantically pull each other's clothes off.

There are two beds, but that doesn't matter. The sight of his bare chest still takes my breath away. The necklace rests against the base of his neck. He puts his hands on either side of my face and kisses me slowly.

"I've wanted to do that all day," he says.

"Me too."

We grin at each other as we move toward the bed. When we get there, he gives me a light push, and I fall backward. His expression turns serious as he takes his shirt the rest of the way off, and then gets onto the bed with me. He falls onto me, his lips meeting mine with just the right amount of pressure.

It's official now.

Today has been perfect.

"I've been thinking about something," I say. We're side by side, facing each other on the bed in the hotel room. We're only in our underwear, and I am draped over Erik so that we have about as much skin-to-skin contact as possible.

Even though I'm as close to naked as I've ever been with him, I barely feel self-conscious at all. Erik is wearing black boxer briefs, and even though his underwear is so simple, seeing him in them? I don't think I've ever seen anything sexier.

I wasn't aware that contact like this could be so blisteringly hot and so comfortable at the same time. It took a little while for us to find a position that works, and the best seems to be him on his back, with me pressed against him, my head resting in the crook of his neck. I run a finger over his chest, past the angel wing pendant to his stomach. I think he might be tensing, but I hope he isn't. It's not his muscles that I care about right now, it's him. The kind, thoughtful guy who makes me feel like I can do anything. That's what I care about.

He brushes a strand of hair away from my forehead. "Did you know you make the most adorable little face when you're thinking?"

I prop myself up and scowl. "I do not."

He laughs. "You really do. It's like this."

He mimics scrunching his face up.

I scowl, pretending to be outraged.

He puts his arm around me, moving me closer. As he does it, I'm struck by how remarkable this feels. We haven't known each other that long. How can we be so comfortable around each other? I'm not exactly known for being comfortable, especially around guys.

"Come on," he says, as he starts playing with my hair. "Tell me what you were thinking about."

Like they have been all day, my thoughts were drifting to my plans for my future. The more I've thought about it, the more I've realized just how much I enjoy being in Mitanor, and how much I would like it if I could stay here. I still want to finish school in America, and I don't think there's any way that Mom or Mike would let me move here until I graduate. But after that, I can't see them having a problem with it.

"I think I'd like to stay in Mitanor after I graduate."

He sits up. "Jamie, that's huge."

"I know," I say. "I can't decide, though. I love my friends

and I'm worried I'm going to miss stuff if I stay here. But I don't know. Being here, it sort of feels like what I'm meant to be doing. Does that make sense?"

"It does," he says. "I know I've said this before, but you're a natural at this. You've only been a prince, what, a few weeks, and look at all you've accomplished. Have you told your parents?"

"Not yet," I say. "I wanted to be sure before I tell them. What do you think?"

"I think it's a great idea," he says. "Mitanor would be lucky to have you."

"And I know you have to go back to Sunstad. But here's a lot closer. So we could, like, keep doing this. If you wanted to."

"I'd like that. I'm not saying this just because I would like it if you lived closer to me, because I would like that. I truly think this country is better with you here."

What he says means the world to me.

I've made up my mind.

Once I graduate, I want to live in Mitanor.

Chapter Thirty-Six

Erik

I've always been terrified of good things.

It's as if they can't last, and my brain is sure there is something terrible lurking around the corner. Jamie is beside me, the blanket pulled up to his waist. He's breathing softly, asleep. His chest rises and falls with each breath in a steady rhythm. In the soft, early morning light, I study his face. He looks at peace, and he's so beautiful.

Last night was something like a dream. We had dinner with Alexander, then Jamie and I spent some time talking in the pool hot tub, staying until they kicked us out. Then we came back to the room, ordered room service for dessert. We made out while we waited for the cakes we ordered to arrive, then we sat up in bed and watched Netflix and ate what can only be described as a copious amount of cake.

I wore the necklace he gave me the entire time. I hid it under my shirt when we had company. I never want to take it off.

At some point, we decided to call it a night. We fell asleep with his body pressed up against mine, and for a few hours, it was possibly the best sleep I've ever had. We didn't go any further than we usually do, but still, sleeping next to him felt amazing. It felt so easy and comfortable to share this space with him. I even found his soft snoring completely adorable.

Then I woke up, and felt the worst anxiety I ever have.

All I can think about is how to make things work. I want to see where things can go with him. I don't want any more secrecy. I want to properly be with him.

For that to happen, I need to tell Gran, and get her permission.

Which I can do, but it's incredibly risky. If she tells me what I think she will, then I will have to break up with Jamie. The thought of doing that is heart-shattering, but it's what I would have to do. I simply don't have a choice in the matter.

But I'm stuck. After the wedding, they will find someone new for me. And I don't want that. I can't even imagine it.

The only guy I want to be with is him.

He told me he's been thinking about moving to Mitanor after he graduates. The way he said it, it seems he's already made up his mind. And he should stay. He's incredible at this. The people love him, and he's already had such a positive impact. He's won over almost everyone he's met. What else could he achieve if he stays here?

The problem is, it brings up the question of us. Gran didn't approve of us as a couple, and it's possible that hasn't changed. I have never, not even once in my entire seventeen years on this planet, seen her change her mind.

I keep bouncing back and forth between those two realities. What I want, and what has to be.

No matter how hard I try, I can't think of a way to get them to line up.

It was easier to explore this with Jamie when we both had things keeping us apart. He was going back to America, and I had my issues with my family. Now, it seems like his issue is resolved, which means I am the reason we can't become boyfriends one day. It feels uneven, like it is now up to me to be the one to sort this out.

Maybe it always has been.

Jamie softly opens his eyes. The first thing he does is smile. I feel an intense swell of affection for him.

"Morning," he says.

"Morning."

He sits up. "Is everything okay? You seem nervous."

"I think I owe you an apology."

"For what?"

"I haven't told my family about you yet."

"I know," he says. "It's okay, I don't expect you to. It's fine."

"I don't think it is," I say. Every word feels like it could have devastating consequences. But still, I fight against the urge to give Jamie a diplomatic answer. He deserves the whole truth.

"I really like you," I say. "And Jamie, I want to be with you. As your boyfriend, I mean."

It feels like the world hangs in the balance as I wait for his answer.

"I want that, too," he says.

"But for me to date I need permission from my family," I say.

"I know."

"And I want to talk to them about us, but I'm really scared they're going to tell me I can't be with you."

"They might've changed their minds."

I shake my head. There's no chance of that.

"All we know is they told you to stay platonic with me, right?" he says. "That doesn't mean a relationship with me is, like, forbidden or anything."

"It might," I say.

"Hey," he says, pressing a kiss to the side of my head. "Talk to me, what's going on?"

"I want to be with you," I say. "I want it so badly."

He starts to smile. "I want that, too."

"But I can't," I say. "Not yet, anyway. And Jamie, if they forbid me from seeing you I won't have a choice."

"Sure you do."

"That's not how this works."

"Are you sure?' he asks. I seem to have annoyed him, which is fair. He might be great at being a prince, but he doesn't understand the lengths to which I am controlled.

"I wish I could tell you otherwise," I say. "But it's the truth. If they don't approve, I can't be with you."

He's quiet. "Are you breaking up with me?"

"No!" I say, taking hold of his hands. "I'm just trying to be honest with you. I've let this go too far, and it was unfair of me, and I'm sorry. But I think we've gotten to a point where we both need to know if we can properly be together or not."

"So what are you going to do?"

"I'm going to talk to Gran," I say. I'm trying to project confidence I don't feel, because the thought of standing up to Gran is utterly terrifying. "You deserve someone who can be with you with no reservations. If it's not me, it's going to break my heart, but it's what's best."

He chews his bottom lip. "This sucks."

I press my forehead against his. "I know."

"But okay," he says, swallowing hard. "I think this is a good plan. You tell them, and if they let us be together, we will be together. And if not . . ." His breath hitches.

I get it. I don't really want to think about that possibility, either.

My phone buzzes loudly on the bedside table. Jamie grabs it and hands it to me.

It's a message from Gran.

Erik, we need you to come home. A car will pick you up from your hotel in forty minutes.

See you soon.

Love, Gran

I read the message again, and feel a nearly overwhelming bout of terror. She knows. It's the only explanation. We messed up somehow. Maybe someone saw the kiss in the pool back at the palace, or a photographer caught me looking at Jamie affectionately while we were at the festival.

They know. They know and they aren't happy about it. I knew something like this would happen. I *knew* it. They're going to tell me that I can't be with Jamie, and I am going to hurt him.

"What's wrong?" asks Jamie.

I show him my phone. He reads the message.

"I think she knows about us," I say. "And I don't think she's happy."

"We don't know that for sure," he says. "It could be about something else. I don't want you to go."

"I don't want to go, either."

"I have an idea," he says. "Let's pretend none of them matter. Until your car gets here, it's just the two of us, and we can do whatever we want. What would you want to do?"

"I'd want to stay here," I say, scooting closer. "With you."

"I want that, too."

"Then let's pretend," he says. He sets a timer on his phone. "We have that long, at least. Until this goes off it's just us, okay? Nothing else matters."

But it does matter. It'll tear us apart.

"Is that what you want?" I ask. "Knowing everything?"

He puts his hand on the side of my face. "What I want is you."

I kiss him, and it feels different.

It feels like a last kiss.

The time passes quickly, and when his timer goes off, Jamie pulls me closer. I let myself linger for a moment, trying to ignore the blaring alarm.

"I need to go," I say.

I get up, and quickly get dressed. "You'll have to tell Alexander what happened," I say.

"I will."

Jamie gives me a kiss, then hugs me tight. I'm going to fight for this, I think. I'm going to fight for us.

I force myself out of the room and down to the lobby. When I get there, the car is already waiting. I compose myself, then approach. The driver opens the door for me, and I climb inside.

As the car drives away from the hotel, my resolve hardens.

I'm going to fight for us with everything I have.

Chapter Thirty-Seven

JAMIE

Every minute feels like a lifetime.

Erik and I have reached an agreement. On one hand, it's amazing. He wants to be with me as much as I want to be with him. But there's still a giant hurdle in our way, which is his family.

Either they will let us be together—properly together, with no more secrecy.

Or we will break up.

The thought is frankly terrifying. How I feel for Erik is more intense than any crush I've ever had.

And it could all go away.

After Erik left my room, Alexander invited me to breakfast. So even though I'm very much still processing what is happening, I'm trying my best to maintain a decent level of composure.

We're in the hotel restaurant now, with security standing by the door and by our table. Nobody has bothered us. Most of the other people here are middle-aged tourists, I assume in town for the festival. They certainly seem curious about our presence, but they haven't come over and said anything.

There's a full breakfast, and my plan is to drown my feelings in food. It's a tried-and-true way of dealing with negative shit, and I'm very much hoping it comes in clutch today. I load my plate high with slices of bacon, scrambled eggs, and toast, then make my way back to the table, where Alexander is already half-way through a bowl of *desayuno dorado*.

I go back to the table where Alexander is sitting. He's near the back of the restaurant, with a security guard keeping watch beside him.

I wish we could be together, without all of this.

"You seem troubled," says Alexander. "Did you have a fight with Erik?"

I poke at my eggs. I need to be careful. Even though I am feeling a lot when it comes to Erik, I can't give him away. I still don't know with complete certainty that they do know about us. Something else may have come up.

"No," I say. "I'm just tired."

"Ah. The famous 'tired.' Tomas used to say the same whenever there was something he didn't want to talk to me about. Fair enough, I will let it be."

I take a bite of toast.

"How's the food?" he asks.

"Great, how's yours?"

"Delicious," he says. "This might be the best *desayuno dorado* I've ever had. Don't tell the palace chefs that."

He winks.

I remember what I spoke to Erik about last night. About my plan to stay here. Even though things with Erik are complicated right now, my resolve in that idea hasn't changed.

"I was thinking about something last night," I say. "I was wondering how you would feel if I moved to Mitanor after I graduate."

His eyes light up and he starts to smile. "You would like that?"

"I would. I love it here, and I think there's more work to do. Hope House feels like just the start. I know this is a lot to ask."

"It's not," he says. "You are my son, and you are welcome here as long as you would like. We would need to talk to your parents, of course. Have you asked them?"

"Not yet."

"Ah. Well, it depends on what they have to say. But I think it's an excellent idea. Mitanor has some of the best colleges in the world. You could become an Oakwood student, like I was!"

I imagine going to a college here, the same one my father went to. Yes, I would miss my friends and Mom and Mike horribly, but it would also be so exciting.

"I'd like that."

"Talk to your parents, and I'll see what I can do. I must admit, nothing would make me happier than you staying here. But it's up to them, of course."

That settles it. I can stay, if I'm allowed.

All I need to do is ask.

CHAPTER THIRTY-EIGHT

ERIK

An aide is waiting for me on the steps of the palace.

People have often said that Hjornborg Palace is beautiful, a jewel of the city, but I'm having a hard time looking at it that way now. It's monolithic, the aged stone exterior reaching high up into the sky, the gothic sense of style so out of place compared to the gleaming glass and metal buildings that surround it.

It has never felt like home, no matter how long I've spent here. It's too large for that, too much like a workplace.

Home for me is my dorm room at West Hill. Not here.

I shove all that down as I make my way up the steps. High above me is the Sunstadian flag, whipping violently in the wind. The blustery weather matches my feelings, and it's yet another stark reminder that my time in Mitanor is over. My summer with Jamie is over. Whatever freedom I felt there, the chances I had to explore being someone outside of the role that my family have always wanted to force me into, is done.

Now, I am home.

The car pulls to a stop at the front of the palace entrance, the tires crunching on the white gravel. It's not unusual for this time of year, so I'm trying not to read too much into it, but it was raining when I arrived back in the country. It's one of those relentlessly gray days, where the sky is dark and the rain comes down hard. The rain has kept up the entire drive back to the palace, coming down in heavy diagonal sheets. One good thing is that the roads have been quieter than usual, people fleeing the weather by staying inside.

I get out of the car. The aide hurries down, opening an umbrella to shield me from the rain until I'm under cover. Once I'm done, he shakes the excess water off the umbrella and snaps it closed.

"Your grandmother would like to see you in her office," he says.

I try to read into his tone. Anything could be waiting for me in Gran's office. Inside, it's freezing, the air-conditioning icy. Usually, I'm used to it, but after a week in Mitanor, where it's always lovely and warm, I need to readjust.

Home sweet home. My walk across the palace is nearly silent, with the only sound being the pounding rain outside. When I get to Gran's office, her door is hanging ajar. She's sitting at her desk, reading something.

"Erik," she says. "Take a seat."

I do as she asked.

"We have a problem," she says.

Here it goes. I've also spent a lot of time during the journey trying to figure out what I would do if she tells me that she knows about me and Jamie. I decided quickly that I wouldn't lie, because that would only land me in more trouble.

"Have you seen this?" she asks.

She places a magazine in front of me. It's a glossy magazine, *Royals Daily*. If I'm remembering correctly, it's the magazine that first broke the story about Jamie and Alexander.

ROYAL FEUD: GET THE INSIDE SCOOP INTO THE SIBLING RIVALRY OF THE CENTURY

She throws down another magazine.

BROTHERS AT WAR

And then another.

STEFAN'S FURY: BETRAYED
BY UNGRATEFUL ERIK

Looking back at me is a picture of me scowling, juxtaposed
with an image of Stefan looking forlorn. I can recall exactly
when that picture was taken, when I was on a school excursion to
the Solheim museum, and there were press waiting for me outside. I let my façade drop for a second, and my displeasure at their
appearance read all over my face. The picture of Stefan seems to
have been taken from our holiday in Greece, as he's tanned and
his hair is shorter than it's been for a while.

None of that matters. The pictures next to each other, as well
as the bold red text, tell a complete story. I've dealt with stuff
like this for my entire life, but while I've been in Mitanor I've
felt separated from it all. I haven't had to look at what the press
are saying about me. I haven't had to think about my perception,
or how my actions could be spun in any direction. While I was
there, I let myself stop caring.

Gran tosses down a magazine. It's like a slap to the face.

"It's all anyone is talking about," she says. "People are saying
that you spent time in Mitanor because the pair of you needed to
be separated."

"But that's not true," I say.

My emotions got the best of me, and I see the fear of that reg-
ister on Gran's face. I've been in Mitanor too long. It's changed
me, turned me into a completely different person, one I can't be.
I can't be this emotional. I need to go back to the old me, the past
Erik.

In the back of my mind, I'm relieved. This is worrying, sure,
but at least they don't know about Jamie. I can tell them when I'm
ready, and I won't get in trouble for keeping a secret.

I was wrong. I wasn't called back because of Jamie.

Our secret is still safe.

"I know," she says. "The truth doesn't sell magazines as well as fiction, unfortunately. It's why we needed you back. I need you and Stefan to attend some events together, to show everyone you're a supportive, loving brother. Can you do that for me?"

"Of course."

"Good. I'm sure you're tired, so get some rest. Tonight, you and Stefan will be attending an opera premiere." She tosses the magazines into the trash can beside her desk. "And thank you for spending some time in Mitanor, with Jamie. From all I've heard, your trip was a roaring success."

I have to tell her about Jamie. I know I do. But my fear is too intense. My instincts are practically screaming at me to stay quiet.

"Is there something on your mind?" she asks.

"No," I say. "I was going to say I missed you."

Her features soften. "Oh, Erik. You big softie. I missed you, too. Now, go, you look tired."

I head toward the exit. Behind me, Gran gets back to work.

I stop in the doorway.

"Actually," I say, turning back. "I need to tell you something. I should've told you this a while ago."

I hesitate for a moment. I don't think I've ever been this scared to say something. This is nothing like me. I know I have to do this, and it gives me strength.

"I'm interested in Jamie. Romantically. If you can give me your blessing, I would like to pursue him."

Gran rubs her temples like she has a headache. "I thought I had made myself clear, I don't think that you and Jamie are a good match."

"Why not?"

"The two of you are too different," she says. "It will never last. He will always have his ties to Mitanor, and to America for that matter."

"Are you telling me I have to love someone from Sunstad? Don't you know how limiting that is?"

"No," she says. "But Erik, trust me. Jamie is not the right partner for you. In fact, now that you've mentioned it, it's time we talked about Sebastian."

"What about him?"

"I've spoken to his family, and all agree he should be your date to the wedding. I'm sure you won't have any complaints."

Tears prickle my eyes. I can't recall the last time I teared up in front of Gran, or anyone in my family.

Not only is she telling me I can't be with Jamie, but I have to go to the wedding with Sebastian. It's like I'm trapped within a nightmare.

"Gran," I start.

"No," she says, her voice rising. "This conversation is over. You will cease your relationship with Jamie and you will attend the wedding with Sebastian. Have I made myself clear?"

I stare her down. There is fire in her eyes at the moment, and I can tell I will only make things worse for myself if I continue to fight. The decision has been made, and there's nothing more I can do about it.

"You have," I say.

"You're dismissed," she says.

When I get back to my bedroom it all catches up to me. I feel the necklace Jamie gave me around my neck. This is why I didn't want to tell them. Because now, I can't be with him. I simply can't be. If I did that now, it would mean I am going directly against their wishes, something I cannot do.

I have another heartbreaking thought.

I need to tell Jamie.

Actually, it's more than heartbreaking. It's completely devastating. I can't do it. I simply can't.

Being with Jamie, the way he has made me feel, has made me happier than I have ever been in my entire life. I've never felt so free, never felt more like my actual self. Spending time with him, I have felt the persona I've built up around myself slowly start to chip away, revealing the real me. I know I've got more work to do. I know I've twisted and changed myself for so long now that it will take time to rediscover who I truly am.

But now I feel all of that slipping away. My time in Mitanor was just a holiday. Now that I'm back home, I already feel myself slipping back, and I can't think of anything to stop it.

I am becoming the royal version of me again. I have to do what I'm told, even if I don't want to. I try to think of any way around it, any way I can change this. This is the way things are in my family. I do as I am told. Keeping the peace is the most important thing.

I have to break up with Jamie. Even if it breaks my heart.

I don't have a choice.

CHAPTER THIRTY-NINE

JAMIE

I've been waiting for my phone to ring all afternoon.

I can't stop checking it. Erik is probably back in Sunstad now, and I hope that means that he has spoken to his family about us. Any moment now, I will know if I we can be together, or if it's over.

I've been in my room for the past hour or so, searching for any distraction and finding none. I've tried reading, I've tried watching videos on YouTube, I've tried messaging Amara, Ren, and Spencer to see what they are up to.

Nothing has even slightly helped, because I know, at any moment, I'll get the call I've been waiting for.

It feels as if the entire trajectory of my life hangs on this. If it goes the way that I want, I'll be on my way to having my first boyfriend: a guy I am super into and really want to be with. We'll have to figure out how to be long-distance, but I know it'll be worth it.

If not, well, I don't want to think about that too much. Just the thought is like a lance through the chest.

My phone starts buzzing. Erik's name is on the screen.

I accept the call and press my phone to my ear.

The heavy pause on the other end of the line gives me my answer. Erik told them. Erik told them and he was told no.

"What did they say?" I ask.

"What I was afraid of. Gran said we can't be together."

I try to think of a way out. Of some way I can make this better. This can't be it. There's no way. I have to do something to fix this. I'm not ready to give up this easily. Still, the detached tone in Erik's voice is already making me feel like there's nothing I can do. I'm sure he fought as hard as he could, and if there were some way to make this possible, he would know of it. He is the one who has been royal for his entire life, after all. He knows a lot more about this than I do.

"I'm so sorry," he says. "I let things between us go too far, I should've known better."

"Hey," I say. My voice cracks. "It's okay. It's not your fault."

It's not in any way okay, but hearing him sound this hurt is ruining me.

"It is. You deserve someone who can be with you fully. I wish it was me, but it's not."

I sit on the end of my bed as the heartbreak sinks in.

It's over. It's over and there's nothing I can do about it. I am being broken up with. I'm sure most of the time there is some anger involved, and maybe that will come in time, but at the moment all I feel is completely helpless.

I feel tears well up in my eyes. "Is there anything we can do?"

"I don't think so," he says. "I'm so sorry, Jamie."

"So what now?" I ask. "We go back to being strangers?"

"Maybe in time, we could be friends."

Friends?

I don't think I could ever be just friends with him. My feelings toward him are too strong. But what's the alternative? Cutting him out of my life completely? I don't want that, either. In truth, I don't want any of this. I want this to have gone differently. I want his family to approve of us as a couple, and for them to allow us to be together.

"I'm sorry," he says.

I can't bring myself to answer him.

"Are you still going to stay in Mitanor once you graduate?" he asks. "Please don't tell me this changes anything."

I know what he means, but still. I can't tell him that because this does change everything.

"I am," I say. "I told Alexander, all that's left for me to do is tell my parents. As long as they say yes, I'm going to."

I have so many emotions, and a part of me wants to break down. The other wants to yell, to beg Erik to fight for us. I'm not sure if that will do any good. From the sound of things, the decision has been made, and it's final.

"Please," I say. I start to cry. "There has to be something we can do."

He sighs. "I think I should give you some space. We'll talk later, okay?"

"Will we?"

I hate how bitter I sound. But I can't help it. I'm not upset with him, I'm upset at his family, for stopping us from being together.

"Fine," I say. "I'm hanging up."

He doesn't object, so I end the call. I don't know what to feel.

It would be one thing if Erik doesn't want to be with me because that's what he wants. That would still be difficult, I'm sure, but this seems worse. He wants to be with me, and I want to be with him. But we can't, because of his family.

I don't want to dismiss that. He's told me how difficult he's found being royal because of the amount of control that has been held over him. I'm not saying that's not real, because I'm sure I would struggle if I were in his shoes. He has been raised his entire life being told he must always do as he's told and behave in a certain way.

It takes longer than a few weeks to break free of that.

It will take more than meeting me to break free of that.

I feel tears bubbling up again and I try to force them down.

I knew there was a chance of this happening. I've known the entire time that maybe, just maybe, I could've been burned in exactly this way. He always made that clear, and it always hung in the back of my mind over every kiss, over every glance.

Every time I felt myself get lost in how sparkly and fun it felt, I was distantly worried something like this could happen.

The problem is I'm not sure I completely believed either him or the voice in my head. I thought that it would work out. It was all theory, because how could he ever end things with me after all the things we've done together?

He knows how well we work. He does. I've seen it, and there's no way that he doesn't feel at least some degree of what I feel. And he can't fight for it?

I blink a few times, trying to stop the tears from taking over.

It's really, truly over.

I can't fight them anymore, and the tears surge up. It's been a while since I've cried like this, and I'd forgotten how painful it is, and how it's completely out of my control.

I'm never going to be with Erik.

It's over.

I haven't spoken to anyone for an entire day.

I've basically spent the past twenty-four hours in my room. I have only left a few times to grab food, and that was it.

I don't have the energy or mental space to do anything else. I picture Erik smiling at me and my heart threatens to break even more, something I wasn't sure was even possible.

I grab a bunch of tissues and blow my nose. I'm honestly glad nobody can see me, because I'm sure I look like an absolute wreck. I haven't showered so my hair is a mess, and I feel gross. I am sure that a shower would make me feel a little better, but that would take some effort and I'd rather stay in bed and wallow.

I'm pretty sure Mom and Mike know something has happened,

as they've been walking around on tiptoes around me, giving me space. When the breakup was brand new, there is no way that I wanted to speak to them, but now that a little time has passed, I think I'm ready to talk.

I wish I could speak to Max, but we're still fighting, so that isn't an option.

Any time I think about Erik, it brings on a fresh wave of tears. I know we haven't known each other all that long, and I know this reaction doesn't exactly help anything. I think that's the biggest issue. Nothing will. I can't see any way forward, anywhere to go from this. His family have forbidden us from dating.

That's not the most heartbreaking thing, though. Erik deserves to be able to make his own choices. If he simply didn't want to be with me because he doesn't, that would hurt, but it might be easier to accept.

Right now all I can think about is him being trapped in a life that isn't his choosing. It's so messed up and unfair, and I don't really know how to deal with it.

I roll over and bury my face in my pillow. I can't tell if I want to scream or cry.

"Jamie," calls Mom through the door, her voice wary. "Can I come in?"

My door is locked, so I go over and unlatch it. Then I go back to bed and drop back down onto it. I don't have the energy to stand up anymore. Every few seconds, I think about Erik. I think about meeting him for the first time. I think about our lessons, with him teaching me to bow or the correct way to eat. I think about riding horses with him and kissing him in the pool.

I will never get to do anything like that with him ever again.

Being with him felt like an adventure. It made everything so exciting. And what do we have now? The thing is, I still want to talk to him, even though I know I can't.

"Fine," I call.

Mom comes in. Mike follows after her, holding a steaming cup of hot chocolate.

Mike puts the hot chocolate on my bedside table. It does smell good, but I'm not at all in the mood. That's how I know it's bad—even one of Mike's Mitanorian hot chocolates isn't appealing.

"What happened?" asks Mom.

I nearly burst into tears again at her asking that. I'm sure she already knows about Erik and me, because I have turned into the sort of mess that's only possible due to heartbreak. Mom and Mike are both very intelligent, and they know me.

"Erik told me we can't be together," I say.

"Oh, Jamie," says Mom. "I'm so sorry."

"I really liked him," I say. "Or I still do, I don't know. You can't tell anyone about this, by the way."

"We won't," says Mike.

"I'm sure you did," says Mom. "And I'm sure what you're feeling right now is incredibly painful. But it will pass."

"It always does," adds Mike.

I'm not so sure. I can't see myself ever being over this. I can't see myself ever not wanting to be with Erik, or being totally fine with how our relationship ended.

Now they know about Erik and me. I guess that doesn't matter so much now, both because he's told his family, and because things between us are over.

"I promise you," says Mom. "Whatever you're feeling right now, it will fade."

I'm not so sure about that. I don't even know if I want my feelings for Erik to fade, and I can't even imagine being okay with this.

The room goes quiet.

"I've been thinking a lot," I continue. "And I think I'd like to move here once I'm finished with school."

They glance at each other. I think they're having one of their couple-telepathy conversations.

"Well," I say. "Thoughts?"

"That's a big decision," says Mom. "And we have time."

"Plenty of time," adds Mike.

"I know," I say. "But I've made up my mind. I want to finish the school year at home. After that, I think I should live here."

"Want to talk us through it?" asks Mom. She sits beside me on the bed.

"I feel like I belong here," I say. "I have so much to catch up on. I've gone seventeen years without knowing Alexander. If I live here, it'll be easier to get to know him. Plus, there are great colleges. And I could keep working with Hope House, and . . ."

Mom interrupts me by giving me a hug.

"Why is this happening?" I ask.

"I'm so proud of you," she says. "I think you moving here is a fantastic idea. As long as it's after high school."

"And you follow through with your college plan," says Mike. "Just because you're a prince doesn't mean you can skip out on an education."

Even though it's still a year away, I feel a huge surge of emotion that brings tears to my eyes. This is my future, and I need my family to support me on this, and from the looks of things, they do.

I know it must be hard on Mom, as I'm sure she is finding it difficult to know that I plan on moving to a different country once high school is over.

"We suspected this might be the case," she says.

"You did?"

"Of course," says Mike. "You're killing it here."

"We can figure something out," says Mom. "You could live here during the term, and at home during the holidays. We can make this work, Jamie."

I'm still devastated about Erik, but this is good. For the first time since he broke the news, I feel a flicker of hope for my future.

"Group hug," suggests Mike.

We huddle together, with me in the middle. I trust Mom. I hope that this will pass, eventually. It might take some time, but finally, I will feel better.

I do trust her, I realize.

This will be difficult, but I can get through this. It'll just take time.

"You should talk to Max," says Mom. "She'll help."

"But she's mad at me," I say. "And she's not wrong, I messed up."

Mom rubs my arm. "She's your best friend, and friends fight sometimes. I'm sure if she knew what you were going through she would show up for you. Would you do the same for her?"

"Of course."

"Then there's your answer," says Mom. "Tell her."

She's totally right. It still feels dangerous, but I think this is a big enough deal for the two of us to put aside our differences. If anything like this had happened to Max, I would want to know about it so I could be there for her.

"Thank you," I say, giving Mom another hug.

I type a message to Max on my phone.

> Hey, I know we're fighting right now
> and I'm really sorry for what I did, but
> I need you. Can we talk?

I hit *send*.

The screen changes. I'm getting a call from her.

I swipe and answer the call.

"Hey," she says. Her voice is soft and full of sympathy, a far cry from the last way that we spoke with each other. "What's wrong?"

I can't hold it back anymore, and I start to cry.

PART
THREE

"Nothing matters but love. Nothing."

—KING ALEXANDER

Chapter Forty

ERIK

"Why do you keep checking your phone?"

I glance up at Sebastian, who is watching me, his dark eyes able to read me with seemingly no effort. We've spent most of the past week together, and I have come to appreciate a lot about him. He is keenly intelligent, and very savvy in the way that public figures operate: by having two distinct identities. One public and one private.

I can learn a lot from him.

We're at the opening of a new exhibition at an art gallery in Solheim. It's nice and all, but it's hardly my idea of fun. Not that anything is exactly fun for me currently. I'm simply trying to survive.

Sebastian looks immaculate in his dark suit, and we know exactly when to smile in a way that makes it seem like we're a loved-up couple. It's all fiction. As much as I appreciate Sebastian, I can't get myself to really like him. I can't get myself to forget the way he spoke to me when we first met. How he told me that our entire relationship, no matter what, will be nothing other than transactional.

Plus, he's not Jamie.

Even though we're, at least according to the public, official boyfriends, I hardly know anything about Sebastian. The closeness is about the same as looking at someone's social media profile.

I know some things, but only the parts of himself he wants me to know.

"No reason," I say, sliding my phone into my pocket.

"Ah, Jamie," he says. Sebastian often looks at me with disdain, and I know it's not because of Jamie. It's Sebastian's general way of being: he wants me to know every single second we're together that this is a purely strategic partnership. "Are the two of you speaking again?"

"No," I say.

He moves a little closer. "We promised to be honest with each other, my prince."

He says it so bitterly I nearly wince. But then someone walks past and both of us switch on, any animosity between us instantly melting away.

"We're not talking."

It was decided that Sebastian and I should attend this opening to show the support of both our families. The rest of my family are too busy preparing for the wedding, and made it quite clear that I am being sent because I am considered helpful, but not essential. Stefan is here as well, and he's actually having a good time.

"I'm going to get a drink," says Sebastian.

My heart aches. I wonder if this would be easier if I could get myself to simply like him. I wonder if we could forge something a little less painful if I felt genuine affection.

The thing that grates at me is that this is my life.

Forever.

CHAPTER FORTY-ONE

JAMIE

"No," says Max. "No freaking way."

I'm in my bedroom at the palace, on a phone call with her. I've just asked her if it's too soon for me to reach out to Erik about being friends.

Given the outrage in her voice, I've received my answer.

I know there's a saying that time heals all wounds, and I am getting sick of waiting for that to happen. I still think about him nearly every second, and no matter what I do, I can't stop.

As much as it hurts, I still miss him more than I've ever missed anyone. Even if a part of me is sure that I'm not ready to be just friends with him, the alternative is not seeing him at all, which is killing me.

"Might I remind you," says Max, "he stomped on your heart. Besides, isn't he dating that Sebastian guy?"

Even though I know dating Sebastian is Erik doing what he feels he has to do in order to keep his family, it still breaks my heart. I've been trying to be strong and avoid looking him up online, but sometimes, usually late at night, I break down and decide to do it. There are always new pictures of Sebastian and Erik, posing for the cameras. They look perfect together, both so handsome and polished. I have to remind myself that the happy-looking people in those pictures isn't the full truth.

It's all for show.

The thing is, I know it's not Erik's choice. He doesn't want to be with Sebastian. It's just that he can't fight his family.

"Hey," says Max. "Listen, if you want to message him, you can. But if you want my advice, I think you should steer clear until you're sure you're ready."

"Noted," I say.

She's probably right. If one good thing has come out of Sebastian ending things with me, it's that Max and I have finally gotten over our drama over me posting the video. Tackling this is already impossible, so I'm grateful I don't have to do it without my best friend.

"Aw," she says, "I'm sorry."

Silence falls for a moment.

"We're okay, right?" she asks.

I flinch. "What do you mean?"

"I mean, you know, our falling-out."

"We're good," I say. "We're friends, we fight sometimes. It happens."

"Yeah, but I was pretty shitty," she says.

"So was I," I say. "I'd say it was fairly even. I really should've asked you before I posted the video."

"I should've been there for you instead of being so worried that I was going to lose you. I was so scared, and I lashed out. Seriously, I'm so sorry."

"It's okay," I say. "I get it, the whole royal thing was a huge shock. But I love you, and it's totally okay. I'm just glad we're back to normal."

"Me too, because I was actually hoping to ask you something. I've written another song, and I was wondering if you'd like to be the first person to listen to it?"

That's the way things always used to be.

Maybe Max is right. I am not really ready to talk to Erik again, and the smartest thing to do might be to leave it be.

That chapter of my life might be over.

It's for the best.

Chapter Forty-Two

ERIK

After the gallery opening, a car picked me up and drove me back to the palace.

I went straight to my room and have spent the past hour lying in bed, listening to music, constantly checking my phone, hoping for a message from Jamie, telling me he's ready to be friends.

It's not what I want, exactly, but I'll take what I can get.

There's been nothing yet, and I'm starting to lose hope. I've never missed anyone as much as I miss him. It's like there's an enormous hole in my life, and nothing I can think of can fix it.

I get a notification, and I see that the pictures from the gallery opening have been sent. I open it, and find the picture of Sebastian and me. I try to imagine what anyone who looked at it would think. They would simply see a happy couple, I know it.

There have been some people online who have speculated that my relationship with Sebastian is political, but they're a small minority. Even the royal tabloids think we're a real couple.

My thoughts return to Jamie. I'm sure he's doing well, because it's Jamie and he's smart and totally capable, and he is truly the best royal that I have ever met. He doesn't care about status or wealth, all he wants is to help people as much as he can. I would say that's a much better skill than knowing about etiquette.

The truth is he didn't need me to teach him anything.

My phone buzzes, and my entire body reacts. Is it him? I grab my phone from my bedside table.

Please, please let it be him.

It isn't. It's a message from Stefan.

Hey, Elise and I were wondering if you would like to come over? Elise has baked a cake and wants your opinion.

Elise and Stefan want to see me? There must be a reason, and it must be a bigger one than a cake. Like when he drove me from school to Gran's place. There must be some news they are going to break to me.

I'll see you soon.

I go to the bathroom, it takes me a split second to process what's looking back at me in the mirror. As a side effect of the misery I've felt, I've stopped my skin-care routine. That, in combination with my lack of sleep, has had a horrible effect on my complexion. I have dark circles under my eyes, and I am even paler than normal. I look unhealthy. It won't help, but I splash some water onto my face, then head out.

Stefan and Elise live in an apartment on the other side of the palace. As I cross it, passing by the countless doors, hiding barely used rooms, I find myself missing Jamie more than ever. I really made a mess of things with him. As fun as it was, I now feel as if I should've done everything differently. I shouldn't have let things progress past the point of friends. I should've kept that distance. I knew it was the right thing to do at the time, but I was weak, and I let myself indulge.

And now the worst thing has happened. I've lost him. Probably forever.

He will, apparently, be coming to the wedding. How will I be able to handle seeing him again if he doesn't want to talk to me? What are we going to do, treat each other like we're complete strangers? I think of seeing Jamie across a crowded ballroom and him ignoring me.

My eyes nearly well up at the thought.

I reach Stefan and Elise's apartment and ring the doorbell.

Stefan opens the door a few moments later, stepping aside to let me in. Their apartment is one that has historically belonged to the future ruler of the country before they're married. Mum lived in this very apartment before her wedding to Dad, although Stefan and Elise have modernized it since then. It's clean and airy, with white furniture and only a few royal touches: the heavy blue-and-gold curtains and Fabergé eggs kept in a glass cabinet near the window.

I go into the kitchen, where Elise has baked what has to be the most perfect-looking chocolate cake I have ever seen. It's a few layers high, and she's surrounded it with piped white and red roses. Seriously, is there anything she isn't truly exceptional at?

"What do you think?" she asks, beaming proudly. She's wearing a slightly dirty apron, and her face is sweaty. She's also made an absolute mess of the kitchen, as it's covered in cake pans and mixing bowls and cracked eggshells.

"It's perfect," I say. "I didn't know you could bake."

"I started a few weeks ago. It's a good way to deal with wedding stress."

I sit at the kitchen island. "I bet. How are you feeling about it?"

"Only slightly terrified." She smiles. "How are you?"

"About the same. I'm sure it'll be great, though."

Stefan and Elise glance at each other. Oh boy, here it comes.

As amazing as the cake looks, I seriously doubt the reason I've been asked here is to look at what she's made.

"We wanted to talk to you," says Elise, as she cuts me a piece of cake. "About Jamie."

I can't contain the surprise quickly enough to stop it from showing on my face. I thought that, to everyone else, Jamie is nothing but past news.

"What about him?"

Stefan clears his throat. "We heard about the talk you had with Gran."

I stare down at the tabletop. I was not expecting them to talk to me about this. As much as I love Stefan and Elise, we don't really talk about things like how we seriously feel in this family. For the most part, feelings are treated as annoyances that should be contained as well as possible, especially when they contradict the plan.

The plan is that I will attend the wedding with Sebastian. Anything other than that doesn't matter.

"We wanted to say that we're sorry," says Stefan. "I know how hard it must've been. We could tell you were struggling with something, but we didn't know what it was until last night."

I start picking at my fingernail. I love both Stefan and Elise. They're family. But that's part of the problem. The thing keeping me from being with Jamie is my family. I have to be careful with what I tell them, because word could always get back to Gran or Mum and Dad.

"You can talk to us," says Elise. "You have our word that we'll keep whatever you say a secret."

I'm not sure how true that is. But I want it to be. So maybe that's enough.

"I'm having a hard time," I say. "I get that it's the way things are done with our family, but it's been really hard to move on."

"Move on from what?" asks Stefan.

"Jamie," I say. "I really liked him. I felt like I found someone who was special. I know we didn't know each other that long, but I don't know. It felt different, I can't explain it."

"Did it feel like you'd found your person?" asks Elise.

I nod.

"Oh, Erik," she says, moving around to give me a hug. "This is so unfair."

"It is," says Stefan. "I remember the feeling well."

I go totally still. I see so much of myself in Stefan right now. I can see him fighting an internal battle, one where he is trying his best to be careful and make sure he doesn't say the wrong thing or something that could come back to hurt him.

"You don't know this," he says. "But when I first met Elise, Gran didn't approve."

This is the biggest bombshell of my life. It leaves me speechless.

What?

There's no way. I've been told the story. My family considered Elise perfect from the moment they met her.

"Why?" I say.

"They already had a woman picked out for me. She was the daughter of a media mogul, and they thought that me being with her could ensure some positive press. So when I met Elise, they told me I couldn't be with her."

I try to keep up with this information, which is difficult because it feels like the ground is shifting beneath me.

"What did you do?" I ask.

"I told Elise," says Stefan. "And she gave me the single best piece of advice that I have ever received."

I turn to her.

"You have to fight," she says. "This world is filled with people who will tell you what they think you should do. But I've seen what happens when you simply do what everyone wants you to, and trust me, it is a recipe for misery. If you have something you care about, then you need to fight for it with everything you have. You can't give in. You simply can't."

Fire catches in my chest. What if she's right? What if I actually can fight for this? I didn't think it was possible, because I didn't think it was a fight that could be won.

"What should I do?" I ask.

"You should arrange a meeting with Gran," says Stefan. "And you should fight for Jamie. If you know he's your person, that is."

I am. If anything, the time away has only confirmed this.

"It might be too late," I say. "Jamie and I aren't talking."

"Do you think he feels the same way about you?" asks Elise.

"I think so," I say. "He did, but I've handled this so badly."

"If you think there's a chance, you need to take it," says Elise. "You'll always regret it if you don't."

"You have to try, bud," says Stefan. "Trust me."

"I'll call Gran now," I say.

Elise shakes her head. "Don't do that. Surprise her. Don't give her a chance to say no. You need to be ruthless."

I didn't even know that was something I could do. Now I see that it is a good move, though. If I give her a warning, she might simply ask not to see me. Or she will be prepared enough that I won't be able to get what I want. What I need is to show up at the palace unannounced and ask for a meeting.

I'm her grandson. I might need to wait for a while if she is busy, but I doubt she will outright reject me.

This might work.

Stefan grabs his keys. "I'll drive you."

It's technically breaking a rule, as we aren't supposed to travel in the same car. It's one we've broken only a few times before.

I'm okay with it.

Chapter Forty-Three

Jamie

"Surprise!" says Alexander.

I'm not yet sure what the surprise is. Alexander has taken Maria, Mom, Mike, and me to an empty hallway on the west side of the palace. We've just stopped in front of a plain-looking door, and I doubt a visit to a random hallway is the surprise Alexander is so excited to give me. He's practically buzzing with energy.

Wait. It clicks.

There's no way.

Alexander reaches into his pocket and pulls out a key card. Then he offers it to me.

"It's yours," he says. "I filled in the paperwork this morning. This apartment is officially, and legally, yours."

I look at the key card. On it, in small cursive letters, are the words APARTMENT 42.

"I don't know what to say," I say. "Thank you."

"Go on, open it," he says. "I thought I'd let you do the honors."

I tap the key card against the panel. The light flashes green, and I push the door open. All the air gets knocked out of my lungs.

Just when I thought I had gotten used to life at a palace and being royalty, something like this gets thrown my way. It's the nicest apartment I've ever seen, although I might be biased since this one now belongs to me. It's similar to the apartment Erik stayed in, as it has a lot of the same features: modern kitchen, hardwood floors, crystal chandelier above the living room. Yet the layout is different, and this one isn't furnished.

We go into the middle of the room. This place is huge. And the view! I can see all the way out to the mountains from here. I look up at the ceiling. The edges have a golden trim to them, and it makes the whole place look even more expensive.

How much does this cost? I know they own the palace and nobody else lives here, but still. This apartment anywhere else would be worth millions. And I, a former part-time Cinnabon employee, now own it.

"We decided unfurnished would be better, so you could pick everything you like and make it truly your own," says Maria. "I thought it would be a fun project for us."

"I'd love that," I say. My voice sounds a little raspy, because I am still not fully comprehending what has just happened.

"You have space for an office, too," she says. "We've got a lot of work to do."

"I know it's early," says Alexander. "But after our talk on the coast, I got so excited. This apartment is yours. You can stay here whenever you visit, and if you still want to, this could be your home after you graduate."

"It can be whatever you want it to be," says Mom.

I walk around going into one of the bedrooms. I don't know what to say.

"What do you think?" asks Alexander. He's clearly put a lot of thought into this, and cares a lot about my reaction. "We worked together to pick one we thought you would like."

"We all want it to be perfect for you, bud," says Mike.

Seeing them speaking like this nearly makes me cry. I might have one of the strangest family combinations on the planet. I wouldn't change it for anything. Them all working together like this, to do something simply for me, is so nice that I could cry.

I wish that I could tell Erik. What would he think? I'm sure he'd love it.

"Of course, you could stay in a dorm when you go to college," says Alexander. "But this will be waiting for you whenever you want to visit."

"And we hope you do," says Maria. "We love having you here."

"I love being here, too. This is so nice, I don't know what to say. Thank you."

I give Alexander a hug. He holds me tightly. I remember the first time I hugged him. That time, it felt slightly awkward. Now it doesn't.

I look around the apartment again. It's so lovely, and it's mine. I hope that, wherever she is, Emilia would be happy for me. I think she would be. Nobody has tried to control me, and everything I've done has been my choice.

I'm so lucky.

All right, Jamie. Game face on.

My life lately has been filled with almost exclusively new experiences. And I have survived them all. Even the times that have felt impossible, like the earth was going to open up and swallow me whole.

I have no reason to think my first-ever televised interview will be any different.

I'm ready to go. Physically, at least. I've got a face covered in makeup and I'm wearing a suit. The finishing touch, a gift from Maria, is a golden lapel pin that shows the Mortenallo family crest.

I check the time on my watch. For the interview, I swapped out my smartwatch for a Richard Mille, a present from Alexander. My hair is swept back and neat. I shaved, and my shoes are brand new.

I think I look the part of a Mitanorian prince.

I leave the bathroom, and find a new, unfamiliar person waiting in the tea room. It's a young guy holding a clipboard and wearing a headpiece. As they've been setting up this interview, I've seen a few members of *The Lens,* the program that won the bidding war to interview me, getting everything ready.

"Ann is ready for you," he says. Then he bows his head and ducks out of the room.

I try to forget the fact that last week's episode of *The Lens with Ann Lee* was viewed by three million people. It's a weekly news show that covers stories across Europe, and airs in multiple countries.

I have already pledged to donate the eye-watering fee they are paying me to Hope House, and I hope to mention it while I am on the air. I button the jacket of my suit, and go out to the Blue Room, where the interview will be taking place.

Ann is already seated on one of the ornate chairs, and everything around her has been set up. There are two cameras, as well as dozens of lights placed in front of one of the lounges that usually sit up against the wall. They've angled the shot so that one of the portraits, this one of King Robert, my great-grandfather, is within view if the camera were to pan out.

Out of nowhere, a strong emotion nearly overwhelms me. My sadness over what happened between Erik and me has been difficult to contain, and tends to rear its head at the most inopportune times.

Like right now.

"Jamie," says Ann, bowing her head and offering her hand at the same time. "It's a pleasure to meet you."

We shake hands, and I remember what Erik taught me during our first lesson. Eye contact, strong grip. I can't break down now, there's too much on the line. Doing this interview will raise almost a million dollars for Hope House, and also give them televised exposure. That's what I'm doing this for. I can break down about Erik later.

"I've been watching your interviews," I say. "You're amazing."

Truly, she's a shark. Her questions are always insightful and get the truth out of whoever she's interviewing. There's a reason so many people tune in to watch Ann Lee's interviews every week.

I take a seat opposite her.

"This is your first TV interview, correct?" asks Ann.

"Yes, it is."

"Are you nervous?"

"Of course," I say. "But I'm happy to be here."

"Good, good. Let's start, shall we? Tell me, how has your life changed since your mother told you the truth about your parents?"

"Well, it's changed a lot," I say, getting a rare smile out of Ann Lee.

I start to feel at ease. Even though the cameras are on me, and I'm aware of the pressure, I don't feel as if I'm out of my depth. I can do this. I can represent myself, both my countries, and the crown.

I can do this.

Chapter Forty-Four

ERIK

"Good luck," says Stefan.

I think I'll need it.

I unclasp my seatbelt. We've been driven across the city, and now we're parked at the side entrance to the palace where Gran is working today. It towers over us, grand, imposing, and gorgeous. I unclip my seatbelt and force down the nerves threatening to take over.

Gran is in there, and she has no idea that I'm coming. This behavior is simply not the way things are done in this family. I'm breaking the rules in a way that will land me in hot water. It goes against all my training, and a loud voice in my mind is telling me to stop, and that no good can come from facing Gran like this.

Then I think of Jamie, and know I simply don't have a choice. Following the rules isn't working for me. This past week I have been miserable, and I can't see that changing unless I do something about it. Even if Jamie decides he doesn't want to be with me because of the way that I acted, I still need to go through with this.

I can follow the rules in other areas of my life. But not who I love. That is my decision, and my decision alone.

A royal aide opens the car door for me.

"Remember, be strong," says Stefan. "I love you."

"I love you, too."

"Now go show Gran you're not someone who can be pushed around."

I couldn't be more grateful to have a brother like Stefan right now. He is going to get married in two days. He could've easily shut me out and let me deal with this on my own, as he has so much on his plate right now.

What gives me strength is that Stefan had to do this very thing. Maybe this is the way that things are done in this family and I just wasn't aware of it. It might be that this is a test that my family puts everyone through in order to make sure that they've found the right partner—someone that they will fight for.

I make my way into the palace. Timothy is standing by a large oil painting, speaking to an unfamiliar man in a suit. As I enter, Timothy turns to me, his eyes going wide with surprise. He breaks away from his conversation and strides over to me, seemingly in a hurry.

"Prince Erik," he says. "What are you doing here?"

"I was hoping I could see Gran. Is she available?"

The shock on Timothy's expression doubles, to nearly comical levels. It's clear that he hasn't had the same training that I've had, and isn't as good at hiding how he feels.

"My apologies, but I believe she is in meetings all day. If you had arranged a time, I'm sure she would've loved to see you. Is there any chance you could come back, say, tomorrow?"

I stand my ground and shake my head. "It needs to be today. Please, I really need to speak with her."

Timothy sighs. "I can't make any promises, but I will see. Wait here."

With that, he turns on his polished shoes. I watch him go. This might be a strategy on his part, to leave me standing here. There are countless waiting rooms in this palace, and someone as experienced as Timothy would've invited me to wait in one of those if he had wanted to.

The more I think about it, the more I know this is a strategy, as I arrived unannounced. He wants me to be uncomfortable. I go farther down the hallway, one that still gives me a good view of the entrance. Underneath an oil painting of waves crashing against the Emerald Cliffs is a lounge chair.

I take a seat. No matter what, I'm not giving up. I'll wait here as long as I need to.

After about half an hour, Timothy returns. I stand as he draws closer.

"Good news," he says. "The queen has agreed to meet with you right away. She doesn't have long, so make sure whatever it is you want to say, you say it as swiftly as possible."

Easily done. I have spent the past half hour practicing, going over what I'm going to say, and preparing my responses to any of her counterarguments.

Familiar pangs of anxiety are still rooted deep within me, but they aren't strong enough to get me to change my mind. I'm not sure anything is. I had to force myself to break up with Jamie. With this, it's the complete opposite. With every passing moment, I am finding myself feeling even more sure of myself and what I'm doing.

I follow Timothy across the palace, going down the hallway until we reach the central stairway at the heart of the palace. We climb the marble stairs to the top level, then follow the long, quiet hall until we reach Gran's office. Timothy opens the heavy door for me and we go in, passing Gran's receptionist. She waves at me, then seems to sense the gravity of the situation, as she lowers her hand.

"She's expecting you," says the receptionist. "You can go right in."

Here we go.

Gran is sitting at her desk, writing something by hand in a

notebook. This isn't that rare for her. She treats computers like they are a necessary evil, and only uses them when she has no other choice. She doesn't react. This is normal for her. She always finishes what she was doing before giving anyone any attention. She places her pen down and finally looks up as I reach the desk. I bow, and she smiles graciously.

"Erik," she says. "What an unexpected surprise. Take a seat."

I pull out the chair and sit. I feel as if I am up against a force of nature, and I'm going into a battle that I can't possibly win. Still, I feel a steely amount of resolve. Even though I'm anxious, I have to fight. As scary as this moment is, the alternative—being forced to be with someone I don't truly love for the rest of my life—is far worse.

"You wanted to speak to me?" she asks.

Even though I've gone over what I want to say to her countless times, I find my words getting stuck in my throat. I only have one chance at this, only one shot to get the life that I want. One misstep, one false word, and it's all over.

"I wanted to speak with you about Jamie," I say.

The room goes silent.

"We've spoken about this," she says. "You're dating Sebastian."

"I am," I say. "But we both know that's not real. With Jamie I've found someone who I can truly be with, who I can genuinely feel something for. I want to be with him."

"I wasn't aware the two of you were still in contact."

"We aren't. I did as you asked, and ended things with him."

"That's good, at least."

"But Gran, please listen to me. I know you think that I'm being petulant, but I'm not. I have never felt anything as strongly as what I feel for him."

"Emotions are tricky things," she says. "I've found it best to keep them to yourself."

"Please," I say. "Give Jamie a chance. I know you have your reservations about him, and you want to teach me a lesson about following the rules."

"Do I?" she asks, her voice rising. I've clearly made her upset, and now I feel a strong urge to back down and let things go her way. I remember what Stefan and Elise told me. I need to fight. Gran takes her reading glasses off. "You do know the wedding is in two days."

"Yes."

"And now is the time for our family to show stability. If you change your date now, then people will talk, and we can't have that."

"But there's always something," I say, trying my best to keep any emotion from showing in my voice. I don't feel like shouting, but I'm dangerously close to tearing up, and if I do that it may as well all be over.

"You do it because it's what you've been told," she says. "We know better than you, and you need to listen to us."

I shake my head. "Respectfully, I can't. Not with this."

She holds my gaze for a moment. I can sense her searching for any signs of weakness or cracks in my resolve. But she won't find any. I am nervous to confront her, but I know in my heart this is the right thing to do. It's the only thing I can do that has any chance at making me happy.

"Do you love him?" she asks.

Of all the questions I was bracing for, I wasn't expecting this one. Do I love him? My brain tells me that I haven't known him long enough for that. I think of love as something like Stefan and Elise have. Yes, there might have been infatuation from the start, but love is something much more steady, built over time. And yet, with Jamie, it's different from any guy I've hooked up with or even found attractive. It's soft and gold, and just thinking of him fills me with warmth.

"I think I could," I say. "I don't want to be with anyone else."

She sighs. "I had thought having children would be the biggest difficulty of my life. Turns out grandchildren are far more of a headache. Very well, you have my blessing to date Jamie. On one condition."

"Yes?"

"Can you wait until after the wedding? I don't want any disruptions, and I want your focus to be purely on making sure your brother's wedding goes perfectly. Do that, and you have my blessing."

Those are her terms. While they aren't exactly what I would like, because I would prefer to be able to tell Jamie right now, the wedding is only two days away. I can make it that long, if it means I have Gran's blessing. It will be difficult, but I can do it.

"I'll wait," I say. "I'll tell him at the reception."

It's settled, then. I can be with Jamie.

I've never been happier than I am in this moment. I can barely contain my smile. I fought for what I wanted, and I got it. It's real. I have permission from Gran. There's now nothing stopping us from being together, if that's what he wants.

"May I be excused?" I ask.

"You may."

I rise from the chair.

"And Erik?"

I stop in the doorway, and look back at her.

"Good luck," she says.

I tap the doorframe, then leave.

Chapter Forty-Five

JAMIE

It's been weeks since I've seen Erik. Since I've spoken to him, even.

And today I will. During a televised royal wedding.

I'm in a private jet, looking out the window. We're not too far from landing right now, so the green stretches of land I can see out the window must be Sunstad. Erik's home.

I can't believe I'm visiting his country while the two of us aren't even speaking. How is today even going to go down? Are we going to speak, or not?

I'm sure he has a lot going on right now, so he's probably not even thinking about me.

"Pretty, right?"

I turn, as Tomas returns from the bathroom to sit in the seat beside me. He returned home from his Florence trip yesterday, and we had dinner as a family. It was really nice, and I do wish that I had gotten to spend more time with him this summer.

There are plenty of chances for that in the future.

"It's incredible," I say.

"Can I get your advice?" he asks.

I bob my head.

"So I was seeing this girl, right," he says. "She was in one of my classes, and we really hit it off. And I really like her, but now that the summer is over . . . "

His shrug fills in the blanks. I get it. He's asking where things can possibly go, seeing as the two of them live in different countries.

"You could try long-distance," I suggest. I was willing to do that with Erik if his family hadn't come between us.

"You don't think that's too complicated?" he asks.

"It might not be the easiest thing in the world, but if you like her enough, I think it's worth a try."

"You're right," he says. "So what about you?"

"What about me?"

"Are you interested in anyone?"

"Nope," I say. "I had enough on my plate given the whole 'surprise, you're a prince' thing."

He laughs. "That's fair enough."

The flight attendant emerges from the front of the plane.

"We'll be landing soon," she says. "Please fasten your seatbelts."

I look out the window again. We're nearly in Sunstad. I just need to get through today. After that, everything will be easier.

It's just one day.

The scene in the city can only be described as pandemonium.

Thousands of people have taken to the streets for Stefan and Elise's wedding. A lot of them are dressed in the light blue of the Sunstadian flag, with matching temporary tattoos stuck to their cheeks, and a lot of them are waving miniature flags. Loud music is playing, and the atmosphere is one of a city-wide party.

I can practically feel the joy of the entire country. Their prince is getting married, and they are getting a new princess.

We're in a car trying to get to the hotel so we can get ready for the wedding, which will be starting in less than two hours. We should've been at the hotel an hour ago, but the traffic has slowed our pace nearly to a standstill. Through the front window of the limo is a view of streets filled with cars.

"I'm sorry," says the driver of the limo. "The turnout was much higher than anticipated."

I can see that; the entire city is gridlocked. A police officer on a horse rides past right by my window. None of the cars are moving, and a few of the drivers have taken to blaring their horns, as if that will get things moving.

"We should walk," suggests Mike. He's on his phone, which has a maps app open. "The hotel is only two blocks from here."

There is one security guard in the limo with us. He is armed, and his muscular frame fills the light gray suit he's wearing. He certainly does not look like the sort of man one would want to mess with.

"Can we?" I ask him.

He gives a short shake of his head, giving us our answer.

"We're going to miss it," I say. "We need to go."

The hotel is within walking distance of the church; so as long as we get there, we'll be fine.

"All right," says the security guard. "Jamie, keep your eyes down, and don't stop no matter what."

"I won't."

I open the limo door, and it's like being hit with a wall of sound. People are cheering and screaming. As I step onto the sidewalk, I catch someone noticing me.

"Oh my God!" he screams. "That's Prince Jamie."

I'm not sure I'll ever be used to being called that.

"Let's move," says the guard, taking me by the arm and moving me across the street, away from the guy who noticed me.

I keep my head down as we push through the crowd. It earns us a few double takes, and the security guard is probably drawing more attention, but we move so quickly nobody stops us. We cut through the crowd and find ourselves in an empty street. This one mustn't have a view of the procession. We rush down it, then cross another block until we find ourselves at the entrance of the hotel.

We made it.

Hopefully from now on, it will be smooth sailing.

I remind myself it's just one day. One difficult day, but that's all it is.

CHAPTER FORTY-SIX

ERIK

Funnily enough, I've never been in a horse-drawn carriage before.

A few people at school have assumed it's a common mode of transport for us.

It's not.

Still, looking at the one that has just pulled up to drive us through the city as part of the royal procession, I wish I had ridden in one more often. The carriage is a work of art, coated in a brilliant, lustrous gold. Sitting in the driver's seat is a man in a traditional military uniform, with a group of similarly dressed guards surrounding the vehicle. Two horses are already attached to the carriage, and are standing at the ready.

Stefan and I walk down the steps of the palace toward the carriage. This morning has been surreal, with all the pieces falling into place without any issues.

Stefan is wearing a light blue military jacket with a golden sash over his chest. My suit is much simpler, although it's still one of the nicest things I've ever worn: a three-piece tuxedo. Neither outfit is really designed for this weather, and I can feel the sweat already building under all my layers.

I think we both look the part. That makes it worth it.

A part of me feels slightly selfish that I can't focus only on the wedding. I am genuinely so excited for Stefan and Elise, and seeing Stefan act like a giddy schoolboy even under all the pressure warms my heart. But I can't stop thinking about telling Jamie that we can be together. I can hardly wait.

I know it's for the best. If I wait, we will have Gran's blessing.

One of the men in uniform opens the carriage for me, and I climb in. Stefan follows me inside. Sebastian will be meeting us at the church, and I spoke with him last night about my plan. I felt too guilty not to tell him. I apologized profusely, which he was gracious enough to accept. He thanked me for my honesty, and agreed to go through with the ceremony because it will be great for his family and his future career. After that, he said we should part on good terms, so that I can announce my relationship with Jamie.

The carriage suddenly lurches forward.

It's happening. The wedding is starting.

The carriage moves with a surprising speed. We pass by the main gate, and start heading toward the city. There are red curtains on both sides of the window. I pull them back and look out at the view.

"What are you thinking about?" asks Stefan.

"This," I say. "I can't believe it's finally happening."

"I know," he says. "Strange, right?"

"So strange. I should probably check and make sure you're not getting cold feet?"

"Me? Never."

I knew that would be his answer. The thought of Stefan not wanting to go through with this is impossible to imagine.

"When are you going to talk to Jamie?" he asks.

"At the reception," I say. "If that's okay?"

I don't think he will object, but think it would be best to check, given it is his wedding.

"Of course it is," he says. "I'm excited for you."

The carriage turns a corner, and the first parts of the crowd appear. I've tried my best to avoid looking at the news, but I've overheard conversations at the palace saying that public turnout is far higher than anticipated, and the city is scrambling to catch up. That must mean there are thousands of people out on the streets, and we're headed right toward them.

My chest suddenly feels tight. I suck in some air, then exhale. It'll be fine.

I look out the window again to watch the crowd, with people in camping chairs sitting out to watch the procession. Stefan starts waving out of the window. I do the same.

The carriage follows a path through the city, and the closer we get to the church, the more people there are. The streets are now filled, people crammed together like it's a concert mosh pit. It reminds me a little of the crowd that showed up to see Jamie when we visited Hope House, only on a much bigger scale.

We reach the street of the church, and I have never seen this many people in my life. It's hard to comprehend the magnitude. It's clear the people love Stefan and Elise. It's not something that's forced. They can see that they are good people who have the country's best interests at heart.

The carriage rolls to a stop. I wish that I could pause time. I don't feel ready. This is the moment I have been the most anxious about. The walk from the carriage up the church steps. It's televised, and if I stumble, it will be something that clings to me for the rest of my life.

One of the guards opens the carriage door. I step out. The crowd starts to scream and cheer. I wave a hand. Up above, by the tall spires of the church, are two black helicopters.

Stefan emerges from the carriage, and the crowd cheers even louder. He comes over and claps me on the shoulder. He leans in close.

"Ready?" he asks.

I nod.

We go up the steps of the church until we reach an archway of flowers that has been placed around the entrance. This very spot is where Stefan and Elise will kiss as they greet the public after the ceremony. According to Mum, this picture is pivotal, as it will be the image that people remember the most about the wedding. It will be printed on mugs and plates and sold as merchandise for years. It's another thing they have to get right.

Under the flowery archway are two church priests. They bless Stefan, then me.

We go inside.

I keep my attention forward, to the front of the church. Hundreds of people are seated in the pews, and I know they will all be highly important. There will be celebrities, politicians, and royalty from both Sunstad and other countries. They aren't who I am thinking about right now.

Jamie will be in here, somewhere. But there are too many people here to spot him.

I go down the aisle until we reach the front. Mum and Dad are already here, and sitting in the front row. Mum is already crying, and seeing Stefan brings on a fresh wave of tears. I take a seat next to Sebastian as Stefan speaks to the priest standing to the side.

Who knows, maybe in time Sebastian and I could find a way to be friends. I simply can't pretend that I feel something for him that I don't. I don't do that anymore.

Orchestral music starts to play, and a hush falls over the crowd.

The ceremony is about to begin.

CHAPTER FORTY-SEVEN

JAMIE

I can't get over how Erik looks.

Everything about him is *perfect*. He's a prince out of a story-book.

I'm trying my best to keep a brave face, but internally, I'm falling to pieces. As much as I thought I had prepared for what it would be like to see him, I was in no way ready. The second I saw him enter the church, all my defenses withered away to nothing, leaving me completely unprotected.

What makes it worse is I still want to be with him. I'm pretty sure I always will. I can't imagine my feelings for Erik ever changing, or ever going away.

We're technically in the same room at the moment, but he couldn't be further away. We're seated on the second level of the church, looking down. I have a great view of everything, but I'm far enough away from Erik that he hasn't spotted me.

Not that he's looking. It might be in my head, but it seems as if he is actively trying to stop from searching for me. And then there's Sebastian. Even knowing their relationship is fake, seeing them sitting together broke something within me. I even saw Sebastian whisper something to Erik.

What if they like each other now?

Weirder things have happened. Me being here is a testament to that.

I try to focus on the crowd. There is a shocking number of famous people. Like the king and queen of England, as well as the copper-haired prince and princess. The prince is around my age, and is covertly messaging someone on his phone, something I'm only able to see because I'm above him. He lifts his head and catches me looking. Before I look away, he shoves his phone back into his pocket and winks. His mom scolds him, and the prince grins and leans back against his seat.

Did I really just have a moment with the prince of England? Wild.

The orchestra swells, and an opera singer starts to sing, her voice high and perfect.

A hush falls over the crowd. I look back at the front of the church to see Stefan and Erik are now standing at the front of the church, beside the priest.

The ceremony must be starting.

People turn in their seats to look at the back of the church. Around the corner comes a girl who I'd guess is about five. She's in a white dress and her hair is in tight rows of braids. There is no missing the family relation this girl has to Elise. She walks down the aisle, dropping pink and white flower petals as she walks.

Next is a man and a woman who has to be Elise's sister. They go down the aisle. This proceeds until the entire wedding party is standing on the stage.

A hush sweeps over the crowd as Elise, accompanied by a man who I would guess is her father, enters the church. Her dress is flawless; a long-sleeved white gown covered in intricate detail work, as well as a long veil that reaches all the way to the floor. It shimmers when the light hits it. Breathtaking is the only way to describe it, and I'm not sure the word fully encapsulates how stunning she is.

She looks straight down the aisle at Stefan and smiles. It's clearly not a put-on smile. It's genuine, her eyes lighting up at the same time. I turn back, and find Stefan smiling, too, and tears have welled up in his eyes.

Elise makes her way down the aisle, her train trailing behind her. Both Maria and Alexander start to cry quietly. Despite my instincts telling me not to, I turn away from Elise in order to see Erik.

He pushes his shoulders back, and I notice there are tears in his eyes, too. It does something funny to my chest.

I can never be with him. As much as I want to be, it's never going to happen.

I know I can't, but I wish that I could get out of here. I can't handle it anymore. I simply can't.

Elise reaches the front of the church and stands in front of Stefan. The music grows quiet. Even with all this spectacle going on around them, it truly seems like Stefan and Elise don't care about anything else right now. It's just the two of them, and they're all that matters. The priest starts making a speech, but for me, and I would be willing to bet a lot of people in the crowd, it's background noise.

Once the speech is done, Stefan says something quietly, just to Elise, and she laughs. To the side, Erik blinks a few times, but he is otherwise completely stoic.

I start to wonder about Stefan and Elise. Were they controlled like Erik was? It doesn't seem to be that way. Looking at them, it seems apparent that they are genuinely in love with each other.

I can't stop thinking about Erik. I need to leave. The thought of being at the reception and seeing Erik with Sebastian, even if I know it's fake, is too much for me to handle. I need to go.

Stefan and Elise exchange vows, and almost everyone around me starts crying tears of joy. Then it's time for the big moment.

"I now pronounce you man and wife."

Finally, mouths Stefan, and he kisses Elise.

Like Elise's dress, the kiss is a showstopper. It's so genuine, and a little more passionate than I was expecting. It's clearly a kiss shared between two people who love each other with everything they have.

And that's it.

They're officially married.

"Are you okay?" asks Mom.

I can't lie anymore. I shake my head. "Can we leave?"

She looks at me for a long moment.

"I'll see what I can do," she says.

Chapter Forty-Eight

ERIK

I'm finally free.

The ceremony is over, and almost everyone else has moved on to the reception. I have spent the past hour with the rest of the wedding party. We must've taken hundreds of photos in various locations around the palace: by the lake, in the fields. I'm happy to have done this, and I'm sure the pictures are going to turn out great.

But now I can finally talk to Jamie.

I enter the ballroom, where the main party is already in full swing. Hundreds of people, all dressed in their finest clothes, are milling around, drinking and talking.

I look around for him. I've done what was asked of me, and I can't wait any longer. I need to tell him what's happened, how I feel, and find out once and for all if we are going to be together or not.

My first sweep for Jamie proves fruitless. I do, however, make contact with Sebastian. It reminds me of something I felt at the wedding. As excited as I am to speak to Jamie, it can wait a few more seconds. I approach Sebastian.

"My prince," he says, his voice dark.

"Listen, I need to apologize," I say.

He lifts a perfect eyebrow. "For what?"

"The way I've handled things. I'm sorry, truly. I wish that I had been strong enough to stand up for myself before you were involved. Still, it was unfair of me to include you in this mess."

He laughs to himself. "I think you're giving yourself a little too much credit. I do recall telling you that it was fine for us to see other people, as long as we were honest with each other. From where I'm standing, you've always done that."

He's right. Maybe I can let some of the guilt that I'm holding onto go.

"Are you sorry you didn't catch feelings for me?" he asks. "Oh, sweetie. Don't be, I'm perfectly content with the way things are. I've already gained thirty thousand followers. Plus, if we're being honest, there are a few guys here I've got my eye on." He steps closer. "Have you heard the rumor about the prince of England being gay? I might have to have a word with him. Talk about an upgrade."

He winks.

From one of the side entrances, I see Alexander and Maria enter. If anyone is going to know where Jamie is, it's them.

"Go," says Sebastian. "Get your man."

I break away from Sebastian and cross the ballroom to catch up with Alexander and Maria. Stefan and Elise have just arrived, and they've made a swift beeline to the dance floor.

"Erik," says Alexander. "Looking sharp, as always."

"Have you seen Jamie?"

"Not since the ceremony, but we've only been here a short while."

I get an idea.

"Could I use that favor?" I ask. "If you see Jamie, can you ask him to meet me in the Blue Room? I'll be waiting for him there."

"I will," says Alexander. "I'll call him now."

I leave the ballroom and go straight to the Blue Room. The doors are already open, but the space is empty. I go inside, and stop in the middle. This is it, the moment I've been longing for. It's finally here.

I check my phone. As I was taking the wedding pictures I

messaged Jamie, asking him if we could talk. He hasn't replied yet, nor has he even seen the message.

A few minutes pass, and I start to get worried. What's going on? My phone vibrates. I've received a text from Alexander.

I'm so sorry, Erik, but Jamie decided not to come to the reception. He's already on his way back to Mitanor.

I stare at the message as it sinks in. Jamie isn't coming. I was too late.

I'm barely here.

I've gone back to the ballroom, and I've been pretending to have a good time. This is Stefan and Elise's wedding, and I don't want to bring them, or anyone else, down with my mood. After I was told Jamie isn't coming, I waited for a little while as it truly sunk in that I had screwed up, yet again. Of course he wouldn't want to go to the reception and see the guy who broke up with him. I should've expected that.

My phone vibrates.

Where are you??

It's from Jamie.
I feel my heart pounding against my throat.

What do you mean?

Alexander told me to meet you in the Blue Room, but you're not here?

I get up from my seat and rush across the ballroom. I don't care if anyone sees me and thinks I look ungraceful. I start running down the empty corridors until I reach the Blue Room. I stop by the entrance, and take a moment to catch my breath. Then I tug down the ends of my jacket, and walk inside.

Jamie is standing by one of the windows. I clear my throat, and he turns.

His smile is the best thing I have ever seen.

I stop myself from hugging him. There are things we need to talk about, things we need to go over to make sure we're on the same page.

"So," he says, dragging the word out. "You wanted to see me?"

"I talked to Gran," I say. "About us."

Both his eyebrows lift.

"And I totally understand if you have changed your mind after the way I've handled things," I say. "But I want to be with you. That's what I talked to Gran about, and she changed her mind. She said that we have her blessing, if being with me is still something you want."

"She said we can be together?" he asks.

"Yes," I say. "She said that seeing me fight for you is what she needed. Because how I feel about you, it's stronger than anything I've ever felt before. And if you do, then I want to see where this could go."

"I want that," he says. "I want that so badly."

I laugh. "Yeah?"

"Yeah."

He draws closer, and the walls we had between us melt away. Before I know it, his hands are on the sides of my face and he's leaning up to kiss me. His lips meet mine. It is, without a doubt, the best kiss of my life. Because there are no issues now, no doubts, no danger of me not being able to be there for Jamie.

Because that's what I am. Completely and utterly there for him.

"Can we tell people?" he asks.

"We can," I say.

"In that case, we have a reception to go to."

His hands leave my face, and he takes hold of my hand. Sparks run up my arm as he pulls me toward the door. We go back through the palace, until we reach the ballroom. As we enter, people turn to look at the two of us, holding hands. I don't let him go.

Jamie leads me to the dance floor. He puts his arms over my shoulders.

"I can't believe this is happening," he says. "It feels like a dream."

I lean down and kiss him. People are watching us, and I know everyone will know that we're together by tomorrow morning.

It won't be a secret anymore.

And I couldn't be happier.

EPILOGUE

JAMIE

Dear Diary,

I guess birthdays aren't that bad. Today, for one, has actually been pretty good, and not because I've been spoiled rotten. I must say, having two families is excellent in terms of gifts. Everyone went above and beyond, and I feel so lucky. Erik's presents were also PERFECT. He got me a copy of Serpent's Claw, *which I've been waiting to play for ages, and a shirt I referenced liking weeks ago. PLUS he wrote me a card which has maybe the sweetest message I've ever read. I nearly cried reading it.*

Anyway, what else? Oh, we're all in Mitanor at the moment, and Alexander and Maria are throwing me a ball for my birthday. It should be really fun, I can't wait. Simon made me a new suit and I'm obsessed with it . . .

"What are you doing?"

I close my journal and spin around on my chair.

Erik is leaning against the doorframe to my room. He's been growing his hair longer, so a few golden strands fall over his forehead. It's a good look. A great look, really.

Although I must say, pretty much everything looks good on my boyfriend.

"I was trying out journaling," I say. The leather-bound journal I was writing in was a gift from Maria, and Alexander gave me a matching pen with my name engraved on it. Like I wrote, everyone has gone above and beyond for my birthday this year.

I kind of get it. I mean, you only turn eighteen once.

"What do you think?" he asks.

"Of journaling? I like it. I think I'll keep going."

"I think that's a great idea," he says. "Sorry to interrupt, but I do have another gift for you."

There's a blur of movement past him, and Max rushes into my bedroom. Before I can even come to grips with her being here, she's hugging me.

"Happy birthday!" she says. "God, I love you so much, and you're eighteen! You're so old."

I scowl at her. I decide to let that comment slide, because my best friend is here.

"Erik invited us," she says, answering my question before I can even ask it. "We wanted it to be a surprise."

"Wait, us?"

Amara, Spencer, and Ren all enter. The last person inside is the newest addition to the group—Blake, aka the cute boy from Anchor Bros, who is now Ren's boyfriend. Ren has thanked me so many times for the whole royal secret reveal, since without it, he and Blake wouldn't have ended up dating. However, seeing how perfect they are together, I think there's a chance they would've found each other no matter what.

I feel the same way about Erik. We are meant to be.

"I can't handle this," I say.

"Surprise," says Erik.

I can't stop myself from smiling.

I get crushed by Ren's bear hug and then hug Spencer.

"Well, go on," says Ren. "Tell him your news!"

"What news?" I ask.

"You know that agent I had the meeting with a little while ago?" asks Max.

"I do."

"They offered to represent me."

"What!"

The meeting Max had was with one of the biggest agencies in the industry, an agency that represents some of the most famous singers and bands on the planet. I'm not surprised, because I have always known how talented Max is. But I am truly delighted.

"When?" I ask.

"A week ago."

"Why didn't you tell me?"

"I wanted to tell you in person," she says.

I give her a hug. "That's awesome!"

I've been thinking a lot about my life path lately. If my secret had never gotten out, or Mom had told me earlier. If I somehow had the power to change any of it, I wouldn't because it all led me here. That's a good sign that I'm on the right track.

"We need to get ready," says Max. "See you soon?"

"You will. I can't believe you're here. And you have an agent! Ah!"

Max hugs me again, and then they all file out of the room, moving past Erik. Ren winks at me before he disappears down the hall. When they're gone, Erik makes his way over. I can see a part of the angel necklace I got him poking out against his shirt. He rarely takes it off.

"I did well, right?" he asks.

"You did amazing. You always do."

He nuzzles his nose against mine. "You deserve it."

"I love you," I say. We said it for the first time after dating for about three months, and now we say it daily. Dating long-distance has been tough, but we see each other in person whenever possible. Because it's not a secret anymore, Erik is allowed to stay in my apartment.

"I love you, too," he says.

He kisses me. Who would've thought a year ago that I'd be standing here right now, madly in love with a prince?

Half an hour later, Erik and I enter the ballroom. I spot Mom and Mike. They wave me over.

"Where have you two been?" asks Mom.

"We were just talking," I say. We were making out, but they don't need to know that. "Where's Dad?" I ask. I've been calling Alexander "Dad" for a while now, and I still remember how overjoyed I was when I first called him that. He's earned it, too. He's been so gracious and kind and is always there to talk to me, about anything.

"I'm not sure," says Mom. "I haven't seen him anywhere."

"What about Grandma and Octavio?"

Over the past year, I've gotten incredibly close with Emilia's parents. My bio-mom doesn't feel like a blank space in my life anymore. I visit Grandma and Octavio whenever I visit Mitanor, and we have dinner, and they tell me stories about Emilia.

The lights in the room dim. Dad walks out onto the stage.

Everyone in the ballroom goes quiet. The king is about to speak, after all.

"Welcome," he says. "I want to thank you all for coming. It is funny to think that, a year ago, Jamie and I did not speak."

To the side of the ballroom is Tomas and Maria. Beside them is Talia. Hope House has been reopened for a year, and our continued fundraising efforts mean it's never going to close its doors again. For the past year, we have been working together almost nonstop, and have managed to open two new centers, with a few more in the works.

John Valencia hates our guts, which I'm perfectly fine with. I would be worried if a man like him was ever pleased with me.

"I wanted to take a moment to appreciate my son on his eighteenth birthday. In a short space of time, he has done incredible work, and I couldn't be prouder. So please, everyone, raise your glasses to my son: His Royal Highness, Jamie Johnson!"

Everyone around me lifts their glasses.

"To Jamie!"

Erik steps a little closer.

"There's one more surprise," he says.

Wait, another one? How many more of these can one guy take?

His fingers link with mine, and the music in the room fades. I don't think this will be a bad thing, though. This isn't going to change my life as radically as Mom telling me the truth. Or maybe it will.

"Can we go to the balcony?" asks Erik.

He pulls me across the dance floor. As we leave, I catch Max's attention. She blows me a kiss. Still holding hands, Erik and I climb the stairs until we get to the second level and go out onto the balcony. The palace garden stretches before us, and I can see the hedge maze where we first kissed, and the gazebo where we first met in person. That feels like a lifetime ago.

Erik takes his hands in mine, and we face each other. In the same way it's hard to imagine not knowing my father, it's hard to believe there was a time in my life without him.

He clears his throat. "I'm going to get sappy for a second, if that's all right?"

"It's encouraged," I say.

"This year has been the best of my life. You've taught me so much and made me better and happier than I've ever been. I feel so lucky and grateful to be your boyfriend."

I can barely contain the happiness bubbling up within me.

"I feel the same," I say.

"My news is that I heard back from Oakwood. Jamie, I got in."

"You did?"

Oakwood is a college in Mitanor where I'm going to study psychology. Erik applied as well, and I knew he would get in, because he's brilliant. But I got early acceptance and he didn't, and I'd be lying if I said I wasn't starting to panic.

"My parents helped me," he says. "I told them it's what I wanted, and they made it happen. Gran sent a letter of recommendation to the dean."

"That's amazing," I say. "Are we really going to go to the same college?"

"I think so."

He gives me a little smile. I can't hold back anymore. I rush forward and press my lips against his. He kisses me back just as hard.

"So what do you say?" he asks, resting his forehead against mine. "Us, at the same school. Would you like that?"

I can picture it. No more long-distance. Studying together. Kissing in each other's dorm rooms. Making friends, going to class. Erik can join the swim team, and I can cheer him on in the bleachers. We can go to house parties together. We can just *be* together.

Would I like that?

I can hardly wait.

ACKNOWLEDGMENTS

Behind every book is a huge team of people who give it their all in order to make the best book possible, and I am so lucky to have a truly incredible team working with me on *The Rules of Royalty*! They're all rock stars, and I hope they all know how much I appreciate their hard work.

First up, to my agent, Moe Ferrara, who has been there from when this book was just an idea all the way until now. Your support and guidance have meant everything to me. Thank you!

To my editors, Lisa Bonvisutto and Vanessa Aguirre: the two of you have done incredible things for this book, and I am so grateful for every brilliant note, comment, and revision suggestion. To Lisa, thank you for always being so willing to talk with me on the phone in order to hash out plot things, and for your amazing editorial letters. To Vanessa, thank you so much for all your help in the final stages of editing. Your first-class notes were so insightful and kind and made the final stretch a joy. Special shout-out for your enthusiasm about Erik and Jamie and for the nice notes throughout the manuscript! It made me so happy every time you thought a joke was funny or a moment was especially cute.

A huge thank-you to the amazing people at Wednesday Books. I know you've all worked really hard, and I appreciate you all so much. This book wouldn't be possible without Eileen Rothschild, Sara Goodman, Soleil Paz, Devan Norman, Althea Mignone, Brant Janeway, Zoë Miller, Kelly South, Melanie Sanders, Sara Thwaite,

Gail Friedman, Steve Wagner, Emma Paige West, and Isabella Narvaez. Thank you all so much!

To Olga Grlic and Petra Braun for the jaw-droppingly adorable cover! For a long time I have wanted to have a blue book, and this is the kind of cover an author dreams about.

To my friends and family, thank you for always being there for me, both when I am excited to talk about something book-related and when I am struggling to figure things out. Nick, I love you! You have been so supportive that it's difficult to imagine doing it without you. I'm so appreciative that I can always talk to you about book stuff, and your perspective is always spot-on. You're truly the most incredible boyfriend a guy could ask for, and I love you so much.

Mum, Dad, Kia, Shaye, and Selam: I feel lucky to have the most amazing family ever! With this one, I will have dedicated a book to each of you, and that's honestly one of the things about my publishing career so far that I am proudest of. It's been a secret goal of mine for a long time, and I'm so happy it's a reality.

To my friends, thank you all for the support you've given me. Callum, Ryan, Mitch, Fraser, Finella, Lauren, Dean, Michael, Jaymen: I am so lucky to have you in my life, and I hope you all know how much I appreciate you! Huge special thanks to Kia and Callum McDonald for giving me fantastic editorial notes on the first hundred pages of this!

To Sophie Gonzales, thank you for always being there for me to chat about all things publishing (and a bunch of other things). Your insight, drive, and talent are truly so inspiring to me, and I'm so happy we're friends.

To my author friends: David Slayton, Becky Albertalli, Tobias Madden, James L. Sutter, Shaun David Hutchinson, Kosoko Jackson, Jordon Greene, L. C. Rosen, Julian Winters, and Adib Khorram. I look up to each and every one of you so much; thank you for being so kind to me and for your incredible books!

To all the bloggers and people online who have ever supported me: thank you!! I truly appreciate whenever you take time out of your day to make something related to my writing, whether it be an Instagram post or a review or a piece of art. Your support means I get to keep doing this, and I'm so grateful.

And to you, for reading this: whether this is the first book of mine you've read or the fifth, I hope you enjoyed it, and thank you so much for supporting me as I follow this wild dream of mine. THANK YOU!!!

ABOUT THE AUTHOR

© Shaye Beth

CALE DIETRICH is a YA devotee, lifelong gamer, and tragic pop-punk enthusiast. He was born in Perth, grew up on the Gold Coast, and now lives in Brisbane, Australia. He is the author of *The Love Interest* (a 2018 Rainbow Book List selection) and *The Pledge,* and coauthor with Sophie Gonzales of *If This Gets Out.*